THROUGH HER EYES

I hope all your dreams come true

Sophie Fahy x

By

Sophie Fahy

First Published in 2019 by Blossom Spring Publishing

Through Her Eyes Copyright © Sophie Fahy.

ISBN 978-1-9160320-8-8

E: admin@blossomspringpublishing.com

W: www.blossomspringpublishing.com

Published in the United Kingdom. All rights reserved under International Copyright Law. Contents and/or cover may not be reproduced in whole or in part without the express written consent of the publisher. Book cover copyright © Blossom Spring Publishing.

This is a work of fiction. Names, characters, places and incidents are either products of the author's imagination or are used fictitiously. Any resemblance to actual events or locales or persons, living or dead, save those clearly in the public domain, is purely coincidental.

Grace, this book is for you and every other angel that cut their life too short. Though you cannot read it or have your very owned signed copy, I just want you to know that the love you had for writing inspired me.

Fly high, sweet angel x

Prologue

I've lost count of the number of parties I've attended since starting high school. My party invitations seem never-ending; even ticking them off on all ten fingers wouldn't cover it. If I told you the exact figure, you would think I did nothing but party all the time.

If you'd told me a party would be what ripped my world apart, I probably would have laughed at you. It wouldn't be a wholehearted laugh, either. I would probably give a harsh *you're out of your mind* sort of laugh.

I had no idea a party would be my destruction and would force me to rearrange all my goals and dreams in life.

Only one burning conquest made it to the top of my to-do list: *revenge*.

The desire to get even.

No pain, no gain. That night was my pain, and it was the sort of pain I could never forget. Revenge would be my gain, and I was ready for it.

I was the girl who loved to read, sit on the rooftop all night, and admire the bright shining stars. I wanted to travel the world, see the Eiffel Tower, cherish mouthfuls of Turkish kebabs, and swim in the shallow Caribbean water—but all my ambitions disappeared into the distance because *that night* made me no longer *that girl*.

I was swallowed into what felt like the depth of darkness.

My soul was high in my body, waiting to be released.

One

Noelle Carlisle: a girl who is prestigious in her own right, who takes pride in her long blond locks, and who is much more popular than me. Even so, she cares—cares enough to make me vegetable soup if I'm suffering from a cold and to hold my hair back so delicately when I'm puking my guts out down the toilet. She is the most loving best friend anyone could ask for.

When Noelle throws a party, she always makes sure they are the most out-of-control nights of the year. The house is filled with bodies, all crammed in and clammy from the summer heat. There's dancing and gyrating outside her front door, on her back porch, even in her bathrooms. The alcohol flows. The drugs are passed around, allowing the cokeheads to get their fix. She would never guess that the craziness would spiral and go terribly wrong. In her eyes, the party is going to be bouncing.

Situated in a small town twenty-five miles from Detroit, the sound system is on the maximum setting playing the music so loud the high heavens can probably hear it. It's so loud I can imagine the neighbors dancing along with us—that or calling the sheriff. Teenagers everywhere are shouting over the beat, and hands are covering the ears of those standing too close to the speakers.

Vallyeont, Michigan, has a population of only seven thousand people, and a house party like this one is all the rave. It's all teenagers can do in a small town where the nearest movie theater is a twenty-mile drive away.

The jocks of Valley View High pick up the cheerleaders and place them over their shoulders. They jump up and down, cheering along with each other. There's always that one guy, the one who swings the cheerleader around too much while they're intoxicated up to their eyeballs. He and the cheerleader lose their balance, and it always ends up the same way for both of them: collapsed on the floor, passed out.

I look around; there is glass everywhere, and empty bottles are lying on their sides. Red cups are piled high in all the rooms. They're in the sink, on the armchair, up the stairs, and even balancing on the lampshades. The maid will have her work cut out for her, but that's what Noelle's parties are all about: loud, chaotic, and messy.

No adults.

No rules.

No regrets.

Just a whole lot of alcohol and drugs and memories that will last me a lifetime.

The crowd starts chanting, "Off, off, off!"

"Take it off!" someone yells.

Then there's a whistle and, "All of it!"

Sweat trickles down my forehead as I drop down low, putting on a show.

Imagine yourself standing on top of your best friend's living room coffee table—which, I might add, isn't the biggest of tables—and then imagine yourself moments away from becoming a full-blown stripper. Now, continue to picture yourself with just your underwear on and your dress flying into a cheering crowd predominantly made up of drunken high school students, with the odd college student dotted around.

I'm not sure whether to tell you this yet as it's pretty embarrassing, but that girl, the one who's close to flashing her private parts and dancing away like it's the 1960s—that girl is Alyssa Darlington. Oh, and one more thing—did I mention that girl is me?

I'm as wild as they get when it comes to parties, but stripping is something I'll definitely place my hand on my heart and say I don't do. I can also tell you I'm terrible at it. Stripping will most likely never be the way I pay my bills.

"Come on girl, don't keep us waiting!" hollers Ashton Marston, a soon-to-be senior hottie. He wolf-whistles, aiming it toward me, and elbows his sidekick, Ethan Hale, in the side. The two nod in my direction and laugh while picking up their beer bottles. I hear the *clink* as their bottlenecks connect; it's like a chime on a porch. I glance their way and watch as they guzzle down their beers. Ashton's big brown eyes sparkle below the disco lights and travel along my body, starting at my tanned legs and hesitating on my delicate black bra, which accentuates my well-proportioned breasts.

His gaze lifts to my face.

I'm about to unclasp my bra, ready to throw it toward the guys, who resemble hungry animals, seeking their prey in the crowd. There's a buzz in my head. The smiles and dancing are making me aroused. I tease the guys as I pull my hand away from the clasp and leave my bra in place. I tilt my head backward and laugh. I jump off the table, grinning at the attention my admirers give me. I stroll over with my chest puffed out and chin held high. I wink at the nearest guy and his eyes twinkle.

I twirl an auburn strand of hair between my fingers and smile. "Hi, guys."

I grab Ashton's hand and pull him farther into the crowd. A massive grin appears across his face as I place both of his hands onto my bare hips and listen to his jagged breathing drifting into my ears. Slowly, as we dance, his breathing grows quicker, turning heavy against my neck—and, may I add, that's not the only thing that grows.

The room is dark and the only light shining through comes from the multi-coloured light system. Surrounding us are underage wasters who are dancing as if there's no tomorrow. My hips swerve side to side with the rhythm of the music. Ashton grinds seductively and slowly against me. The heat builds up between us, on the verge of bursting, until finally it radiates off him. I try moving back because the warmth starts to become too much, but he won't let me go. He holds me tightly, suffocating me.

This isn't me. The way I'm acting, it's as if I've gone into Alyssa the hooker mode. Normally, I'm not this girl. I'm generally the quick-witted, one-liner girl, the one everyone knows and adores. I know parties turn me wild, but I would never have guessed they would turn me *this* wild.

Then again, there's a first time for everything.

Someone taps my bare shoulder. Before I have a chance to turn around, Ashton abruptly pulls me away and blocks my view.

"Get lost," he sneers. Someone taps his shoulder again and Ashton turns around, glaring. "You really know how to spoil the moment, don't you, Noelle?"

She smiles curtly. "I wouldn't say spoiling. I'd go with…saving." Her eyes catch mine. "Alyssa, come on." She grabs my wrist. "Let's go get you dressed and decent."

"Bitch." Ashton spits, and it lands inches away from Noelle's feet.

She winks at him, keeping hold of me. "I sure am, and don't you forget it." Ashton attempts to pull me away but fails.

Noelle's been my best friend since I moved over to America from England when I was eight years old. On my first day of school, she was there, waiting and ready to take me under her wing; I called her my guardian angel. She's always picking up my pieces and guiding me. To lose her would be devastating, something I would never want to experience.

Noelle drags me out of Ashton's hold. Hand in hand, we leave the living room, and she leads me through the house, still in my underwear. As I walk, I make sure to swerve my hips seductively, side to side. The guys in the room have their eyes upon me and I smile to myself, pleased. I overhear the girl's snide remarks, one after another.

"What a whore."
"She's such a slut."

The girls laugh, and I'm sure the word *desperate* comes to mind.

Noelle squeezes my hand. I don't care about the name shaming; they can call me everything under the sun and it won't bother me, because I know what happens at parties, stays at parties. So, tomorrow, everything will be forgotten. I know I'm not a slut. I'm not easy—far from it.

To be honest, I don't blame Noelle for interfering in my love life. If she left it to me, I'd be falling in love with a druggy rock star who loves his crack more than anything else. I'm gullible when it comes to falling in love. Anyone who watched Ashton and me could clearly see his hands were starting to grab me in more places than I appreciated. I'm just too blown away from the alcohol to stop him.

That's why, guys and girls, you should never drink—Alyssa's number one tip.

When walking behind Noelle, my ass gets more taps than a ping pong ball. I'm aware of being violated, but I'm not sure if it's reality. It's like I'm floating, like it's more of a dream than real life.

I glance at the back of Noelle's shiny, soft, long locks and hourglass figure. I smile. She opens her bedroom door and pushes me inside. Red beer cups are tipped upside down and beer is spilled all over her grey wooden floor, right beside her white bedframe. Noelle throws me my dress and with a swift motion of my hand, I catch it.

"Get dressed," she states flatly as she picks up the red cups and places them on her dressing table. "I need to go get something to wipe all this mess up." She slams the door behind her.

I sit on her bed. Looking around, I notice three dresses hanging on the outside of her wardrobe. The dress I hold in my hands would still be hanging there if I hadn't taken it as a present.

Not long after, she re-enters the room with a cloth in hand. I sheepishly grin to try to lighten the dim mood that's already been set.

"Don't smile at me like that, Alyssa…" She bends down and wipes up the beer. "I didn't realize my friend is a slut." She hesitates and looks up at me. "Well?"

I snicker. "Woah Noelle, I'm sorry."

"Don't Noelle me—"

"Why are you being so harsh?" I laugh. "You're the one who told me to go a bit wild tonight." I raise my eyebrows. "What was the phrase you used? *Let my hair down.*" I slur my words and flip my hair defiantly.

Noelle stands up and stares at me, the beer-soaked cloth still clutched in her hands. We both look at it. She tosses it onto the dressing table, wipes her hands on her dress, and slowly sits beside me.

"Nothing to say, my dearest Noelle? I thought I'd at least get a hooray or a pat on the back."

Her hands fly up into the air. "Yeah, Lyss, I just didn't want you to slut it up around my house, crikey."

My mouth drops, and I gape at her. *How dare she mock me?* I always know when she does; it's not in her tone, but the language she uses. Although American, Noelle uses British terms I've taught her. *Crikey* is just one on the endless list.

"Look, get dressed." Standing on her feet, Noelle walks to the door. "Find me when you become my best friend again." The door slams shut, and I'm left alone.

I try to process everything that's just happened, but the copious amount of alcohol I've consumed is making it hard to think.

I hold my black-sequinned bodycon dress between my fingers and look down at it. If it wasn't for Noelle, I wouldn't have had a beautiful outfit to wear. The way it clings to my frame, showing me off to everyone, even my own mouth watered when I looked in the mirror. She wanted to help me grab the attention of Conan Dwight by giving me a breathtaking dress to wear, and I blew it up, like a time bomb.

Maybe I did go a little too far tonight. Maybe Noelle has a point.

Conan Dwight: king of popularity. I first laid eyes upon his short, tightly curled head of hair in middle school. He was such a sweet guy, always holding doors open for teachers and girls—*especially* girls. We were friends until high school, and now we're more strangers.

I glance at the chest of drawers at the far side of the room and sitting on it, is her family portrait. Noelle's face is gleaming, smiling broadly at the camera, and her arms are around her dad's neck. Her head is lazily rested on his shoulder. Her mother's beautiful porcelain face is looking at Mr. Carlisle with so much admiration, I'm jealous. Noelle's brother, who is a thousand miles away at college, is slouched on the couch next to their mom, looking ruggedly handsome.

The Carlisle family is like royalty in Vallyeont. They have the looks and the money, and they have what's known as the perfect family. Just looking at this picture is all the proof you need. Mr. Carlisle has millions of dollars, and I'm so lucky to be involved in Noelle's life at all.

I place my arms into the sleeves of my dress and stand up, helping myself to wiggle into the tiny garment. Once it's on, I zip up the dress and prepare myself to go back out to the party.

Outside Noelle's bedroom, two people stand playing tongue twister against the wall. I keep my head down, concentrating on the woodwork beneath me, but as I attempt to walk past them, my eyes catch the attention of Conan Dwight. I try to shuffle by, excusing myself, but I stumble. I would've fallen flat on my face if he hadn't caught me. My cheeks flush. "Sorry."

He's still got a hold on me, stopping my fall. "No worries." Conan lets go and moves his date to one side, out of my way.

"Always in the way, Alyssa," she pipes up. It's a girl with short bobbed hair in the grade below us.

I ignore her comment and keep my eyes on my feet, crossing my fingers that I don't trip. Tears roll down my tanned face, smudging my black eyeliner. I dab my cheeks and lick my plump red lips with caution. I hope that I look okay and that they didn't see me breaking.

I slowly pass people as I walk down the stairway, sliding my hand along the wooden rail. Arriving at the bottom, I find Tommy Henderson talking to a girl with a cheeky grin on his face. I make sure my face is free of tears before holding my head up high and poking him in the shoulder.

"Hi, handsome." He turns around to face me and I kiss his cheek. I wink at the girl behind him, known as Charlotte Summers.

Tommy places his hand on her upper arm. "Charlotte, could you please give us a moment?" He rakes his hand through his short brown wavy hair and ruffles it, making sure it still bounces, just like it always does. He turns back around to stare at me.

"Yeah, I guess. I'll go get us a drink," Charlotte says—*Yeah, Charlotte, run along like a good little princess!*

The fact that I haven't seen Tommy for most of the night dawns on me. If I didn't feel guilty before, I certainly do now. It's consuming me, sitting heavy on my heart.

Tommy Henderson, the boy I've known since I believed my light-up sneakers were the height of fashion, he's the guy who will undoubtedly do anything for me, including coming to a party he didn't want to attend. It was just before the party when he was telling me to skip it and go see a film with him.

~

"*I think we should go catch a movie, preferably one with Jason Statham in it.*" Tommy grinned at me and helped me out of the car. He shut the passenger door and placed his hand on my lower back, guiding us to the footpath and leading us to a night we weren't ever going to forget.
"*Tommy, you're such a bore. You'd rather watch a film than go to party?*" I couldn't stop laughing at him. I didn't want to believe my ears.

~

The look he gave me then was certainly ten times nicer than the way he's looking at me now. I remember the way he looked at me at the beginning of the night; he made steady eye contact as I spoke, and his pupils were large as he listened attentively. He gazed at me with admiration. He made me feel beautiful as he guided us toward Noelle's front lawn.

~

"Course I'd rather see a movie. It's different for me, Lyss. I can't exactly drink." He reminded me of the heads and tails game we'd played back at my house. Unfortunately for him, he'd lost. "Never mind, I suppose I will have to keep an eye on you all night."

"Tut." I slapped him. "Don't be silly—you'll have all the girls swooning over you. Trust me, you won't want to stay by my side all night." I hesitantly laughed, and he swung his arm around my shoulder, squeezing it gently. In that moment, the redness crept *up my cheeks. I dipped my head quickly and avoided his gaze. The tops of his ears turned red and he shoved his hands deep into his pockets as we waited at Noelle's front door, ready to party.*

~

I'm jolted back to the present as Tommy scratches his neck. "What do you want, Alyssa?"

"Don't be like that, Tommy." I giggle, grabbing his upper arm, feeling the pure muscle underneath his blue shirt.

"You haven't wanted anything to do with me all night—why now?" He shrugs and starts to walk away.

"Tommy, wait, don't go!" I grab his wrist, using all my strength to stop him. "Okay, fine." I hold my hands up in surrender. "I'm sorry—you're right." I touch his upper arm gently and my eyes widen. "Please don't leave me."

Why he doesn't pull away, I'm not sure. I left him earlier on in the night. I didn't stay when he asked me to stay...I just walked away. When we got into Noelle's house, she pulled me away from Tommy, and when I looked behind, I found him standing alone. He stared openly at me and threw his hands up. All I could do then was send him an apologetic smile, knowing he would be perfectly fine.

It was far from the truth. He's not fine. Standing here with him, trying to get him to stay shows me exactly that. I'll tell you now, he's pissed off with me, but who can blame him?

I certainly can't.

"That was a nice performance you put on earlier," he says. "Real classy."

I groan, throwing my head backward so I'm looking up at the high ceiling. He pulls his arm away from me. "Not you too. C'mon…" I laugh awkwardly. "It was just a bit of fun."

He clenches his jaw. "See you around, Lyss. I'm going to go let all the girls *swoon over me*—especially one specific girl. Don't wait up." He looks behind us toward the girl with light hair, one he knows I can't stand. It's like chalk and cheese—never going to happen.

Charlotte flipping Summers.

He leaves me standing there like a raw, unwanted, definitely sour lemon.

He's so pissed, and so am I, in more ways than one.

The night becomes dull, but everyone is still partying. Drinks are being placed into my hands, one after another, and each time, I don't hesitate to throw them back. I know it's the only thing that can get me wasted, and that's all I want. I walk along the hallway and pass several people who ignore me. A red cup floats between two heads and I grab it, the liquor trickling down from my tongue and into my stomach in one gulp. It makes me remember why I love parties so much.

I enter the second living room—apparently one isn't enough for the Carlisle family. From the couch behind me, a voice becomes louder with each syllable. I stand alone, trying to mind my own business.

"A.D.," Ethan Hale, a blond-haired bombshell, slurs. "The only girl I've been excited to see. Yeah baby."

I let out an audible sigh. "Of course." I place my left hand on my hip and sway the cup in my right side to side, knowing exactly where the conversation is leading.

His lips form a smirk that most likely makes any girl swoon. "You're so be-au-ti-ful."

I'm not just any girl, and I assure you, the only swooning I'm doing is from too much alcohol consumption.

I smile sweetly, turning my red-painted lips up at the corners. "Come on, Ethan, don't you get sick of being such a flirtatious twat?" I cock my head and tap my index finger against my cheek. "All that hard work trying to get girls into bed must be exhausting."

"Alyssa. Alyssa Darlington," he sings. "One day, doll face, you will be one of the five best girls I've ever had in my bed. Girl, you'll be wearing that smile all…night…long." Ethan puts his right hand out and starts slapping the air, mimicking someone's ass.

I roll my eyes. *Gross.*

Vomit sits at the bottom of my stomach, ready to make its way up, but I shake it off.

"I would only be in your best five?" I slap my hand against my chest, over my heart, in mock disappointment and pout. "Oh, Ethan."

"What can I say? I've had a lot of girls." He grins. "How about we go upstairs…I'd love to see you naked." He winks.

Bile travels from the depth of my stomach all the way up my throat. I cough and stand with a stiff posture, an air of readiness about me. I keep a strong eye in his direction while allowing myself to recoil and cringe on the inside. My smile slides off my face dramatically and I lean down, placing my arms on either side of him, our noses inches apart. I give him the infamous Alyssa smirk and notice his face believing it to be his lucky day. He starts leaning toward me, the smell of alcohol drifting up my nostrils, coming from his breath. My stomach churns and I pull away from his gleaming face.

"Look pal, I wouldn't come near you even if we were the last ones standing," I slur.

I stand up straight, keeping my eyes upon his twinkling blue ones, and relish his shocked expression. Before I walk away, I blow him a teasing kiss and laugh along with our audience, who overheard his failed attempt to get me into bed.

I stumble away, ending up on my hands and knees, crawling past a keg with a dozen guys standing around it, shouting and playfully punching each other. Everyone reminds me of those glass bottles around the house: useless and empty.

Tears roll slowly down my cheeks, my eyes swollen with a redness underneath each. Every time I touch them, a sharp pain travels through my face. I haul myself up so I'm standing and drag my intoxicated body forcefully through the emerging crowd and into the kitchen. I get a glimpse at the black speckled countertops and can barely make out the pattern due to the mess of food and booze scattered across them. The glossy white cupboards have red sauce smeared all over. Noelle's house is a Goddamn mess, and her parents are going to kill her.

I latch myself onto a blond hottie. My arms are around his neck before even knowing his name, and he begins to swing me side to side in time with the music. Although I'm enjoying myself, it's impossible to ignore the obviously annoyed and disapproving glare from Noelle, who's standing in her kitchen doorway. She storms toward me, and all I want to do is run in the opposite direction.

"Alyssa!" she hisses.

The blond hottie is about to pucker up and kiss me—no kidding.

Noelle grabs my elbow and forcefully pulls me away, leaving the guy looking like a fish. My feet are tripping over one another as she starts to recite the ninety-nine commotions that will haunt me in the morning. "You know you're going to regret all this, right? This is so out of character, and you really need to grow the hell up, Alyssa." I know she has a point. "Why are you being like this?"

If *he* had just noticed me, none of this would have happened. All I want is the attention of Conan Dwight. Then again, it always comes down to a boy, doesn't it?

The boy you love.

The boy you hate.

The boy who thinks you're invisible.

At the end of it all, every girl becomes infatuated and heartbroken, and I bet we all know who causes it. Oh, what a surprise: *a boy*.

"You're right," I say.

"You should see yourself." Noelle ignores my admission. "You're making yourself out to be a boyfriend-grabbin—"

I pull out of her grip fiercely and she gawps at me. "If you would shut up for a second, you'd have heard that I just agreed with you. You're right, Noelle!"

Her porcelain doll face is radiating annoyance. "Just because you want him to notice you, it doesn't give you the right to be a bitch to me." Before I have the chance to tell her to wait, she walks away toward a group of girls who are waiting for her.

I'm left standing in the middle of the kitchen, alone, and being alone makes me reflect on how drunk I actually am. My head buzzes and hums, and it worsens when I move. My eyes barely stay open and my stomach churns so badly, it's like the inside of a washing machine on full spin. I feel like I've just ridden a roller coaster, repeatedly.

All I want to do is close my eyes and go to sleep. It's time to put the party to rest and go home, because if I don't, Noelle's right—I'll regret everything. I've already made a fool out of myself.

I look for my ride home, but I don't find my designated driver anywhere. Tommy's disappeared and most likely left with Charlotte.

I step forward and lose my footing, my arms latching onto yet another boy. "I'm s-s-sorr-" I try to finish my sentence, but the words won't form on my alcohol-soaked tongue.

"No worries." Ashton turns and holds on to my arms, helping me stay upright. Just when I think he's playing nice, he slowly slides both of his palms onto my ass and caresses it. He's after one thing: *sex*.

I swat his hand away.

"I know you're into me, Alyssa. C'mon, we'll go upstairs?" He raises a dark, thick eyebrow. I shove him backward, but his fingers are still wrapped tightly around my wrists, jerking me closer to him.

Everyone around us is staring, but they don't help.

"Please. Please stop," I yell loud enough for him to hear, yet he pretends I didn't say anything. "Ashton, stop. Let go of me. You're hurting me."

"Alyssa, shhh. I know you want me. You shouldn't be such a tease, dressed in that short black dress, defining every single curve of your body." He licks his lips. Like I said earlier: *animal*.

I'm unable to think straight.

"I'll never understand why guys try to get into your pants when you just tease them like this, but you can tease me all night long as long as I get a little, okay?"

"No—" I drop to my knees and he picks me back up again. He leads me through the crowd and up the stairs. All I'm able to do is listen to all the drunken whooping. I try to resist, but I can't; I'm too drunk.

Right now, I cannot even tell you my name, never mind shout out.

My mind is like a blank sheet of paper: white and clear all over.

Two

I awake, lying with rumpled white sheets twisted around me. I painfully open my eyes and realize I'm in a bedroom. The layout is different than Noelle's. Walnut furniture surrounds me, and the walls are a shade of light lavender. My dress is above my stomach, but my knickers are still on.

Good sign.

My head is pounding so hard, I want to close my eyes again; music blares in the distance, which tells me I'm still at the party. The last thing I remember is Ashton bringing me to this room, but I don't know what happened.

Don't panic.

"Ashton?" I say.

There's no answer. I'm alone.

I'm not sure how long I was passed out, but I do know I need to get out of this room, *fast*.

I stand and pull my dress down. The room is spinning, making every step difficult to take. It's like déjà vu as I stumble out of the bedroom and into the upstairs hallway, but this time there's no Conan playing tongue twister, no Tommy at the bottom of the stairs.

In a haze, I make my way downstairs and ignore the looks and whispers. At some point I end up sliding through a side door next to a large planted pot and continue my way into a dark room.

I'm wondering what happened between Ashton and me in that bedroom while I was unconscious. Vomit starts to threaten again from my stomach. *That asshat.* I want to ring my hands around his neck. I try to get my bearings, but my head is still fuzzy and I'm weaker than my mom's cuppa teas.

Distantly through the dark, I recognize a parked red Ford GT, the same car Noelle's mother is seen driving around town in. I instantly realize I'm in a garage, which is not what I expected. My head sways to one side, feeling heavy on my neck. I take a step forward on the hard, concrete floor and lean against a different car. It's black…a black Mercedes. I lean against the passenger side and use all my energy to stay on my feet. I try looking around to see what else I recognize, and as I do, I duck to the ground. I turn to the door I just walked through and watch two shadows emerge. There's laughing, as they—whoever they are—walk away from me.

They didn't notice me.

Violently, I curl over and throw up; vomit is everywhere, all over my dress, my right hand, and the concrete floor. I want to go home. I want to be in my bed ready for the day ahead of me. I reach for my phone and remember I left my bag in Noelle's bedroom at the beginning of the night. *Why didn't I just pick it up after our argument?*

I try to focus on the blurry lights shining into the garage from the window opposite. The rattling of old engines sounds outside, the booming echoing in the large garage, and the backfire of an exhaust followed by a vroom makes me jump. It's taking all my concentration…it's too much, and my eyes begin to shut slowly. I feel the need to keep them closed and fall asleep, to let myself drift away. My head drops forward an inch, as if someone has just placed a ton of bricks on my neck.

I try to open my eyes. The ache in my body throbs hard, making the pain override my mind. Dread starts from the pit of my stomach and swirls itself around. I whimper at my lack of energy, and soon all the events seem to spiral into a blank remembrance.

Light, thudded steps get louder; one step, two steps, three—I have company. *I'm going to be okay.* I use my last ounce of energy to try to look at the stranger towering over my body.

"Help me." My voice breaks. "Help me, please."

They make no movement to help. The darkness hovers over us, making it hard to know who stands before me. They remain very still, very still indeed.

"What are you doing?" I croak.

Suddenly, not only are they consumed with darkness, but the dark overrides every sense I have. They pick up a large object, something I don't recognize. Before I'm able to catch my breath, a wet, slippery substance is being poured all over me. It smells like soap: fresh and clean. If it had been under different circumstances, the smell would have been appreciated, but at the moment I'm aching from the inside out.

I try to look around, try my hardest to catch my breath. I turn my head side to side, trying to make the substance disappear, but it just keeps on coming. I'm too weak to scream, to tell them to stop. My eyes burn, so I squeeze them shut tightly, hoping it will take the sensation away. Whatever substance they're using, it's making me feel drowned. I can't catch a breath to be able to shout for help. It keeps coming continuously, and I grab their leg, tugging at them and wishing they would stop. When that doesn't seem to work, I try to move, to crawl away, but evil just keeps on following, keeps pouring, keeps laughing—a deep, malicious laugh, one I'll never forget.

I've gone numb from exhaustion, and soon, the liquid stops. I try my hardest to open my eyes. As I do, grey trousers and black shoes appear. The person throws the empty bottle behind them and at the light thud, I pray it's over. I close my eyes. They walk away from me and I sigh in relief. I hear whispers: a girl, a boy, a man, maybe even a woman. I hear them rummaging through work tools. It doesn't sound good.

I try to move, but I struggle. Echoes of footsteps come closer and my heart rate doubles in speed. I stiffen at the loud screech bouncing off the walls. It's as though a nail is being scraped across a blackboard. Before I open my eyes to see, there's a blow to my head, the impact hard, making me go lifeless on the cold, hard floor. Before passing out completely, I fight through the pain and open my eyes. They're walking away, two of them. All I can think right now is: *why me?*

Time passes by, and I start to regain feeling. My legs twitch slightly, but my arms are sprawled out above my head, unable to move. My cheek is against the concrete and it's filling with pins and needles, traveling to my neck. I try to peel it away, but I struggle.

    The stench of vomit mixed with the aroma of tuna from my dinner wafts up my nostrils, and a whiff of blood tickles my nose. It smells like I've died, but I know I'm still alive, still breathing, still surviving. Every instinct I have is telling me to open my eyes, but it seems impossible. They simply won't open; instead, they're clenched in agony.

    Every inch of me is on fire: my head, back, and legs. My eyes and skin are burning.

    I fight through the pain and attempt to move my hand, stifling a groan as my limbs protest at the movement. Slowly, I manage to touch the sticky wetness that's matted and curled into my hair. The damp, cold slime transfers onto my fingers—blood, sweat, and tears. My hand falls to the side and I shake uncontrollably; I think I'm having a fit.

I stop.

I don't know where I am.

I'm exhausted and all I'm able to do is listen and hope and pray someone finds me. I no longer feel, no longer understand, so I let myself drift off to sleep, trying to forget it ever happened.

A high-pitched scream like a banshee wakes me up.

Someone at my side breathes heavily. "Oh no."

Footsteps echo around the room. People are whispering, hands are touching me, prodding me, lifting me. I want it all to stop.

"Don't just stand there—call an ambulance you idiot!" Noelle screeches. "Alyssa!" I hear her voice, but I don't respond. She shakes me, willing me to move, but I can't. I can't move.

"Sweet Jesus, there's so much blood—" someone whispers, a girl, I think.

A man's voice interrupts. "How long has she been like this?"

I hear a ticking. I think it's just in my head, ticking away until my death. *Tick tock, tick tock, tick tock.*

"What time is it?" The question flies outward.

"Four a.m."

"She must have been here a few hours. Let's just hurry up and get her some help," Noelle demands, sounding aggravated.

I try to stay awake, but with my eyes remaining closed and my body becoming weaker by the minute, I drift back to sleep.

Minutes later, I wake to the sound of machines. I lay uncomfortably on a slim, metal-framed bed, and I shiver, tightly clutching the blanket that's spread over me. I pull it snugly around my shoulders, bringing it up farther under my chin, hoping it brings warmth. I breathe in the fresh air through the open doors of what must be the back of an ambulance, and I hear the hiss of pressurized air.

This is just one tremendous nightmare.

No. Everything that happened is traumatically real, which means I did kiss all those guys and I did wake up in a bed with my dress to my breasts and I really was brutally attacked in that garage. I don't suppose my night can get any worse.

"Wait, don't leave yet—I think she's waking up." There's an urgency in his voice. "Alyssa, you're safe. You're with an emergency team, and we're taking you to the hospital, love." *I know that voice.* I recognize the sharp British tongue to be my father's.

I don't make any response because I'm not sure what to say.

"Alyssa, can you hear me?" he asks.

I keep my eyes closed and stay quiet.

My father strokes the top of my hairline, moving all the dry, bloody strands away from my eyes. "You don't think she's lost her hearing, do you?"

"Alyssa, do you know where you are?" the female paramedic asks from where she sits at my side. She picks up my wrist, placing two fingers just below a vein, and starts counting under her breath, checking my pulse.

My father's hand starts to shake. "They're saying she was out cold for at least a few hours before they found her. What's going to happen?"

"Her vitals are showing she's okay, Mr. Darlington. That's a good sign. We can't ask her any questions until she's ready to reply, therefore the best option now is to go straight to the hospital where they will thoroughly examine her. I assure you, your daughter is in good hands."

I take my arm out from under the blanket and use all my strength to touch my father's knee for reassurance. I push against his leg and sit up, still clutching the blanket to my chest with the other hand. "I can hear you, Dad," I whisper, barely getting the words out, each one burning as they form a sentence. "What are you—"

"Steady." My dad holds on to my shaking arm until I'm comfortably sitting up. "Noelle rang me, and I came as soon as I heard."

"Alyssa, can you open your eyes for me please?" the paramedic politely asks. "I'm going to shine a bright light and it's going to irritate them a bit, but it will be over before you know it. After, I would like you to tell me how many fingers I'm holding up, and then we are going to take you straight to the hospital, dear." I bring my hand up to my hair and touch the flaky blood knotted between the strands. "The bleeding stopped, and you're stable. We had to bandage the back of your head, but the doctors will be able to tell you more."

I scrunch up my face and rub it with my palms, dropping the blanket into my lap. I start from my cheeks and move up to my temples then back down again. I open my eyes quickly and look around. The shadows of the crowd are glinting within my view, and what look to be people wobble around me. There's constant barking in the distance. My nose floods with the stench of distilled spirits and the stale aroma of tobacco. The fumes are strong, and it's definitely coming from me. I know I smell vile.

I look around, and with help of the ambulance's bright lights, I make out the reflections on the dark, wet street. I study the flashing lights farther down the road, where police cars have parked, probably investigating the underage drinking. The noises around me are abrupt and sudden; my head begins to spin so fast, it intensifies my hearing.

I recognize the anger in my father's voice as he shouts at everyone standing around the ambulance door. "What the hell is everyone looking at? Haven't you all got bedtimes to be getting to?" His voice, harrowing and dire, is followed by howling sobs, which makes the situation even bleaker than it already is.

Everyone's looking for answers, even me, the girl scared and shaken, someone who doesn't want to hear the truth, because deep down, I already know what's happened. I know light will never look the same as it did this morning, and I know this afternoon was the last time I got to see the clear, exact image of my family's faces, just before leaving for a high school party—*big mistake, don't I know it.*

"Alyssa?" I look at the paramedic. "I'm going to shine a light into your eyes, and I'm holding a finger up. Please follow it side to side."

I try to concentrate on the finger, the outline of it defined in so many ways. I follow it as best as I possibly can and flinch as the light becomes brighter.

"Awesome." I think she's smiling, and my father squeezes my shoulder. "I'm about to hold up some fingers. Please tell me how many you're able to see and tell me if they're a blur or clear."

My head's pounding so hard, as if it's about to explode. I concentrate on the dark shadows of two long fingers, trying to focus on them so I'm able to see the pink skin, but it never appears; the fingers just stay shadowed. I clearly see there are two, but in terms of detail, none is apparent to me. The sharpness and clarity vanish, and the image looks like a big ball of blur.

I glance down at my hands, holding them out, palms facing upward. I feel weak at the thought of seeing only shadows; I look back up at the unfocused image of the paramedic's hand and tell her exactly what she wants to hear.

"Two." I hesitate. "There are two fingers." Just after they let out a sigh of relief and the hand on my shoulder relaxes, I continue. "The image is dark and unfocused. There's an outline but no color, and I have to concentrate really hard to know there are two of them."

Whether their mouths drop open or not, I can't tell. All I know is my life has changed, and there's nothing I can do about it. It's happening all because of a dumb, useless party where alcohol became more important than my health and well-being.

Both the paramedics and my father stay quiet. It lingers in the air around us. I know they have their suspicions about what may be wrong with me, but I understand it can't be confirmed until I reach the doors of the hospital and have been seen by a qualified doctor.

I may be made of organs and bones, but I'm not sure I can tell—all there is inside of me is emptiness.

Three

Life is either a rainbow leading you to a pot of gold, or it's full of darkness: scary and lonely. You know that gold can change your life, but you'll always underestimate how much the dark consumes you—until it finally does.

The nurse's cold icy touch on my right shoulder shocks me. She's holding a massive needle in her other hand, ready to take more blood. "More tests, Alyssa."

I swear this is going to be my thirty-five-millionth test, and it's going to try to explain how I—the beloved Alyssa Darlington, British sweetheart of Valley View High—found herself here, lying in a hospital bed and expected to eat the terrible food the nurses tell me is supposedly dinner.

Fish fillets, mushy vegetables, and gelatin desserts—*delicious.*

Okay, maybe I'm exaggerating a bit, but there's nothing else to do in this place; I could try to find myself a doctor sugar daddy, but that doesn't sound like the best of ideas with my father in the room.

The last time I was in a hospital, I was ten years old and had broken my leg from falling out of a tree. Noelle, Ethan, Conan, Tommy, and I were playing a game in Ethan's tree house, and when I tried to climb down, I slipped and fell to the ground.

"Ouch. Looks like that hurt," the familiar husky voice of sheriff Lou comments from the doorway. I glance up quickly, still not able to see anything but shadows. I know from the past he'll be wearing his grey and black uniform and his large round hat over the top of his golden blond hair. He's married with a three-year-old son and has the ass of a God: perky and firm.

"Howdy, Sherriff," my father says.

Daniel Lou chuckles lightly. "Afternoon, Mark. Looks like you're picking up that American language, huh." He clears his throat. "Alyssa, I'd like to ask you a couple of questions."

I nod.

Oh crap!

"Can you remember anything from last night? Anything at all?" Sheriff Lou holds a small pad of paper and a pen, waiting for me to answer.

"Not much. I've been told I'll give a statement once I'm better," I say.

"You will. Nothing to worry about. I just wanted to ask the question myself. What happened to you is horrible."

I nod again.

"I also want to remind you you're seventeen years old and there were drugs and alcohol at the party. You were underage drinking."

"Oh, don't you worry, Sheriff—she knows how I feel on the matter," Dad interjects from beside me.

"I know. It won't happen again, sir." I dip my head and my hands become clammy.

"I hope not." The sheriff nods his head in my dad's direction and leaves the room.

I let out a sigh of relief.

It's actually the fourth test I've undergone since somebody decided to whack me over the head using some sort of unknown object. Apparently, it's missing, nowhere to be seen. Wherever it is, it will have quite a lot of blood on it, along with the fingerprints of who did this to me. It needed to be found quickly. It was swung at my head with so much hatred, thus leaving me with what seems to be the ugliest scar to ever exist—which, may I add, feels like a golf ball implanted underneath my bouncy curls.

This scar is never going to let me forget.

We soon find out from the doctor that laundry detergent was thrown over my face, and when left too long in your eyes, it can cause serious damage. It was slimy and sticky, like an unwanted slug. I hadn't understood at the time what it would accomplish, and then my eyes had been burning so badly. My sight is now blurred and understanding it all came very quickly—not just understanding, but also the need to rinse them under water.

It's like living in my own personal black hole of hell. I might as well become friends with Satan while I'm living down here.

Dad grabs my hands and squeezes. "I love you, darling."

Mark Darlington: my father, my hero, my number one fan, and the most brilliant man in my life. He can always make bad situations better, and with this situation being the most difficult of those we've encountered together, he's managing to get us both through it. He cracks jokes, he keeps a smile on his face, and he keeps telling me the silver lining is that I might not have to see his ugly face for the rest of my existence. Of course, he says this while laughing to himself.

I love him for that.

"How do you feel today?" he asks.

I'm unable to find the words, making it hard to reply. My back is against the firm mattress, and soft feathered pillows are underneath my head. I move my hand around the bed to find another one at the side of me, and I place it over my face. My dad coughs awkwardly and sits in the chair next to me. He places his hand on my right arm, the one that is holding the pillow tightly, and rubs it up and down.

I shrug. "I'm not sure." I scream into the pillow, squeezing it hard. "Would you feel great if you were about to find out you're practically blind?"

"Don't say that. You don't know that, and, if that possibility becomes reality, you might only be partially blind."

"Only?" I tease. My muscles spasm and my spine tingles.

"We can work with that, love."

I slacken my grip on the pillow and slowly slide it down from my face to my chest.

I get a whiff of the overused fake tanner from where the cheap brown liquid I used for Noelle's party has started rubbing off onto the sheets. Embarrassing is an understatement.

My eyes remain closed for the majority of time. I keep feeling the need to open them, but I push through it. Why would I want to open them and see what I saw in the back of the ambulance? I don't want to be flooded with disappointment.

Why crush my own hopes?

Dad grabs my hand with both of his quite large, firm hands and rubs gently. "Come on, open your eyes. You can't keep them shut forever."

"Just watch me," I reply petulantly. I remove my hand from his then turn slowly and carefully onto my side so my back is to him. He sighs in obvious frustration and a tear rolls down my face, but I quickly wipe it away.

"I'm going to go get us something to eat or drink. It's past noon and you need *something* since you don't want to eat the hospital food." He laughs. "Maybe it will lift your mood." The chair screeches as he stands up, and his feet tread lightly across the floor, toward the door.

"Doubt it," I mutter.

My relationship with my father is already written out from now on: I'm going to put myself down, continuously feeling terrible about myself, and my dad is going to pick me back up again—just like parents should.

I let my right hand move up to my face, and my index finger traces the dark, blotchy circles around my eyes where they've swelled. I brush past my thick eyebrows and move closer inward to feel along my eyelashes. Nothing feels different. Everything is still the same. I keep having to remind myself that I still have the same shaped eyes, that I'm not abnormal; I'm still *me*.

The funny thing is, I find it hard to feel like me anymore. I'm lost, searching for answers but struggling to find them. I haven't quite come to terms with not being able to gaze intently at a rainbow hiding behind the clouds, to watch it come out and shine. It won't be shining for me, though. Everything will be grey, light grey, dark grey—who even likes grey?

My eyes drip with tears like a dam bursting forth for the very first time. The floodgates have opened, and before I even think about the fact that I'm able to still cry, my body releases as I start to shake tremendously. Brick by brick, my walls crumble, and I let every single pain I've ever felt drift over me. The rawness is real. Everything that's happened to me is an open wound waiting to be healed. I open my eyes while wiping away the continuous trail of tears, and all I glimpse is the fluorescent lighting, blinding me to everything else.

Dad taps on the door gently, the smooth, rich scent of roasted beans piercing through the room and into my nostrils. He comes to my side and sits on the bed, gently, the aroma of black coffee now next to me.

"Everything will be all right, kiddo." He places the cup on the side table. "You'll get through this."

I sit up and rearrange the pillows behind my back. "I'm scared, Dad." I start to scratch my wrist, harder and harder, until finally my dad reaches out and places his hands on the top of mine. "I'm really, really scared," I repeat, my lip quivering. I shut my eyes tightly, my face wet with tears, red and raw.

"I bet you are." He strokes my naturally wavy hair. "So am I. I'm scared for you, because of what you're having to go through, and I'm scared for me, because I don't want to lose my very independent and confident little girl."

With that, I'm instantly relieved that I'm very much surrounded by people who care.

The following day has so far been long and draining. When the nurse picks up my arm, my body flinches at the painful pinch of an IV needle going into my skin, and the flush of the antibiotics begins to hurt as it drifts into my veins.

"You're a very lucky girl. It could have been so much worse," the nurse whispers after checking my blood pressure.

All everyone seems to comment on is how lucky I am. I cannot understand how anything could be worse than not remembering if you had sex or how you got brutally attacked in the same night, and let's not forget potentially losing my eyesight. It doesn't make sense to me. Fair enough, I could be dead, lying in a ditch somewhere, but on a scale of one to ten, I think what happened definitely lands well on the high end.

All I think about is being in that garage, replaying it over and over again in my head. I want to remember. I'd have understood if this had happened to me years ago, because I was an outsider—a British girl on American soil—but years have gone by and I'm now part of American society.

We moved from England, from a small town situated in North Yorkshire. When we arrived, it was a nightmare trying to settle in: the snide looks, the unfamiliarity of school, and the different terms used. Eventually, I made friends, grew up, and became slightly popular, and now, there's no way of getting rid of me or my charms.

    I lay silently perched up against the pillows. Dad's snoring at my side is mimicking the sound of a foghorn. I nudge him slightly and he moves onto his side, snorts, and continues to snore. The phone in his hand starts ringing.

    "Wha—" Dad jumps out of his chair, dropping his phone to the floor. "Who? Hello."

    I burst out laughing. "It's just your phone, Dad."

    He pats my leg, picks up his phone, and sits back down. "Hm, not funny."

    "Soo funny." I laugh.

    "Behave." Dad smiles.

    I raise my eyebrows and turn onto my side so I'm facing him. I watch as he taps the screen of his phone; although I can't see the colors of his black iPhone, I'm able to clearly make out his greyish figure.

    I'm becoming thankful for that.

    "Where's Mom?" I ask, thinking back to when family was the most important thing to her.

    "She visited yesterday, kiddo, while you were asleep." He looks at me, placing his phone on the side table. "She's extremely busy at the moment with work and meetings. You know how she can get." He leans forward and entwines his fingers together. "I don't know if you've noticed, but the flowers on the side are from her. They're very pretty."

I smell their freshness before I picture them, but flowers aren't going to change anything; I know it, and my dad knows it. I look at him and notice his shadow curling over with his head in his hands.

"I wouldn't know—I can't see to be able to admire them." I close my eyes, still picturing darkness.

"What do they look like?"

"They're very bright and colorful." He straightens himself up. "Very beautiful."

"*Great* description."

He laughs. "I know, right."

It's hard to keep up the charade of pretending to be okay. I don't think I can any longer. It's as though I will most likely have another breakdown sooner rather than later, and I'm just waiting patiently for it to happen.

I take a deep breath.

The doctor explained to me yesterday evening that blindness is happening to me gradually. If I had been found sooner at the party, they may have been able to prevent it, but due to me being knocked unconscious for nearly three hours without anyone coming to help me, all this is happening. I know nothing will be the same again, and we're all beginning to realize I'm slowly but surely going blind.

Nobody understands how I feel. Everyone I know has their eyesight and doesn't understand how precious it really is, that the next time they look at their family and friends, it may just be the last time. People take for granted the littlest things—including me.

The familiar sound of vibration buzzing at my side, long and hard, brings me out of my head. It's coming from my mobile, which I completely forgot I have. I glance over at where it sits on the table, then ignore it.

"Noelle and Tommy have been asking to see you," Dad updates me from his chair.

"No." I bite my fingernail. "No visitors." I pull at the nail and touch the end of my finger with my thumb. I slide my tongue over the skin. I don't want my friends to find out, especially if I can help it—not yet, not until I'm ready to tell the world I'm struggling to see it.

"Will you ever be ready to tell them?" Dad asks the question we're both thinking. He's patronizing me. I'm not stupid; I know my friends will find out sooner or later, but for now, they can manage without the truth.

Dad picks up my phone and places it on my lap, "Just in case."

I bite my lip, leaving my finger to get some air. I play with the phone between my hands, hoping it doesn't start vibrating again.

"If you don't want to ring your friends, you could always ring your mom," Dad suggests.

"But—"

"No buts." Dad sighs. "She's your mother—you should be kind to her."

I hesitate, squeezing the solid rectangular object in my hands. I groan, bringing my fist and phone up to my lips. I hold it there, breathing slowly. I start to relax, and I hand the phone to my dad.

"Will you dial her number, please?" I ask in a small voice, hoping he didn't hear me.

Just as I'm holding the phone up to my ear, it starts to ring. *Ring. Ring.* It's still ringing. *Ring. Ring. Ring.*

"Alyssa! Are you okay?" my mom asks from the other end.

I sit silently for a moment, not sure what to say. "Yeah."

"I hope so, because I'm about to see for myself." Just as she finishes, I hear footsteps treading toward me. Entering the room is Melissa Darlington, the woman who gave birth to me, but since moving to America, her work has become the most important thing in her life—that and her prim-and-proper manicure.

Dad looks at the doorway, his expression as gormless as the rest. "Love, we were just speaking about you." He rises from the chair, and I watch their shadows embrace one another.

"Yeah, speaking of the devil." I snort. "Then *pop*, here you are."

"Alyssa!" they both scorn in unison. They let go of each other and my mom looks at me, saying my name as if it'll make my sarcasm go away.

For forty-five, my mother doesn't look bad. In fact, to all the guys at Valley View High, she's a cougar; to the guys back in England, she's a proper MILF.

I study her shadow carefully and watch as she shifts from one foot to another. My dad coughs into his fist, breaking the silence. I imagine her standing in front of me with her long, mousy brown hair, freshly straightened, her makeup applied flawlessly, her green eyes brightly popping from freshly applied black eyeliner, and her feet in black two-inch heels, ready to take on the world. Unfortunately, she never takes on the world for me, just for herself, because for some reason that's her number one priority.

"You look great, Alyssa. You're looking very healthy, better than yesterday."

I ignore the pretence of worry as my nostrils flare and my heart tugs in several directions within my chest. All I want is for the pain to stop. "Why are you here? Surely you have work."

"I'm here, young lady, to make sure you're okay!" She taps her heel against the floor.

Right. Like you even care.

"So?" She walks toward me. She holds the back of her hand, against my forehead, checking my temperature. "You seem to be."

"I wish people would stop checking up on me, stop asking me if I'm okay. Dad, you, doctors, friends—why can't everyone just leave me alone?" I push her hand away from me. I close my eyes and drop my head backward. I then sit back up and throw my legs over the side of the hospital bed.

"We care for you, darling," Mom says.

"Ugh!" I pick up the flowers at my side and throw them in my mom's direction. She squeals, and I hear the vase smash against the wall behind her, all the little shards of glass dropping to the ground. I stand up and walk over to look at the damage I've caused and see the shadow of the water, drifting along the floor; it's just clear, clear as water should be.

"What the..." Mom gawps at me. "Alyssa Annalise Darlington!"

"What?" I throw my hands up in the air and bring them back down just as fast, slapping them against both legs. "What are you going to do, *ground me*? Take away my computer or the television? Do it, I dare ya. I don't care—I can't flipping see it anyway."

I walk backward and sit back down on the bed, hanging my legs over the side.

"Alyssa..." Dad places his hand on my shoulder. I shrug him off, and his hand falls away.

"I wish to be alone," I barely whisper. "Please."

The only thing I'm able to do is plead.

Dad turns toward Mom and guides her to the door. "We will come back soon, and I'll ask a nurse to come in and clean everything up." He looks back at me before leaving and smiles. "We love you, darling." The door shuts tightly behind them.

I never did understand how I managed to turn my relationship with my mom into a dysfunctional one. I remember when we got along, doing what moms and daughters should do together: getting our nails painted, getting our hair done, going shopping. We used to do everything that normally makes a bad situation okay. It's as if once my parents' relationship went sour a year ago, so did ours, and the hatred just kept on building up...so much so that it doesn't want to go away.

I hope it goes away. I *hate* hating her.

Since being in the hospital, I've been asked by several people if I remember anything. Flashbacks keep coming to me, but I still cannot unravel the identity of my mystery attacker. I can't pinpoint their face or who they were walking away with. With time, I know everything may possibly come flooding back to me, and then I'll put the asshole away for good.

Seriously, I need revenge. I need to be okay again, to be normal again, because I'm far from it.

The recollection of everything that happened that night sits at the front of my memory. I practically asked for everything that happened, might as well have written on my forehead: *knock me down a peg or two.*

The nurse sweeps up the smashed glass at the bottom of the bed. I smile tightly and look away quickly, hoping she didn't see. My neck becomes red because of the heat rising up to my cheeks. I pick up my phone, pull back the fresh sheets, and get into the hospital bed.

"Excuse me," I ask politely.

The nurse stops sweeping. "Yes, my dear?"

"I, um…are you able to unlock my phone for me and get me to my voicemail?" I hold it out as far as my arm can reach. "Please."

She takes it off me. "Why not."

"Thanks." The nurse hands me the phone and places my finger over the right button to touch. "Tap when you're ready. I'll give you a few minutes and then I'll come back in to finish cleaning up."

I smile at her, grateful for her kindness. Once she's gone, I place the phone up to my ear and tap the screen.

"Alyssa, hey girl. If you're getting this, I hope you're okay. You've given me nightmares, like, seriously. When I found you on that floor, all that blood…and ugh, the smell. I didn't know what to do. Were you dead? Were you breathing? Like, Jesus Christ, you gave me the jeepers creepers." I laugh. "I can't believe you missed the first day of senior year!"

The automated voice starts speaking. "If you would like to delete this message, please press one. If you would like to return the phone call, press two." Noelle had rambled on so much she'd run over the allotted time. My finger hits the button, hoping it deletes the message and allows me to listen to the next one. "Your message has been deleted."

"I...erm...hi. If you're getting this, you must be okay. Yeah, that sounds stupid. Look, I don't really know what to say. My heart went into my gut when I found out what happened to you. I do truly hope you're okay. You deserve to be okay, Alyssa..." There are a few moments of silence. "I...well...I dunno what I want to say. Talk to you soon, Tommy." I sigh.

"If you would like to delete this message, please press one. If you would like to return the phone call, press two." My finger hesitates. *Do I speak to him?* I groan and drop the phone onto the bed next to me.

There's no question that rumors will have emerged at school. They're going to be brutal—I mean, the kids at school are cruel. Wherever teenagers are, you always have gossip, and let's not forget the bullying and lies. The rumors are probably along the lines of me being a slut and how it's a shame the blow to the head didn't knock me out for good. The funny thing is, they are going to get one hell of a shock, because I might be a stranger to my own eyes, but I'm still me. I'm ready to take one stride at a time and show them they'll have to try harder to knock me down.

If you're going to smack me over the head, make sure it kills me next time, because my revenge is going to be far worse than my death.

I promise you that.

It doesn't feel like a Wednesday, although I can't really say what a Wednesday feels like. The days are blurring into one while I'm still in the hospital. I keep my eyes shut while the nurses prod and handle me. It's starting to feel like a norm being in this routine; even the gelatin dessert is growing on me.

When the nurse finishes, she leaves, and I open my eyes. I look at my dad, and he's sitting with his head resting against his palm. The crinkles at either side of his eyes are defined intently in his skin. He doesn't have to worry about losing his hair due to stress because he's already bald and stubbly. He starts rubbing his chin where his unkempt grey beard is; since being in here with me, it's become the length of my little finger. The dark circles around his eyes aren't just because I see darkness; they're bags forming from the lack of sleep he's getting—that and the ageing.

He notices how I've been tossing and turning a lot while I sleep. Apparently, I'm shouting out, telling someone to stop hurting me and to think about what they're doing. He tells me I'm asking the person to leave me alone. By the end of the nightmare, I wake up, shaking, sweating, and screaming for it to stop. My dad and the doctors call these night terrors. Because of this, he's now constantly asking me to talk about everything, and I mean *constantly*. He tells me he's worried about my mental health, but I don't think he understands. I don't want to talk about it, and it's not even that I don't want to—it's more that I can't.

I have a feeling inside of me and I can't quite explain it. It's like I need to move on with my life, but I'm struggling to find the way to do that. This is how it's going to play out: the nurses will finish with whatever they have been told to do, they'll let the doctors know, and the doctors will crack on with a cure that will solve my problems. Then...then my life will go back to normal.

If you can call my life normal.

Dad continuously says to me it's not as simple as it appears. He says this in his know-it-all voice. Trying to explain that, though, is like talking to a deaf girl, not a blind one...if that's what I am.

I'm a survivor. I've made it this far.
Bring it on.

Fridays: normally the day you get excited about because it's the weekend, the end of the school week, and party central. It's normally the day you go to a house party and get completely blathered. Blathered, of course, means drunk. Fridays to me will now be the day I found out what's wrong with me.

Today is the day I find out my definite results. There's no turning back.

Standing at the bottom of my hospital bed is a doctor with a clipboard, and my dad and I are waiting patiently for her to begin.

She lifts each paper with delicacy. "Miss Darlington..." Her light feathered voice soothes me. "I notice you haven't been active much. Is this right?"

I cling to the clean sheet beneath me and allow the fresh cotton to tickle the end of my nose. "That's right, doc."

"I see." She turns another page. "I've also been told you only open your eyes occasionally. Is there something wrong? Do they hurt?"

"No, it doesn't hurt..." I look at the side of me, towards my dad's hard, lined shadow, then back to where the doctor is standing. "I—I like to pretend...pretend this isn't happening. If I keep my eyes shut, it isn't happening, is it?"

The swirl of her pen against paper etches inside me.

"I'll be right back, Miss Darlington." She walks out of the room and leaves me to sit and wait even longer.

Five minutes pass by then she re-enters the room. I listen closely to her feet shuffling against the wooden floor. I breathe in the air around me and I sniff the doctor's perfume before she even arrives by my side. The scent of lavender drifts up my nostrils, making them flare.

"Would you like to wait for your wife to arrive before proceeding, Mr. Darlington?" My dad's eyes linger on me for far too long, two black circles burning a hole into my head. I make out his outline turning due to the dim sunlight beaming through the window. He looks at the doctor and they stare at one another, longer than I'd like.

"Mom is coming, right?" I start to scratch my wrist, the same place as before. "She is going to be here for the results…right?" I ask desperately.

He sighs. He's always sighing. "Your mom had to stay with Mia." Mia is my cute-as-a-button little sister. "Please, doctor, continue." He gestures for the her to keep speaking.

"Well firstly, we have received the results—"

"Really?" Sarcasm rolls off the end of my tongue. "Here I was thinking you'd come to tell me about the morning weather."

Dad glares at me. "Alyssa, for God's sake."

I notice I'm irritable, uncomfortable in my own skin. "Sorry." I dip my head and keep scratching at my wrist, letting the sharp pain overtake me as I break the skin.

The doctor ignores both of us, and I can't blame her for that. I'm being a bitch, and my dad is practically telling me to give it a rest.

"The outcome of the tests is fantastic. Everything went according to plan and we now know the exact diagnosis and how we will be able to help you." My heart jumps and misses a beat, filling itself with joy and hope. *I'm about to be cured!* "However, I need to point out to you that after sustaining a head injury, you have become—"

"But I'm fine! I'll get better."

She turns a page over. "With the injury and the laundry detergent being poured continuously over your face, we won't be able to resolve what has happened."

"Go on." *Just say it.*

"Although you can partially see now, you will eventually become completely blind."

I can now feel the blood smearing all over my skin. I hide my wrist under the sheets.

"This will not be reversible." The doctor touches my shoulder. "What you have is something that is now part of you. It will stay with you. The harsh reality of this is that the only way you'll be able to cope with it is by accepting it."

My head drops five thousand feet under. I know the laundry detergent was in my eyes for far too long. With that and the forceful hit, I'm not surprised by the outcome, but the outcome suddenly feels more brutal than the attack. Knowing and understanding are two different things, and neither of them can help the pain I'm feeling.

"Surely there is something you can do..." I say innocently, like a small, helpless child. "Anything, please?"

"I'm sorry, Miss Darlington."

I drop my head into my hands and start to shake.

"Your brain is made up of many different nerve cells called neurons. I'm sure you're aware of this, as your father tells me you're a very bright young girl." *Bright young girl, who the hell is she...* "The neurons carry messages from the various parts of the body to a certain section of the brain, and these are then converted into functions."

This doesn't sound good.

"You are aware that sight is controlled by the occipital lobe, which is located in the back of the brain." I sit up farther, concentrating on her shadow attentively. "When you were attacked, the weapon didn't just make an impact on part of your head. It made contact with the back of your head. As the hours passed, you bled out, which then made it difficult for the messages to be carried to this part of the brain..." She places down her clipboard on the bed and walks closer. "You'll find, Miss Darlington, that the rest of the brain is trying to counteract this loss by slowly heightening the rest of your senses."

I look down to...anything. I just want to see something.

"I—I'm..." *Breathe.* "I'm...blind?"

My dad holds on to my visible hand above the sheets. I bury my other one deep between my legs. "Alyssa, I thought you already knew this?"

"If you've noticed, Miss Darlington, you're able to hear a lot more now than what you used to. You need to remember, you aren't blind as of yet. You can still see shadows and people's outlines, and you've still got some sense of where you are."

I lie still, my whole-body stiffening at the thought, trying to take in every word she's spoken. I have noticed I hear a lot better than I used to be able to, but I didn't think it was due to all this. I just assumed when they rinsed my eyes out, it caught my ears, taking away all that wax.

I'm a sucker for letting wax build up in my ears.

"Love, do you want me to explain everything to you, or do you understand?" Dad's hand becomes sweaty in my grasp. I know he's worried about my mental health, and he can't even speak without nearly choking on his words. I feel sorry for him having to be here while Mom sits comfortably at home. I know he wishes he could be there right now, reading Mia a bedtime story; princesses and monsters have to be better than this.

"It's fine. I understand." I lean my back against the pillows, and Dad passes me a glass of water. I take tiny sips, wetting my mouth.

"So, Miss Darlington, this is it. I'm officially discharging you. I just need to fill out some paperwork and then you can get yourself home to familiarity."

The nurse interrupts, "Doctor Loveday, you're needed in the reception area."

"I'll be right there." She nods her head slightly and turns back to me. "Remember, it will be a long process, and as a team, we will get you through this. I'd suggest waiting a week before going back to school, as it's going to be very difficult. Try to get your head around it and take your time, especially now that your friends and teachers may ask questions."

My jaw drops. "What? What do you mean, *ask questions*? How will they even know to ask questions?"

Silence has started to become a regular thing around here.

"I don't think you understand…" She sighs. "You will have to tell peers and teachers. You won't be able to keep this from them. You need as much help as you can get—"

Doctor Loveday is going to come face to face with the wrath of Alyssa.

"No. No, I can't." I shake my head.

"You will need new textbooks, books that are more suitable for your condition, for example, braille.

Counseling will be scheduled into your day because what you've just gone through was a traumatic thing. There is so much support you will need and can receive, but you need to let peers and those around you know." She scribbles her pen across the paper. "You, your family, and your school can discuss everything when you're ready."

Her answer hits me like I'm in a car that's braking too fast at a red light.

"Please..." I try to reach my hand forward to grab her, but I miss. "I can't tell anyone, not yet. I won't be able to cope at school knowing everyone thinks I'm a freak."

Dad's breath hitches in his throat. "Oh, kiddo."

"I just need more time. I'll do anything you want me to. Please just try to...try to find a way to let me save my dignity—like, anything. Please? It's all I have left." I crawl onto my hands and knees and make my way to the end of the bed. I look at her, face to face. My dad tries to pull me back by my shoulder, but I shrug him off. "One month, one month is all I need. Freedom is all I need. After that, I will tell my friends. I'll tell everyone. Just please, please, please...give me this and I'll go to counseling, I'll help the police. I'll even sit through more Goddamn tests!"

"Miss Darlington, I—"

"Please! Technically, I'm not even blind yet." I place my palms together, praying.

She stays quiet.

There's another sigh. "I have rules," she says.

I shoot up onto my knees, and before I know it, I'm hugging her, my eyes wide, surprised. She's stiff in my embrace. "Sorry, sorry…" I mumble. I grin so hard my cheeks stretch to their limit, squeezing at the sides and ready to burst. "Shoot."

The doctor folds her arms in front of her chest. "I will have to tell your teachers—"

"But—"

"No buts. I will explain the situation, as I'm not allowed to let you go into a school where nobody will know. It's illegal, and I could lose my job. I'll run it past the other doctors, but I am happy to pull some strings, just for a month." She sighs again. *I wish everyone would stop with the flipping sighs.* "You will be given a guide dog. I know you may be able to see shadows, but roads are dangerous. Outside of school hours, you will use it. The only exception is if you are with someone who knows about your disability." I nod, like a nodding bulldog, still grinning from ear to ear. "While we're on this subject, I will have to let one of your friends know, because while you are inside the school, you will need a chaperone."

The tiny-framed, skinny but tall woman just told me something that will destroy my relationship with my friends. *Well that's just great.*

Everything's grey.

Four

Giggles permeate the room, squeaky like a tiny mouse. They overwhelm me so much I have to open my eyes groggily.

I'm about to keep them open and then remember, *what's the point?* It's not as if I can see where the soft, musical sound of joyful laughter is coming from.

I have been home from the hospital for a week and all I have done is lie here, in my king-sized bed, feeling numb. The familiarity of home is blissful. I'm no longer eating gelatin dessert or stone-cold mashed potatoes. I'm able to stuff my face with leftover pizza and ice cream. I don't have to think hard about where things are, as I know my dressing table sits at the foot of my bed, just against the wall, under the window. I don't need anyone to guide me around my bedroom; if I place my feet on the floor and step forward three steps, I'll reach a door, and that door is the entrance to my ensuite bathroom.

When we moved over to America, we didn't have a home straight away. We spent months living out of our suitcases, in and out of hotels. Mom and Dad were searching for our forever home and struggled to find the right one. Back then Mom was indecisive. Back then, Dad wanted to make Mom happy, and nothing has changed in that department, because that's all he wants to do now, nine years down the line.

We eventually found the house—this house. It has four bedrooms, two bathrooms, and a white picket fence. It's a place we call home. It's nothing compared to the Carlisle family dwelling, but then wealth isn't everything.

I wish someone would tell my mother that.

The loveable giggles emerge again.

I move my head slightly to be able to concentrate on the bedroom's features. I use my ears, making sure they are wide open so I catch the sound of laughter traveling around me. Several sounds emerge all at once: the constant dripping of the raindrops outside my window, the twitching thud of a branch against the brickwork from the oak tree outside, and flustered voices from downstairs as my parents bicker about their life together. All of these sounds make me more aware of my surroundings.

The giggles stop. I smile slightly, wrapping my fingers around the edge of my mustard and grey duvet. I pull it back, freeing my legs and allowing them to hang off the side of my bed.

The giggles just won't go away, continuing to drift in and out. This time, they emerge closer to me, the sound muffled as if someone is holding their hand over their mouth. I try to look around my bedroom, but no shadows appear, and the light remains off. I study the darkness intently, listening to the bed frame creak from the movement of my legs. The floorboards creak after each giggle is let out, but all I see is the only thing that seems to be surrounding me: darkness.

Before I blink, the loudest snort I've ever heard lets rip from Mia Darlington's mouth, and two small arms wrap themselves around my waist, hurling me backward until I'm flat against the mattress. She climbs on top of me and bounces, using my belly as a trampoline. The giggles and snorting all combine and they are so close to my ear, I start to feel claustrophobic.

I listen closely to her steady breathing and feel the scent of oranges and strawberries attack me. "Mia, you're adorable and all, but you can't keep doing this to me, you little brat." I gently flip her onto her back, tower over her, and start tickling her—the one thing she can't stand—until she pleads mercy. My hands venture around the sides of her body, just under her armpits, and repeatedly move in the same circular motion. Eventually, Mia cries out, and just before I reach for her feet, she snorts a belly laugh and thrashes them.

"Please! Stop! Alyssa, I can't…" She inhales deeply. "Breathe." She releases a puff of air.

I try my hardest not to get kicked in the face. That's the last thing I need, but then again, what harm can it cause now?

I make her squeal louder. "What do you say?"

"You're-the-best-big-sister-in-the-whole-wide-world." Mia rushes the words out so fast, I swear it's done in one mouthful.

I raise my eyebrows and slowly move my hands away from her. "What else, missy?"

"When I grow up to be as old as you—"

I snort, exactly like she did. "Oi! Cheeky."

"I want to be just like you."

My smile widens and my eyes gleam, sparkling at her. There is so much love spread across my face, so much love for her. I lift her up into a sitting position and she perches on the edge of my bed.

"Jeez, Mia moo, you only had to say sorry." I reach my finger out slowly to where I believe her button nose to be and tap it.

I cautiously direct my hands and knees to crawl beside her and sit next to her, her tiny frame so delicate. I brush against the side of her arm, which is barely touching the lower part of mine. I bring my legs from underneath me and wrap them into a cross-legged position. I sit with my eyes open, but the only picture they take in consists of blurry specks of grey.

I need to keep reminding myself I'm not completely blind *yet*.

Mia's heavy breathing is now the only sound in the still room. It feels peaceful to be sitting with her like this—not talking, just being with each other.

Since coming home from the hospital and being on the verge of completely losing my eyesight, my nose and ears are making up the loss by working that much harder. The smell of crispy toast, slightly burnt, swiftly enters my nostrils, mixed with a delightful essence of fresh cotton from the landing. It's coming from the plug-in air freshener Mom keeps just outside my door. Whispers I used to struggle to hear are now so dominant, loud enough for me to be able to catch each and every single word. Sometimes, that's not a good thing, especially when it comes to overhearing how much pressure you're causing for your parents.

  I struggle to see Mia or her face to tell me what she's thinking, but on the plus side, I've known her since she was a twinkle in our father's eye. I know she's thinking about what happened to me.

  I sense her glaring and I don't mind, because I know she's glaring with complete love and fascination. Call it a sixth sense. I also think she's worrying about what I'm going to do to her if I catch her.

  Being the eldest of the two, you're normally the one they look up to, the one they admire, adore, and believe can change the world. That's how I've always seen it to be. My parents have always told me to be a good role model for Mia and If I got that right, I will get anything right. How can I do that now, though, when she knows I've been to parties full of drinking, drugs, and sex? (okay, maybe not the sex part—being six, I hope she doesn't even know the word *sex*.) I just...I'm finding it hard to comprehend the whole *role model* thing. How can I be that for her now? How will I ever be that for her?

My bedroom door bangs loudly against the neutral brown walls. A darkened, broad-shouldered figure is standing in the doorway. Calm down, kids— I'm afraid this isn't where I tell you my knight in shining armor is about to knock me off my feet and carry me away to never-never land. Don't get too excited, unless you like elderly men who have shiny bald heads and grey stubble. That's right: my dad.

"Right, love." He holds his hand out toward Mia. "Let's leave your sister to get ready for school."

I picture her short, ash blonde ringlets shining against the orange morning sunlight and her cute dimpled smile appearing across her face. "But...Daddy, I want to stay with Lyssa."

"To keep tormenting her? I don't think so, kiddo." Dad picks her up off the bed and places her on his back, turning it into a piggyback ride.

"Dur, of course. Just because Lyssa..." Mia pauses. "I'm not going to treat her any different to how I normally do, Daddy."

Just because I'm disabled.

See what I mean about being a role model? That idea can kiss my ass and fly. Even my sister can't admit I'm disabled. She's six, yeah, doesn't understand, yeah—but she understands what's wrong, and is that so hard to say in front of me?

Everything about that night is going through my mind, time and time again. I'm dreading seeing Ashton. What do I do, ask him outright whether we slept together? Because *that* doesn't sound needy at all. What if we did the deed while I was unconscious?

Rip his balls to shreds, Alyssa. I guess that can work.

I don't understand what I did so terribly wrong for someone to cause so much pain and heartache. First and foremost, I wouldn't say I'm a horrible person, and secondly, it's not like I have any enemies, especially ones so psychotic. Who could possibly hate me so much, enough to do *this*?

I know one thing: there's no stopping me until I find that person, and they are going to pay one way or another. I swear it.

I had plans after finishing my senior year: head southeast to college and then travel the world. My plans were huge. I also had hopes to enter my senior year on a high, not to enter it two weeks later, that's for sure.

Today's the first day back for me. You know when you get exhausted from such a wild summer, then it gets closer to the first day of another school year and you actually become excited to see everyone and attempt to take over the school…yeah, I'm not getting that feeling this year. I'm getting a guilty feeling because today, every student I talk to or interact with in any shape or form will assume I'm okay. I can't stand those people that assume. Everyone will rush around the halls all fine and dandy, forgetting that I was attacked. They'll all be innocent-looking, and I won't even know if it was them who did this to me. Let's face it—the scumbag will be walking the same hallways.

My mom's constantly asking me how I'm feeling about going back to school, especially knowing the attacker could be amongst those who call themselves my friends; she doesn't need to be Sherlock to know the answer to her useless questions. I've already had the lecture on how if Noelle's parents had been there, this wouldn't have happened. How she gets off on being a mother, I have no idea. The change from last year to now is crazy—she's a different person altogether, and no one understands why.

My dad coughs, clearing his throat and breaking me out of my trance, yanking me firmly back into the reality of the here and now. He taps his watch. "I know you can't see a clock, but I'm afraid that doesn't excuse you for being late for the first day of your senior year!"

Mia is placed back on her feet and she runs toward me.

"Mia, let's leave her to get ready," Dad says again.

"It's fine." I grab her hands as she leans against my legs. "She can stay and help." I'm not tough enough to be by myself. I'm not tough enough, full stop.

My dad sighs in defeat. "Right. You have half an hour and then your mom wants you both downstairs."

The door shuts gently. I slacken my grip from around Mia's sweaty hands and uncross my legs so they're hanging down.

This is going to be fun.

Heart-warmingly, Mia grabs hold of my hand again. "I'll direct, if ya want?"

"Okay, let's do this, Mia moo." I push up from my bed, and she helps me stand. My legs are like jelly and my brain is finding it difficult to connect the dots fast enough to tell them where they're needed. Mia lets go of my hand and crosses my bedroom floor. The greyscale tone becomes lighter, making it easier for me to see.

"All you need to do now is walk," Mia's sweet voice reassures me, but all I can think about is how it's gotten to this point where I'm being told what to do by my little sister.

Before taking my first step, I take a good look in front of me, and I'm able to make out the dark door frame. All I have to do is take three long strides. *One.*

Mia starts pointing. "Now move that way."

"Which way?" I ask.

"Um, left. No, right. Urgh, I dunno my left and right." She comes over to me and picks up my left hand. "That way."

Why left?

Mia's urging me to move, so I do. As a big sister, I want to make sure she knows I trust her, so I follow her instructions, down to a T. Mia wouldn't use my disability to lie to me, would she?

My feet shuffle to the left.

"Stop!" she shouts.

Two.

"Now what?" I look around in dismay.

"Shuffle a bit more, and you'll be right in front of the door."

I instantly sense the smile forming on her face. I start to understand what she's trying to do. I notice the door far from my reach, and if I take another step forward, I will most certainly be faceplanting into the wall. Of course, Mia will find this hilarious—so I indulge her.

"Right, I trust you Mia moo." I glance to where she's standing. There's a ball of a shadow around her, which makes me assume her hands are cupping her face, silently laughing at me. I lift my foot as if I'm ready to take a step forward and make sure she believes I'll do it, but then I turn sharply and run at her. My arms pick her up in a bear hug and swing her around while she squeals. I concentrate more on my footing than what's around me. The snorting starts, so I place her feet back onto the ground.

A tiny hand with small fingers reaches up to touch my cheek. I smile at her, hoping the reassurance spreads through me.

"Lyssa, if I can, I want to be like you when I grow up, in every way," Mia whispers. "You're the best."

Tears roll down my cheeks, streaming from both eyes, and Mia wipes them away before I have the chance. I embrace her tightly into a cuddle, because no matter how many times I've fought with her, shoved her aside, or wished she'd go away, she's my little sister, and to have a sister who still looks at you, even now, with so much admiration—it's magnificent.

My darling angel.

Suddenly, there's a bang from downstairs. "If you don't both get down these stairs in five minutes, I will feed your breakfast to the dog." Another bang echoes through the house and our mom goes back into the kitchen.

I hurriedly ask Mia to grab my clothes. While she does, I brush my teeth, spray some deodorant and I run a brush through my hair. She hands me a top and a pair of jeans. I slide my jacket on, over my t-shirt, get myself ready, and grab my sister's hand, leading us both down the stairs for breakfast. I might have been imagining it, but I swear I hear Mia chuckling to herself.

Sitting at the kitchen table, I long to see the faces of my family. That longing is pulling at every inch of my body, tearing me apart on the inside because I know it isn't ever going to happen. I reach out in front of me and tap my hand against the table, trailing it across until I'm touching the edge of an empty plate, and I begin to tap the center of it.
"Hungry?" Mom pours herself a fresh cup of coffee.
My stomach grumbles, replying to my mom's tossed-out question. "Yeah."
I listen to the fridge's motor rumbling.
"Sorry love, I told you I would feed your breakfast to the dog if you didn't come down in time. You know that's my rule."
I glare at her then glare at Charlie, our Labrador. There's a steady thump, thump, thump against the cupboard door where he's wagging his tail eagerly.
Greedy mutt.
I would have never imagined my mom could get even more heart-wrenchingly cold than she already was. She opens a box full of wounds, a box full of sadness that's suffocating me slowly. I'm never going to see the sunlight again. I scrunch my face up and shiver, allowing a single, salty tear to run down my

right cheek. I quickly wipe it away with the back of my hand.

My mom takes tiny sips of her boiling-hot coffee, drinking it slowly so she cherishes each mouthful. She taps her fingers against the flowery ceramic cup, and then the doorbell interrupts the beat. "That will be Tommy. He rang this morning and asked if you wanted a lift to school." She slurps. "I said yes."

I picture her sickening smile, like a Cheshire cat. She goes to answer the door for me. I bet she's loving it—my destruction. I panic at the sound of Tommy's voice and shoot a look of terror in my father's direction. "She hasn't—"

As if reading my mind, he answers. "No, she didn't tell him." Dad places his lips on my forehead. "Have a nice day, love."

Mia reaches out and cradles me in her arms. She passes me my bag and I steadily walk toward the open door. Vibrant chatter passes easily between my mom and Tommy; the fact that they get on extremely well irritates me. In fact, I think she gets along with him better than she does with her own daughter.

"Good morning, beautiful." Tommy's voice makes my heart ache. It spreads to my stomach, making me queasy. I hate not being able to see his cheesy grin and hazelnut eyes.

"You kids have fun!" Mom says, pretending to care. I stiffen as she wraps her arms around my neck and cuddles me, showing me some sort of affection.

"Erm…" I pat the top of her shoulder a few times. "Thanks."

Tommy automatically places his hand on the lower part of my back and guides me to his Jeep, and I'm over the moon to not have to direct myself. His hand drops and with a single click, he opens the passenger door for me, just like normal.

"Thanks," I mummer quietly.

There's a beat and neither of us meets the other's gaze; the last time I saw him, he left me standing alone even though I begged him to stay. I finally meet his gaze intensely, baring my soul and searching deep into his, trying to figure him out. You would think nine years of friendship would allow me to do this quickly. I recognize his figure, using the shadow to my advantage, and I know two little crinkles appear on either side of his mouth as he smiles. That smile always made my face go deep red.

He sits in the driver's seat and breaks the silence. "I haven't heard—"

"I'm sorry—"

"—from you," Tommy finishes.

I awkwardly laugh. "Sorry, go on."

"No, no, I'm sorry. You start."

"Where have you been?" I ask him, not sure if I want his answer. As long as Charlotte Summers' name isn't included in his reply, I think I'll be assured.

"I tried to visit you while you were in the hospital. I was worried…" The backs of Tommy's fingers brush my bare cheek. I turn my head away, my face turning beet red. "They told me you didn't want to see anyone, so I guess I just decided to wait until you came home."

"Oh." I played with the silver bracelet around my wrist—the same bracelet he bought me when we were fourteen years old.

"I left you a voicemail…did you get it?"

"I got it," I reply bluntly.

"Oh good." He dips his head. "Well, anyway, when I heard you were coming home, I knew everything was going to be okay."

"From who?"

He looks back up at me. "Your mom." He keeps his eyes steady. "Everything is okay, isn't it?" I recognize the tone of his voice—he's happy to see me, but that doesn't stop me from crying. "Oh God, no. Don't cry. Why are you crying, babe?" Tommy quickly leans in toward me and wipes away the tears, tears I wish had never emerged.

My best friend is caring about me, but he's too late to jump on that ship, as that ship sailed two weeks ago. Where was he at that party when I needed him the most? Oh, that's right, nowhere to be seen. I have so many questions for him that need answers, but I have no idea where to start, so instead, I lean back against the passenger seat.

"It's nothing. Don't worry about it." I sniff and turn my head to make it appear like I'm looking out the window, like a normal teenage girl would.

Tommy puts the car in drive, allowing me to feel the pull as his car drives farther away from my house and closer toward my social hell.

Along the way he reaches for my hand, making me relax. He squeezes gently, and it starts to feel nice. I decide Investigator Darlington can wait to come out to play another day.

The brown shoulder bag my mom bought me just after the attack hangs at my side, and my leather jacket is wrapped around my body like a safety net. Principal Williamson stands within the crowd of students, near the entrance.

"What does he want?" Tommy asks while we walk toward him.

I loop my arm through his. "Huh, dunno."

My name continues to be bellowed above the loud and excited high school chatter. Shadows are dotted around, which makes it harder than I ever thought it would be to recognize my classmates. Everyone's got the same fuzzy outlines; the only thing that makes it possible for me to tell the difference between the guys and the girls is that the guys have broader shapes while the girls are a lot more petite—that is, if you're dismissing the larger, more proportionate girls, which I'd never do.

"Welcome back, Alyssa." Principal Williamson greets me kindly, hovering his hand gently between my shoulder blades. He guides me in the right direction and does it so casually that anyone watching wouldn't suspect a thing. "Will Mr. Henderson be joining us?"

"Um..." I glance at Tommy behind me. "Nope," I say to Principle Williamson. I wave Tommy off. "I'll see you later."

He doesn't argue, agreeing to leave me be, and heads off in the opposite direction.

We're walking through the hallways, listening to the hustle and bustle as kids barge into us, slam their locker doors, and run along in various directions, afraid to miss first period.

"We decided to put you into counseling before going into your regular classes. As a team, we think this is the best option to help you adjust," Principal Williamson tells me with an uneven voice, speaking a bit strangely, as if he didn't get a say in the matter.

An odor wavers under my nostrils, and there's no doubt two large circles have formed under his armpits from the constant sweats he's known to get.

Kids torment him for it, every day, yet he keeps coming back. I actually feel sorry for him.

"Hey, Alyssa." Lindsey Montelowe passes us by. She's the captain of the Valley View cheerleaders, the queen bee.

"Miss Montelowe, I'm glad to see you're in high spirits. I hope you're heading to class," Principal Williamson sternly suggests.

"Of course." I assume Lindsey's wearing her red and white cheerleading Go View! outfit and is flipping her highlighted brown hair. "Glad to see you're healthy, Alyssa. We were all very worried about you."

"Mmhmm." I nod my head. "Better than I'll ever be," I lie.

I have to give her credit—she's very good at acting. The show she puts on could possibly pass as London's West End material, but she doesn't fool me. Lindsey Montelowe worried about me? Is that a pig I've just seen flying across the sky? She and her cheerleading squad all hate me. In fact, I think they despise me, all because Lindsey's ex-boyfriend and I had ten minutes in heaven in junior year. The thing is, nothing even happened. If there are people who'll never love me, it's them; otherwise I'm known as the beloved one—at least that was what I thought.

I continue walking, nodding my head slightly and smiling, hoping my peers don't think I'm ignorant. I keep placing one foot in the front of the other, putting all my trust in Principal Williamson to guide me to my first session. As we walk along the corridors of Valley View High, the hushed whispers are close enough for me to hear.

"I heard through the grapevine she's wearing a wig—they had to shave her hair off to be able to do an operation on her head." Isabella Langley, a junior cheerleader, snickers.

Her friends join in. "You can tell. Like, did she even brush her hair this morning?"

I quickly and defensively run my fingers through my auburn strands. The girls laugh louder, loud enough to grab the attention of every single person standing in the hallway. Because of the bigger person I believe I am, I continue walking and don't look back.

Well, I heard through the grapevine that this school sucks.

Principal Williamson brings us to a stop. "Right Alyssa, we're here." He claps his hands together. "So, just go straight in and head for a seat. I know you can see shadows, which will help you find your way." He starts to look around, the shadow of his head moving sporadically. "I must go. Please, come find me if you need anything."

"Thanks." I push the door open with a light shove and slip into the silent office.

Coming through the open window, a light breeze swirls around me, making me shiver. I tighten my jacket around my waist and rub both my arms. I detect a whiff of dried fruit and cinnamon, so I pinch my nose, hoping to get rid of the smell. I look around the office and see a shadow sitting behind the desk with a chair opposite, so, without any hesitation, I sit myself down. Quietly, I wait for the guidance counselor to start speaking.

"Hey to you too, you ignorant bitch." Unfortunately for me, it isn't who I expect it to be. Noelle scrapes her chair backward. "What the hell are you wearing, Alyssa?"

I look down at myself, forgetting I dropped my jacket to hang loosely around my waist as I sat down, putting my t-shirt on display. "Um…"

"Care Bears. You're wearing Care Bears, Lyss." She laughs harshly. "Really, that's what you decide to wear? How old are you, six?"

No, but my sister is.

One sentence after another gets tossed at me and I'm unable to get a word in edgewise. It's my senior year and I'm wearing a Care Bears top. I'm going to kill Mia and dig her grave myself. "I—"

"What are you doing here? I didn't know you did counseling—I didn't even know *I did* counseling. I was asked to come, too. Strange, huh?" She huffs frantically. "What a load of—"

The door creaks open, cutting her off.

"Ah." There's a sigh of relief as the third person walks in. "Wonderful." She walks toward us, her stride deliberate. "We're all here then. Thank you for coming, ladies. It looks like we can begin."

Well this is just fan-bloody-tastic.

Five

Noelle strides across the room, headstrong and on a mission. "You...no! You have to be joking. You're jokin—"

She makes everything more dramatic with the huffing and puffing like the big bad wolf. I place my head into my hands, shaking it from side to side and groaning as I think about how this is going to pan out. Pure annoyance drifts through my body from the inside out. I grunt and slap the chair arm.

"Jesus Christ," I murmur under my breath.

The overused spray of perfume—like someone has poured the whole bottle over themselves—lingers in the room. I rub my eyes with my curled-up fists and then place two fingers on my temples, moving in a circular motion, hoping it will help the impending headache.

I think they need to have a lesson on how to apply perfume.

"It can't be true. I don't believe it." Noelle points to the woman sitting across from us and within the shadows, Noelle's palms are now turning upward, and in my direction, her arms and fingers outstretched. "Look at her." Nobody looks at me. "LOOK AT HER!"

I look intently at a short-bobbed shadow who I presume is the counselor. I imagine Noelle's frown big and her eyes in slits as she tells the lady she's wrong one last time.

"Y-You're a-a liar," she stutters.

Only being able to see grey is starting to irritate me. I'm trying to hold on to something that obviously isn't there to begin with. It's similar to walking down the street on a summer day and seeing your own shadow on the pavement; it's larger than it should be, and it's as if you don't really exist, as if it's not you to begin with. That's how I feel while I'm in front of people. It's as though I'm suffocating, like my brain is trying to recognize something but my eyes won't let me.

"Pft, Alyssa's not blind."

I lift my eyebrows toward the ceiling, letting wrinkles appear on my forehead. Noelle's persistence and determination to prove I'm not is annoying, to prove that if I'm blind I'm carrying a disease that's contagious to her, and this moment is the moment I never wanted to happen.

Noelle's standing on her feet and she kicks the table leg while clenching her fists. She starts to pace back and forth, ranting endless words under her breath.

"Noelle, please sit down so we can discuss this. I'm sure Alyssa wants to explain everything to you," Maggie says.

I bite my tongue. I wanted to be the one to tell her. I never wanted her to find out this way.

"What's there to say? She would have told me." There's a piercing whisper from Noelle's lips and my chest tightens at how hurt she sounds; it slides off her tongue like a knife sliding out of her back.

She keeps up the pace, back and forth, each footstep like a drumming heart, echoing around me: one, two, three, pause. Then it starts all over again, the rhythm of the pattern becoming a part of me.

"Just because you're some sort of psychopathic, magic, supportive witch who listens to everyone's bullsh—"

I gasp.

Noelle sighs. "That doesn't mean I have to listen to yours." She sits down and shifts her ass against the cushion of the chair.

I purse my lips and decide against talking—I know there's no speaking to Noelle while she's on a verbal rampage, unless I want to be axed down and buried deep in the forest, along with anyone else who dares to speak out of turn. I want so badly to pipe up and tell her to wind her neck in a little, because that magic, supportive witch is telling the truth. Unfortunately for Noelle's target, I don't have the guts to do it.

"Look at her eyes—they seem perfectly normal..." Noelle moves closer toward me. "They're the same col—" She stands in front of me and her voice breaks. I look around, trying to figure out what's going on. "Your eyes, Lyss," she says, choking on her words. "They're not blue anymore...they're pale grey."

The warmth of her breath circles around my face, her nose inches away from mine, and the smell of peppermint makes my mouth sour. Each word she utters, she utters in disbelief. How can I answer? How do I make everything okay?

"I'm s-s-sorry. I'm sorry, Noelle."

I'm glad blindness is going to overtake me because then I'll never again have to see the shock and horror plastered all over her face. Guilt starts to consume me, eating me up from the inside out. I hear footsteps scuff toward the seat beside me and there's a light thud as she sits down.

Our guidance counselor coughs loudly. "Ladies..." Shuffling her papers, she goes silent for a few moments. "I'll now explain why you're both here." The woman's shadow is very soft, yet her figure stands fiercely in a tall stance, making me aware that she's in charge, always. The hairs on her head stand up on their ends in every direction. Her fingers start to tap the desk, starting with her index finger and ending with her little pinkie; it's Goddamn annoying.

"Noelle." I glance in her direction. "Talk to me, please. Like, you know I'd have told you," I barely whisper. I'm still glaring in her direction but have no luck in getting her attention, not even a slight grunt. My hand reaches out to try to touch her, but all I grab is air.

Noelle's pissed off, but can I blame her?

"Right, listen up ladies. I haven't got all day." Did I just hear her yawn? She picks up her pen and looks at us both. "I'm Mrs. Hall. You may call me Maggie while we are having these sessions, but out in the hallways, I expect respect just like every other teacher. Therefore, call me Mrs. Hall. Got it?"

I turn to look at Noelle again, to see if I can figure out whether she's actually paying attention. All I see is her dipped head. A sweet perfume with a kick of spice mixed with roses surrounds us—her all-time favorite.

"So, Alyssa, I completely understand the hatred and denial you're feeling, especially now that I've just told Noelle the one thing you wanted to tell her, but everything happens for a reason. Your mother called us this morning and thought it would be best if we were the ones to tell her, so we came to a mutual agreement."

It's like someone has just stabbed me in the back with a blunt knife.

I wonder, if my mom says jump, does the school ask how high?

"Now that it's out in the open, we can start to discuss what happened to you." Mrs. Hall—Maggie—comes to stand at the front of her desk, perching so casually. "These sessions are here to help, to help you remember what happened. The school, the police, and all of us want to work together to try to unlock your memory."

"Pick at it, great," I mutter under my breath. "I've already given my statement to the police." I start to bite my fingernails.

"Yes, you have. That's completely right, but now we feel like you're blocking the events out so you don't have to relive them, and if you can let us try to help you then maybe a very important piece will rise to the surface." Maggie taps her fingers once more.

"Why is Noelle here?"

"I'd rather not be," she huffs.

"Noelle's here so you can speak your piece, and then if she understands and is willing to help, we will let her be your guide."

"Her guide?" Noelle grumbles. The contrast of lighting helps me to see her dark, thin brows bowing, and I know she's annoyed. She has no understanding of what's going on.

I stand up and start to pace back and forth. I place my fingers around each object on the drawers against the back wall. I hold them delicately: figurines, papers, pens, and everything an office needs. I run my fingers across the smooth surface, guiding me to the end, and I place my hand over a picture frame; I know straight away by the rectangle shape and the cut-out stand sticking outward on the back that it's a frame, but all the objects I touch are missing one thing: they're missing detail.

"Alyssa, why don't you tell us what happened to you that night and how you feel about it? If by the end, Noelle feels she wants to ask questions, she may do so." Maggie lets the pen swirl across the paper, making me lightheaded.

I sit down, not wanting to share. "Okay." I sigh, turning halfway in my chair, speaking more toward Noelle than Maggie, hoping she'll listen. "I know how drunk I was, and I regret everything. You don't understand just how much. Dancing with all those guys, kissing other people's boyfriends...we both know it wasn't my usual approach. I saw the hatred plastered all over your face, the disapproval of my best friend, and now I understand why you scolded me so much."

I think about how to continue.

"Alyssa?" Noelle whispers.

"Everything you said to me was right. I was being a bitch, but don't worry, it wasn't just you who didn't want anything to do with me—Tommy didn't either. There were people who did, though, and I let them."

My mind drifts from the words spilling out of my mouth, spiralling into my consciousness. Before I can blink, I remember the events like it was yesterday: someone's soft but firm hand gripped my elbow and pulled me away from the crowd I danced amongst. I could hardly stand up. I wanted to say no, wanted them to let me go, but they continued to dance with me. My insides were destroyed, and I knew I could be sick at any moment. I was completely pissed off that I was being treated like a ragdoll, dragged continuously, but I was too drunk to even slur out one syllable.

My arms were thrown over some guy's neck, and they found his dark, unkempt hair. I remember the way his mouth curled up at either side, his grin causing a tug in my stomach, but it was soon gone from the puke starting to boil. I knew who the guy was—he was the guy I'd tried so hard to impress all night. Conan Dwight: the gorgeous, dark-haired, masculine God every girl would kill to have a dance with. I remember him asking if I was okay and I did the worse thing possible—I just grunted.

The sound of Maggie's ballpoint pen tapping against her desk brings me back to the here and now. I automatically reach my hand out to touch Noelle. I'm in shock that the memory even came to me, the memory of Conan dancing with me. In my head, he hadn't spoken to me all night, hadn't acknowledged my existence, but in reality, he had; I was just too drunk to even remember.

"What happened, Lys?" Noelle turns in her seat and reaches her finger up to trace my eyes while waiting patiently for my answer.

I stay quiet, dropping my head to the ground slightly. I ended up alone. "I stumbled into your garage, and I saw the cars. I figured if I stayed there, maybe someone I knew, someone I trusted would find me. I just wanted to go home. I thought you might show up to try to make amends. I knew I didn't deserve that, but I still hoped for the best."

"Oh, Lyss..." Noelle gently pulls me into a familiar, warm embrace. "You're fine now—you're safe."

I hold on to her tightly, hoping and praying I'm not dreaming this. I need her here so badly. I need her to understand it all.

"I'm s-sorry Noelle." I lean up and look at her, seeing a dark-as-the-night-sky face staring back at me. "You're my best friend. I wanted to tell you straight away, I just didn't know how."

"You don't need to explain any more. I understand. I'm here for you, you poor, poor thing." Noelle links her little finger with mine, squeezes, and places her soft lips over the two of them. "Always and forever."

The room is silent; it's finally over, and I manage to let out a massive sigh of relief.

"I'm sorry to break up the love, but I will need you to continue. We're making progress."

I sit back out of Noelle's embrace, unlinking our pinkies. I wipe away the wet, salty tears underneath my eyes and pat my cheeks, leaving red blotches behind. I allow myself to take one big breath.

I reach out for Noelle's hand, finding comfort and support. "I was slouched against a black Mercedes and could see your mom's GT in the distance. It was like the world was ending for me. I looked down at the ground and it looked as if it was moving beneath me. I stumbled backward, and I knew it was the alcohol making me feel that way. I needed to go home, sober up. I had a hard pit in the bottom of my stomach and it felt like something bad was going to happen. I dreaded it." Tears keep rolling down my face like a stream. If I collected them all, I could probably fill the Mississippi River.

I hear Noelle sobbing at my side, sniffling into a tissue, and I hate myself for making her cry.

"Keep going, Alyssa. You're doing great," Maggie says from behind her desk. I'd forgotten she's still there.

"Guess I was right about the bad thing, huh. Imagine that." I half-heartedly laugh, using the back of my free arm to wipe my face. "I wished I could go back into the house with you lot, somewhere safe. I just sat there and prayed someone would come get me. I wanted Tommy to take me home." Noelle rubs her hand up and down my right arm, trying to make everything okay. "Everywhere was dark. Something possessed me to go into that garage, and it allowed my body to break down. The room was quiet, too quiet—creepy quiet. Before I could process the situation I had gotten myself into, I had company, and you don't know how relieved I felt that I had someone there to help me. Then it happened—laundry detergent was poured all over me, making me drown, not only in that but the mixture of my own sobs and my own body substances. I was drowning good and proper, and before I knew it, I passed out."

I wipe my nose with the back of my hand and sniff. Maggie finally hands the tissues to us both. Memories are coming forward into my head and it's too much for me to handle. I'm struggling to compose myself even a little bit. I try to process them quickly, but before I get a glimpse of the first one, a second one arrives, and it's starting to drive me insane.

I remember lying on the cold hard floor of the garage, thinking about everything, everything I had done—everything that had been done to me, including having sex while unconscious.

I lay there, still, and I wanted Tommy so badly. I wanted him to take me home and make a joke about it being another party he only attended for me. I thought about his arms around my body, bringing some warmth to me, making me long for it—not in a sexual way, but a protective way—to keep me safe. My body shivered near the Mercedes and what felt like hours passed me by. Suddenly, I woke up to footsteps coming toward me, and they echoed around the room, making it seem more dramatic than it actually was. The painful throbbing throughout my body overrode my mind. I whimpered at the lack of energy I had left.

In Maggie's office, the events of that night start to tumble out in clear view, onto a blank sheet of paper, allowing me to remember those memories I'd thought to be locked away: my clear, crystal blue eyes had widened, becoming terrified of the large crowbar being held above me. I locked my eyes onto it and was petrified as they swung it back and forth while they cackled.

Maggie and Noelle are intently looking at me. I shiver, grasping the arms of my chair, hoping and praying the session is over soon. I sit still, and all I hear is Noelle's voice repeatedly asking if I'm okay.

"Alyssa," Noelle says. "Alyssa?"

It's like a weight has been placed on my shoulders and now I can't get rid of it.

"Do you remember something?" Maggie asks.

I have to get out of here before I get sick, before I start to block my mind completely, stopping those memories I need to remember.

"No, I don't," I lie. I remember coming in and out of consciousness…I remember as my hand tried to reach out for anybody, anything.

~

My eyesight blurred, burning my view, and my head pounded hard against my skull. It felt like a ticking time bomb, ready to explode. I looked over at the door I had come through and focused my blurred vision. I noticed as he entered the room, but before I could realize what he was doing, he was gone. Looking at me in awe, most likely terrified by my limp body, was Ashton Marston. I reached my arm out toward him, pleading for his help, but he walked backward, out the door. Before falling back unconscious, I said one thing: "Help me."

~

Noelle grabs my shoulders as I start to breath harder. "I think she's hyperventilating." Her hands start shaking me. "People can do that, right?" Noelle asks Maggie, wanting reassurance.

I want to laugh. I'm laughing on the inside, but on the outside my breathing starts to restrict me.

"Calm down, Alyssa. Take deep breaths," Maggie instructs.

Noelle kneels in front of me and takes a deep breath. "In…" She breathes. "Out." She puffs outward. "Do it with me." She shakes her hands in front of her, bringing them toward her as she breathes in and pushing them away as she breathes out. I start to copy her, repeating each movement, and eventually, I'm back to normal—well, as normal as I can be. "Oh, thank the lord." She squeezes me tightly.

"I can't b-br—" I say.

"Whoops." She giggles.

I smile, letting my pearly white teeth glisten. "Thank you."

"I think we need to leave now. Come on, Alyssa." Noelle grabs my hand and forcefully pulls me off my chair. I nearly fall over my own feet. "This isn't helping her. This has brought up unnecessary memories she doesn't need to remember. You think you and the police know how to help her, but you're just going to let her get hurt again. Can't you see? Us kids don't remember things we don't want to—we block things out for a reason." We get closer to the door. "Ya know what, I know what you are—you're a psychotic cow."

My mouth drops open, ready to catch flies, and Maggie glares at us.

Surely that's a detention.

I tug on Noelle's arm. "Stop, Noelle. Please can we just stay? I'm fine, honestly," I lie, not wanting her to get into trouble over me.

Maggie straightens her body, making her taller than I remember. "It's okay—you can both leave." Her feet tread toward us and she places her hand on my shoulder while looking straight at my best friend. "I understand you're annoyed, Noelle, but this is the best way to help Alyssa. The school knows it, her parents know it, the police know it, and deep down, Alyssa knows it too." She looks at me, cupping her hands around my face. "Be kind to yourself, Alyssa."

Noelle opens the office door and starts to drag me out.

"Oh, and one more thing, Miss Carlisle, just while we are on the subject—this is the last time you'll be able to attend these pointless sessions. From now on, it's Alyssa and me—do you understand, or would you like me to go over it in detention?"

Noelle slowly but surely takes the warning, though she clearly doesn't like it; her teeth grind together so loudly it's like listening to a blender. She nods her head and pulls me out of the office, guiding me to our first class.

That session taught me one thing: I have a best friend I'll always be able to rely on. When everything gets tough, she's there through thick and thin. I'm not alone and I never will be. I'm going to survive my last year of high school whether I want to or not. Nobody will even notice that in a few months, I may be blind as a bat. Like Noelle and I always have done, we'll work as a team to stay on top of the social ladder.

This morning, I got closer to finding my attacker. It nearly became a reality—laying eyes on Ashton Marston after the incident that occurred makes my blood boil. Not only did he invade my body, inside and out, he walked away from me while I pleaded for help. He kept walking. I laid there hopeless and scared and covered in a pool of my own blood, but he went running in the opposite direction.

Coward.

I need to confront him, so badly.

I'm preparing myself for a war. I'm not going down without a fight, and this time, I'm prepared.

Noelle holds my hand tightly as we walk along the hallway with our heads held high. She shouts angrily at anyone who stands in our way. She's on the warpath just as much as I am, and together, we are going to solve the puzzle.

Four words and sixteen letters.

Let the games begin.

Six

Imagine being the equivalent girl version of James Bond—that's what I am. Noelle's probably picturing it now while sitting in the gym on the pale brown floor, stretching out our muscles. We're going over the plan I have, and a plan it *is*. I'll definitely say it's not one that's going to go smoothly, but is James Bond smooth while he's soaring through the sky, jumping onto a moving train? Nope, he is certainly not.

The plan is smooth because obviously, I'm a *smooth criminal*. It's a simplistic easy adventure and it starts with getting Ashton Marston to open his mouth and speak out about what he saw that night—and, while we're at it, finding out whether our encounter was mutual. Was it my own fault my knickers went down to my ankles, or do I need to cry rape and be pissed off worse than I am now? I really hope I gave consent and it's just that my mind was swimming in liquor, making me forget.

Either way he needs to pay; either way I was passed out, completely oblivious to the world, and the thought of it makes my eyes sting.

Ashton's your standard stocky, admirable jock every guy wants to be and every girl wants to bed. Unless you're me—then you have standards and pass out rather than enjoy it. Then again, if I remember rightly, I said no.

He's cute, sure. He gets my eyes swivelling as he walks on by, sure, but I wouldn't say he's anything special. He's just a guy that's too high and mighty for his own good, like most guys at Valley View High. Hopefully, thinking too highly of himself will come in handy when I start blackmailing him. *Did I say it's going to be simplistic?*

The basketball team is practicing and the ball swishes through the net, banging loudly against the backboard. The sound echoes around the gym and I recognize the noise so easily, the dribble of the ball from one side of the space to the other. The air is dry, making me swallow hard, and the smell of sweat wanders amongst the room, reeking of testosterone and well-exercised bodies. I part my legs and stretch each side, leaning over to touch my toes.

The hard, brown basketball rolls toward me and hits my ankle.

"Over here." Conan Dwight claps his hands and brings them up in the air, shouting from the other side of the gym. Noelle picks the ball up and throws it toward the group of guys smiling idly.

"Hey! Noelle." Ethan nods over in my direction. "What happened to her—is she blind?"

"Blind and sexy," the guys joke, laughing and bumping each other's fists.

I turn a crimson red and look away, making sure they can't see my face. I know it's a joke. They don't really have a clue—how could they?

Ethan's always been jealous that I look at other guys but not at him. There's nothing wrong with him, with his boyish, chubby cheeks and perfectly styled (like a member of One Direction) blond hair, but I was put in a difficult place: it was either him or Ashton, and back then, as a sophomore, Ashton's brown eyes made me swoon so badly my legs turned to jelly. I was immature and didn't know anything about dating, let alone guys.

Ashton picked me up like the gent he was and met my dad, going even higher up in my standards. He stuttered, said *yes sir* a lot, and kept his hands to himself while we walked to his car. That all changed once we were out of Dad's sight, though. The moment you throw the guy a spade, he'll just keep on digging, and that's exactly what he did. He dug himself a big enough hole to put himself in, and for all I care, he should've stayed there. We drove ten minutes down the road to a popular ice cream parlor, *Eat Me*. It was, and still is, my favorite place to go. My mouth drools each time I enter the parlor for the sweet sensation of chocolate-covered pastry. It fills my nostrils, giving me the need to tuck in. The man who runs it is a cute, elderly little man named Pablo. After a month's worth of visits of drowning my baby fat with sugar, Pablo and I were on a first-name basis.

When I'd introduced Ashton to Pablo, it had taken one second for Pablo to turn his nose up at him and shake his head disapprovingly, in a way a protective grandfather would. I could say the date continued on to be great, but why would I want to make myself out to be a liar? Ashton's attention was more on my breasts than it was on the information coming out of my mouth. Our evening didn't end well; when we left, Pablo's deep grandfatherly voice and his grandson, Lucas, warned him to be kind to me, making it even more awkward.

We were making our way home and Ashton made a detour through a small town south of Vallyeont. Even though he was my age, in my class, and not that much bigger than my tiny frame, he started to scare the hell out of me. He drove past a bunch of bikers known as the Bellevue Motorcyclist Gang. He rolled down his window and made a transaction with a guy who had his ear pierced and was covered head to toe in tattoos. The guy winked at me while his tongue slid over his lips, and I'll never forget his face.

I asked Ashton why we were there. His reply was telling me not to worry my pretty little head. When he started driving back to town, I let my body relax knowing I could soon put the date to bed, and not figuratively speaking—but then he pulled into an empty parking lot, not too far from my house, and it made me uneasy and queasy. Let's just say he was only interested in one thing, which I should have guessed since he was known to be a little sex-crazed. They say leopards never change their spots. The best thing about our date was the swirling breeze as I walked home, leaving him curled over in the driver's seat. I pulled my jacket up higher to my cheeks and rubbed my arms up and down swiftly, hoping for some heat.

They say parents know best. When your dad tells you a guy is a complete *wrong-un*, make sure you believe him, because the way Ashton tried to slide his hand up my dress was daring. The hype he showed was not from eating chocolate waffles; you could tell by the way his eyes glazed over he was a first-class twat that only cared about getting laid and using his nose as a hoover for the white powder he kept purchasing off the Bellevue Gang. Ever since that date, I try to remember to take my peppermint spray out with me—it works wonders when you need to make a swift exit. If I'd had it on me at Noelle's party, I might have had a chance.

I know I noticeably threw myself at him at the party, but it makes me sick to the stomach not being able to remember whether I slept with him or not. It would drive anyone insane.

While we're stretching our bodies, Noelle listens carefully to everything I have to say, everything I want to tell her, and she starts laughing, holding her stomach tightly and curling over. "It's a horrible idea." She catches her breath, still chuckling. "Think of something else. I mean, blackmail? Really?"

I hush her, hoping nobody overhears. "Shhh." I place my index finger against my lips.

She holds her hand out in front of me so I can clearly see its shadow. "Feel it," she demands.

I place my palm on her hand and realize her middle finger is pointing upward.

I swat her hand away. "Har, har." I glare. "Hilarious."

"Anyway, even if you do blackmail him, he's not going to tell you anything, Lyss."

I stand up and stretch my arms above my head. "How do you know? He might be scared."

"Pfft, you're definitely a dreamer."

I look around the gym, watching the shadows huddle together in different corners. The wooden bleachers are covered with people sitting and sprawling out all over them. Everything around me is too bright as the light shines through the window, making it harder for me to see people clearly.

Noelle lightly shoves my back, making me grunt. "Ouch—"

"Smile."

What the— "Ouch, Noelle. Don't be a—"

"Alyssa! So nice to see you're back, and may I say, looking as well as ever!" Charlotte Summers,

Lindsey's best friend, bounces toward me like her feet are on springs. Her dark wavy hair bounces with her. I follow the sound of her voice and smile. I assure you, I am not smiling on the inside. I am most certainly scowling.

"Thanks. I'm happy to be back." *Lies.*

"Like, *oh my God*, you were pretty drunk that night, weren't you?"

Well done, Sherlock Holmes. Her perfect doll face makes me want to punch her square in the nose, with her tiny little figure, tiny little feet, and tiny little face. *Ugh.*

"Do you remember who attacked you?" Another question is flung my way—nosey doesn't cover it. Most people would say she's being a kind, caring, and concerned friend, but she isn't being any of that. She's not worrying about my health and welfare; she isn't even being kind. Charlotte Summers is being a bitch, like always. "Tommy told me you were incredibly stupid, ya know, getting that drunk in the first place." Lindsey's wing woman just keeps on piping up.

My fist curls and I nearly snarl, like a wild, hungry dog. *Just go away.* "Oh, did he?"

"Well that's what she freaking said, isn't it," Lindsey spits out. Who the hell rattled her cage? Of course, when there's one of them, the other follows.

I grab my toes, pulling my foot up to my bum to stretch my muscles. If I just ignore them, they'll go away…I hope. I have nothing else to say. Noelle coughs, smiling at her own thoughts and probably at how ignorant I'm being, but I don't give two flying birds because I don't want to talk about the party with them. I don't want to talk about the person who treated me like I wasn't a human being, and I especially don't want to talk about it with the chuckle sisters.

"Party at my place next Friday. Noelle, you in? Starts around six p.m.," Lindsey says pointedly, while she plays with a highlighted, blond, strand of hair. She ignores me, looking straight at Noelle and left me standing here like an unwanted, bratty child.

"Sorry, I'm busy." Noelle gives her a tight smile.

Lindsey huffs. "Suit yourself." She turns on her heel. "Come on, girls."

Noelle prods me, just below my shoulder. "They're gone." She laughs, the sound very distinct, like a hyena surrounded by a bunch of cows. "That, my darling was brilliant! You were so blunt!"

I place my finger up to my mouth once again. "Shhh."

Noelle glances over to the Go View! cheerleading squad. "Don't worry, the devil children are too far away to be able to hear us."

"What do they bleeding expect, for me to list off a selection of people I think did this to me?" I tilt my head to one side and think for a second. "Oh, by the way girls, you're on my list of suspects." I snicker, raising my voice to match that of my sister's electronic Barbie doll. Noelle laughs even louder, making the entire team glare at us. Several pair of black holes etched into my brain. I copy them and glare at her as well, and I notice the outline of a warm, light shadow. Noelle's lips are pursed and she's gleaming, always gleaming.

Lunch begins to close in and by then, I'm finding my day easier to handle. The hallways are easier to tackle, and my feet feel confident on where they step between classes. I've found I'm not always having to hold Noelle's arm for support, and I suggest that it's better this way, due to the fact that it looks slightly odd that she's not letting go of me, even when it comes to opening my own locker (I had to ask her five times to let go of me...*five*).

    We head toward the cafeteria, walking past the lockers lining the walls on either side of me, against the shabby plastering. I visualize the blue tiles underneath my feet as I tread forward, slowly and patiently, stepping cautiously. I squint my eyes down at the floor, taking in any details around me. A strange odor lingers in the air from all the teenagers crowding the halls, some running, some walking, others hovering at the sides until the path is clear. The majority of them are eager to get to where they need to be, letting life rush by like a whirlwind. It feels refreshing knowing that's not me anymore—rushing all the time. I hear the chitchat amongst them along with the raised voices of those who want to be heard.

I concentrate hard on the dark objects, helping me to step aside and avoid them before I'm shoved out of the way. As I'm walking past everyone, I make sure a smile is continuously on my face, though I don't feel like smiling. I feel like dying.

I knock a few elbows and shoulders, but there's nothing to cause any suspicion because the bodies are compact, all touching one way or another. Two hands hold on to my shoulders, steadying me as I continue to move with the crowd, like a sheep with the herd. I try to shrug the hands off, but they hold on to me tightly. I stop in the middle of the hall and allow people to knock into us.

"Don't just stand still." My shoulder becomes a target from a very angry girl.

I try to get my bearings, but I'm lost. I sniff, smelling sweet almond with a hint of cherry. "Tommy," I say on an exhalation.

I run my fingers through my hair and cross my arms over my chest. He pulls me by my elbow, leading us to the side, no longer allowing people to use my shoulder as target practice, and I'm thankful for that. I remember everything Charlotte said to me in the gym, and instantly the feeling of betrayal replaces it. I hope he doesn't make me a hot topic in their make-out sessions; that's just gross.

Awesome, now I have a picture of them making out in my head. It just keeps going around on a one-way lane. *Bloody fantastic.*

Noelle shouts from farther ahead, leaning casually and effortlessly against someone's locker. "Lyss, you coming girl?"

"I'll catch up with you. Give me two mins, yeah?" I bite my fingernail, nipping it away from the skin. I look up into Tommy's dark holes, where his eyes are, and remember how I used to sink into the light, soft chocolate color.

"Hey." Tommy grins.

I give him a half-smile. "Hi."

"I've been trying to get your attention all morning." He gives a shaky laugh. "How's it been?"

I glare. "I spoke to Charlotte." I look away, purely out of habit.

I can sense his weight shifting from one side of his body to the other as he says, "Oh…"

"Oh?" I repeat.

"What did she say?" he asks quietly.

"I'm sure you know what she had to say." My eyebrows furrow together. I'm fuming. I let my mouth hang open and I set my eyes on his face. I know if I could see him right now, I'd be burning a hole into his head. "How could you speak to *her* about me? You know how much I can't stand her." Anger travels fast inside me, like a flaming bullet. My blood is boiling, bubbling quickly like a witch's cauldron, and I try to calm myself, breathing heavily. Tommy grabs my hand and I pull it away sharply. "How could you, Tommy?"

First-class asshat.

"I've never—" he begins.

"You've never?"

"When have I?" Tommy splutters.

I sigh. "You tell me." *Please.*

"I—"

"Oh, save it. Save the bullshit you've come up with." I raise my hands in the air, high above our heads, and quickly let them fall back down. I slap the locker door at the side of me, hard. "I-I trusted you, Tommy. You're my best friend." I turn away, broken. "I'm going to go to lunch now—I'd say I'll see you later, but I hope I don't."

I start to walk away, and he grabs hold of the corner of my jacket. It pulls tighter around my back, making me stop. "Wait, Lyssa!" He slides his hand through his wavy hair. "I never talked to her about you, not in the way you think." He cups my hands and pulls them up to his mouth, warmth surrounding them. "I promise," he mumbles into our hands.

"You promise?" I whisper. I bring my hands down in front of my stomach and start scratching at my wrists, hoping the burning will start and hoping it causes some sort of pain.

"Charlotte started talking to her friends about how you deserved it. I stuck up for you, told her to stop being so childish." He grabs my wrists, stopping me. "Please don't do that." He brings me into a cuddle, his arms embracing my body, and places his lips on the top of my head. "All I said to her was that you shouldn't have drank the amount you did, and if anyone was to blame it might as well be her, considering she brought the most alcohol to the party and she dru—"

"She what!?" I push myself away from him.

He shifts his weight again. "Never mind, Lyssa."

"Go on."

"Drop it. It doesn't matter."

"Bullshit, of course it matters—it matters to me!" I pull him closer to me, holding both his hands with mine. "Please." My eyes widen.

"Okay," he shouts. "Okay." He pushes me away and waves his hands in front of him in mock surrender. He doesn't look at me. "Charlotte put something in your drink that night, but I don't know what."

I gasp. "Like…" I struggle to breathe. "She spiked it?"

Tommy stays quiet. I pace small steps in a circle in front of him, ready to ring my hands around her scrawny neck. My head starts spinning. My drinks were potentially spiked, and it seemed like no big deal.

"Why am I only finding out about it now? Why only today..." I gape.

I guess in their eyes everything is okay. They don't give a toss that I could hardly move. I place my hands on my knees and bend over, breathing loudly.

"Lyssa, that night, I...you...I mean, I knew. Well, I mean, I just want to say, if I'd have known you were in trouble, I'd never have left you standing alone like I did. I assumed you had crashed out in Noelle's bedroom or something. I, well...when you didn't come looking for me, I..." He sighs, "I know I wasn't around." I stand up straight and open my mouth. He places his hand over it. "No, let me finish. I feel—I feel horrible. I'm so sorry Lyssa." His voice cracks. He splutters each word as if they are his last and my heart tightens, playing tug-of-war with itself on whether I should forgive him or not.

"But I wasn't okay. Whatever she put in my drink made my body shut down. It's because of her I probably ended up in bed with Ashton, not knowing if I had sex with him or not. It's because of her I couldn't move in the garage and felt so groggy, and here I am, all along feeling like it's my fault for drinking so much."

His jaw clenches and his fists tighten by his sides. "You slept with Ashton!?"

I shake my head. "Look, forget it. I understand you're sorry." But do I? I can't be sure. We stay silent and he brings me into another cuddle. I cherish every second.

"Do you want to grab lunch? I'll even sit with Noelle for you." He laughs lightly and playfully taps my shoulder. Him offering to sit with Noelle is like offering his balls on a plate, bare and precious. He *hates* her, and she *hates* him. I know hate is a strong word, but if there was a stronger word for me to use, I'd use it.

I smile. "It's fine. I won't make you do that." *No matter how much I can't stand you at the moment.*

"Phew." Told you. "I hate being around her." His voice strains. "Are you sure you're okay?"

I bow my head and step to one side, being cautious not to step on his feet. "I'm fine." *Just cold inside.*

"You sure, babe?" Tommy gives me a quick side hug and I nod my head. "Okay, well, I'll see ya." He plants his soft lips on the side of my temple, and walks away, catching up with his friends.

My body feels weak, and pains shoot through my legs and my arms, making my whole body want to shut down. I'm completely ready for school to be done with and for me to go to bed, to be content and worry-free.

I feel like a five-year-old, rather than a fully grown seventeen-year-old.

Don't take it the wrong way—everyone wishes they could go back to their younger years and never grow up. But, when you're treated like a child when all you want to be is a woman, it's hard not to feel the bittersweet taste. I don't think I can manage a month of my father standing at the bus stop, waiting for my arrival, especially with half of my classmates on the same bus. I'm not going to try to comprehend the treatment I'm receiving, as if I'm an incapable child, which I know for a matter of fact I am.

Otherwise, how did I end up here?

My first day in the jungle went surprisingly well. I didn't fall flat on my ass or my face, and nobody except Noelle found out I'm disabled.

Everyone believes I'm okay.

Everyone thinks I'm on the road to recovery.

Everyone thinks whoever did this to me is free and clear. They have no idea what I have planned or what I'm going to do when I find my attacker. I'm going to send them down hard, and they won't know what hit them.

I jump, sitting with my right leg over my left, swinging my foot around in a circle. I listen to the rustle of plastic bags.

"Are you okay, miss?"

My head is dipping over, and the voice makes me lift it slowly, allowing me to see the contrasts of lighting change. The railings on the bus turn a slight blur of a grey, while the pitch-black sharpness of the man's probably ironed suit catches my attention. The aroma of stale tobacco, burnt coffee, and expired chicken drifts up my nostrils. I tuck a strand of my tinted auburn hair behind my ear and wipe away the wet, salty tear leaking from my right eye.

I sniff. "Yeah, I'm great." I see the shadow of a small smile cross his lips and he nods his head at me before the bus stops, allowing him to get off. I listen to the scrape of the door opening.

"Bye," he calls behind him.

The engine of the bus booms and shifts into drive then travels a short distance forward. Suddenly, it stops. There's a tap on the window at my side and the chatter on the bus continues, taking no notice.

"Alyssa!" the bus driver yells from the front.

I hear my father's voice. "Thanks Timothy."

I've arrived to where I need to be. I push myself up carefully and grab hold of the bar that's level with my chest. I take small steps toward the front of the bus until I lose my footing, throwing me off balance. I hit a broad, hard chest.

"I'm sor—"

"Watch it, Darlington—don't you have eyes?" Sarcasm rolls off the end of his tongue so naturally, so belittling.

Ironically, I do have eyes, they just don't work. I'm about to say sorry to the obnoxious dick but then think better of it and stay quiet. I try to catch a glimpse of him before he walks ahead of me, straining my neck. I squint my eyes forcefully, only catching his broad, sculptured, definitely looked-after silhouette.

I concentrate on getting off the bus without causing any harm to myself and nod at Timmy, the bus driver. "Thank you," I say.

My father waves from the open door of the bus and grabs my bag out of my hand, helping me down onto the pavement. Before I tell him how embarrassing he is, I'm tackled toward a post behind me as the engine of the bus booms again and it drives away. Panting hard and pushing gently against my stomach is an overactive, furry animal.

"SURPRISE!"

I glance down but am unable to see any shadow, so I use my hands to show me. I pat them around its head, touching the dog's coarse fur. I start to tickle two ears, hoping it's pleasing my new friend.

"Meet Fusco. He's cute, smart, and did I mention cute? And, he's your new guide dog—all armored up for you," Dad jokes lightly. I bend down to stroke the new addition to the Darlington household. He starts to continuously lick me, his tongue gritty against my skin. Fusco is exactly like Charlie, our Labrador.

"What color?" I say.

"Black, love."

"Please tell me he's not wearing that horrible, luminous jacket?" I ask warily.

My dad lets out a deep, hoarse laugh and hands me the end of the leash. "He did come with it, but I thought against it since you're undercover and all that shizzle."

"Please, never say shizzle again." I shake my head with a smile on my face.

My dad continues to laugh as we start to walk. Laughing at his own jokes is something he does regularly. *Someone has to.*

"Good boy," I coo, patting Fusco on the back gently. The walk home turns into an adventurous one: Fusco stops at crossings and the edges of pathways, and he even leads me out of the way of others. He makes me seem normal, not having to worry about where I'm walking. This little furry pal makes it ten times easier, and he's going to be my ticket around town.

I never imagined putting all my trust into one little dog, but when he licks my hand to let me know I've arrived home, I instantly fall in love. Charlie has my heart, but this little guy is going to be my savior, which allows my heart to expand.

I open the white, cracked front door and find the house empty. As I walk in, I shiver. I instantly smell the aroma of spring blossoms swirling around the hallway, filling my head to the brim and making it hard to concentrate.

Dare I ask? "Where's Mom?"

Dad helps me to the bottom step and I take off my shoes. He takes them from my grasp and places them on the shoe rack to the side of the front door. "She's out, love. Just me and you tonight."

"Out?" I scrunch my nose up. "Where's Mia?"

"Mom's at a business meeting, and Mia's at a friend's house."

Mom is always attending business meetings, always away for weeks on end with no phone calls, no emails, not even any presents when she returns—just a mom who comes and goes. After my incident, I began to hope she'd be around more, and I think Dad was hoping too as he clings to his phone every night, waiting for her to contact him.

Obviously being around her family isn't my mom's first priority. *Selfish.*

Fusco follows Dad into the kitchen. "We'll order pizza tonight..." He raises his voice so I can continue to hear him. "Does that sound good, kiddo?" I hear a soft growl from Charlie and a whimper releases from Fusco. "Alyssa?" Dad comes back to the foyer, where I'm sitting silently on the bottom step of the staircase. "We could order something else if not?"

I love him even more.

"Sorry…" I glance up and smile. "Pizza sounds great. In fact, it sounds delicious."

Dad walks back into the kitchen. Standing up, I hold on to the banister and feel along the wall for the entrance to our living area. I find my way to our brown leather sofa and let my body slump down. I bring my feet off the ground and curl them up beneath me. Charlie bounds in to greet me, his tail wagging and tongue hanging out. I pat him gently and Fusco joins, pushing him out of the way, making Charlie growl. They both jump up onto the couch, where Fusco curls himself into my lap and Charlie wraps himself around my feet.

Things aren't so bad.

I just need to get used to this new normal.

Seven

If I told you I look forward to school when I wake up in the morning, I'd be lying to you.

If not for Tommy picking me up—even after our awkward encounter yesterday afternoon—I'm not sure how I'd handle the situation I'm in. I really want to tell him about me being partially blind, but I don't know where to start. Where do you start when you tell someone you've been lying, lying about everything? That the only reason I don't mind his hand on the base of my back is because I can't see where I'm walking? Tommy has been there for me since middle school, just like Noelle, and this is how I treat him? To think he could walk away once he finds out I'm keeping something so big from him—it's unbearable.

Standing alone in the hallway at school feels weird. This time last year I had so many people surrounding me, but that's high school for you—always changing, always cruel. Once you make a fool of yourself in front of everyone, you think no one will remember it, but the truth? The truth is they remember every second. Those friends you thought you once had, they disappear with the click of a finger. It's hard staying at the top of the social ladder, and it's even harder while partially blind.

Since being attacked, I don't have many people coming up to talk to me; invisibility is my new superpower. I might as well be borrowing Harry Potter's invisibility cloak. Is being invisible what I wanted? Hell no, but a blow to the head and a toxic swig in the face sort of changes that, especially when that person is me.

I'm not quite sure *how* to fit in anymore. Trying too hard is hard, but not trying at all seems harder. I don't want people asking too many questions, so I block myself off from others, but as the days go by, juggling a secret like this and trying to socially climb proves more difficult.

Callie McGovern bounces toward me, her bounce always gracious but her hair, not so much. "So, I'm thinking now that you're over the whole *I've been attacked* pity party and all that..." Two round, lined shadows are perching on the end of her nose. "You can help me on the prom committee."

She holds her five books close to her chest and struggles to keep them there. She slants to one side, catching one book before the others hit the ground. She bends down and gathers them all up. She looks at me intently, the light reflecting off her glasses, allowing me to know they're still resting at the end of her pointy nose, and she holds her breath as she waits for my answer. Over the last year, her appearance keeps changing. She went from punk chic to plain and then to a nerdy look. One thing that never changes is her wiry hair, which looks like Hermione Granger if she got electrocuted. It's bushy to the max, and even a hair brush would get lost in the depth of her curls.

"Please say yes." Callie's dark brown eyes are probably pleading with me. "It'll mean so much to all of us." She speaks on behalf of the prom committee.

Even if I wanted to, I wouldn't do it. Last year was hell. In fact, even worse than hell, if that's even possible. Insanity comes in many different forms, and Callie McGovern is one of those forms. She doesn't stop talking, constantly chatting my ear off, telling me what and what not to do. I wanted to punch her even when she just glanced my way. At least now I'm not tempted since I don't have to see her sparrow-looking face day in and day out.

"Ah…" I scratch the side of my face, looking elsewhere, anywhere but her. "I think I'm going to pass."

I hold the heavy lock of my locker in my hand and fiddle with it. Once it's open, I pretend to look at myself in the mirror hung on the inside.

Just act natural.

"The committee just isn't for me, Callie." I smile and pat my bottom lip carefully, using my index finger to plump it up, hoping I don't smudge the mauve lipstick, especially considering it took me four attempts to get it right this morning. I shut my locker door and cross my fingers behind my back.

Please don't be offended.

"Oh." Her mood drops. "I just...I dunno. You're always on it, and I assumed you'd want to be this year. I like having you around, because truthfully you were the only person who liked me last year."

"I do still like you." *Well, I can tolerate you.* Her shadow is light as can be, but her stance is sad. I feel guilty, but I know I won't cope. Being on the committee will not help me, not at all.

"Please, Alyssa—please do it."

"I'm sorry," I say, reaching out to touch the top of her arm. "Maybe we can hang out sometime, yeah?"

I don't want to promise anything, but I notice as her mood lifts. She's back to being her happy, annoying self. I walk away, praying she stays that way.

Callie's right: the committee is something I usually take part in every year, without fail. The idea of being in charge of what theme the school has or how smoothly something so incredible runs and it being all down to me—well, it always kept me on my toes. The smiles that appeared on everyone's faces brought joy to me. It filled me with encouragement to come back each year and make something ten times better than the last.

All that doesn't matter anymore. I'll never be able to enjoy it, and I don't want to burden Noelle to join me. Babysitting me definitely won't be on her agenda for prom, or even leading up to it.

I keep dreaming that one morning, when I walk amongst the halls of Valley View High, color will appear. I wait for it like you wait for a train or a bus to come, slow and draining. I keep telling myself not to worry, that it's just late to arrive. In my gut, it doesn't feel normal or right that I'm hoping so much. It's as though I'm on different planet than those around me, like I'm missing out on something spectacular. I don't feel like I'm part of the world anymore, more like I'm looking in from the outside.

The bell rings, signalling a period change, and the footsteps around me make me aware that I'm late to my counseling session. I run carefully along the side, making sure I keep my hands on the lockers. I touch each door as I pass and look for a round handle. Three doors down, I find it and sigh heavily.

    I open the door quickly and my body collides with another. "Someone's in a rush this morning."

    I jump out of my ghostly skin. *I still need to apply more fake tanner.*

    My hands are planted firmly on his chest. I laugh and retract them. I scratch the back of my neck, bring my hands down in front of me, and rub my palms against the soft fabric of my skirt.

    Crimson travels up my neck and I glance to the floor. "I'm so sorry." I hesitate. "Holy crap! What is wrong with me?" I run my fingers through the top of my hair, shaking my curls out, and I push my bangs away from my eyes. "I guess this year is going to be a clumsy one."

I guess this year is going to be a clumsy one? What the hell Alyssa? Did you not feel that hard chest? Crikey. I half laugh at myself, still not knowing who's standing in front of me.

"Second time in two days, Darlington. It must be fate."

My jaw drops, gaping unattractively. "Yeah...if you say so." I try my hardest to take a reading of his body, but all I manage to see is his bold, dark silhouette. His voice is deep and husky, musically beautiful to my ears.

"Since it's you, I'll let ya off," he says. He reaches out and tucks a stray strand of hair behind my ear. His knuckle touches the bottom of my earlobe and at the same moment, as if right on time, the sun dims through the window behind me and I glimpse his sculpted, hard-lined jaw. His eyes are wide, although to me they're large, black holes. I'm going to guess they're blue—he seems to be a crystal-blue-eyed boy. "Your hair is blocking the view."

Smooth. "Of what?"

He winks at me. "Your eyes." We stand looking at each other for what feels like forever.

I've heard that saying before...when I was thirteen, up in a treehouse. *Conan...*

"Dwight." My body flinches at the sound of Maggie's voice behind me. "It's time for you to go."

I move to one side and my heart begins to double in speed. I try to slow it down but it doesn't work. If anything, it speeds up faster, maybe even louder. My chest feels sore, squeezing as if it's about to burst.

Standing in front of me is the same guy I've crushed on for years.

"C-Conan?" I say, stuttering the word like I'm on some sort of drug. I know it's not our second encounter; it's our third.

"Catch ya later, Darlington." He nods and walks out, leaving me with my mouth agape and my eyes turning.

I slowly lower myself into the chair opposite Maggie and stay silent, my head in a daze. My chest still pounds, making it hard to concentrate. The silence creeps around the room like an unwanted guest. I think knowing I can't see makes Maggie twitchy as she deliberately starts tapping the pen against the wooden surface of her desk. I'm ready to stand and walk out.

"Care Bears, huh?" Maggie chips away at her nails, the crunch as she bites filling the silence. "Tell me, how do you feel about that?"

I raise one eyebrow. "Annoyed."

"What do you mean by annoyed?"

"Annoyed...where you can't be bothered because something's upset you."

"And why do you feel this way?"

"I just do," I reply bluntly. I don't want to be in the room with her any longer. Why should I be in this room answering questions like I'm under interrogation? I assumed these sessions would be helpful in unravelling the mystery of my attack, not full of sitting around and talking about Care Bears.

Maggie leads the conversation in a new direction. "How did you feel your first day back went?"

I tilt my head. "You mean, how did I feel it went while being blind and everything."

"I see you have some confidence back." Maggie taps her chin, once, twice, three times.

I smile. "Confidence is the way forward—isn't that what you like to tell the kids?"

Maggie is a weird woman. Sometimes I believe she loves her job, but other times I think she just puts up with it. The tapping of her pen seems more to do with boredom than anything else.

"Okay, let's start with the basics." Maggie pushes herself backward, still sitting on her swivel chair. "We know you were attacked at the party, whether it was purposely or accidentally."

"You think it could have been an accident?" I stop playing with my fingers.

"Well, can you think of anyone who would want to hurt you?"

"Do you get kicks from listening to kids' problems?" I ask, not understanding why she likes to do this job.

"The question, Alyssa." She ignores my outburst. "Answer the question."

I rub my chin. "Let's see…" I should have joined drama club, never mind the prom committee. "There's Lindsey Montelowe—everyone knows she's a bitch and hates me." I tap the table. "Ashton—let's face it, he might have wanted to shut me up, considering—"

"Considering?"

"I don't want to talk about it." I bite my fingernails. "Pass."

"Okay, anyone else?"

I lean back into my seat, crossing one leg over the other. "Hmm…Ethan Hale." I stare into familiar darkness. "Charlotte Summers, because she has a thing for Tommy but he isn't interested—"

"What about Tommy?"

I drop my leg to the ground. "He's my best friend," I reply, straightening out the bottom of my skirt by sliding my hands across it and ironing out the creases. I sit up taller and wait for her to continue.

"Can you tell me where he was? Could he be a suspect?" Maggie pauses, allowing the idea to sink in. "I understand he's your best friend, but you told me yesterday you left him on his own, so maybe he retaliated by doing this. Maybe he felt angry toward you? Of course, I'm only speculating. We can't know for sure. Only you can answer that."

She's crazier than I gave her credit for. *Wack job.*

"Hang on," I snap. "Are you accusing him?"

Of all the people who could hurt me, Tommy Henderson is not one of them. I must admit, it crossed my mind for a split second because he was there and then he wasn't. But, after thinking rationally, I know Tommy is the type of person who wouldn't even hurt a fly, never mind his own best friend.

"Calm down. I'm simply presenting you with a scenario."

I hate her.

The fear curls up inside me, and she placed it there. "A scenario that doesn't make sense—why would he want to attack me? I've known him since middle school. He wouldn't do anything like this. He has a breakdown when he sees me crying."

Stupid woman.

I hear the opening of a drawer and the shuffling of a pile of paper.

"Maybe you're starting to question it yourself?" There's no emotion in her voice. Now I know why she does this for a living. Maggie stands and walks around the desk to crouch down in front of me. Her hands touch mine, her skin ice cold yet so soft. "Look, Alyssa, I'm not here to accuse any of your friends. I want to help you find closure. Whoever did this to you did an awful thing—an unforgivable thing. I just want to warn you not to be so close-minded. Otherwise, in the long run you will become even more hurt than you are now. You have to think of every possibility. You have to trust your instincts."

"Well, if that's the case, my instinct is telling me Tommy..." I quietly try to convince myself before speaking the words aloud. "Tommy had nothing to do with this." *Since his alibi was Charlotte Summers, doing God knows what.*

A tap on the door interrupts us. "Come in."

I keep my eyes down to the ground, twiddling my fingers to try to keep the feeling of dread in the pit of my stomach from erupting. I stay still and pull the sleeves of my jumper down over my hands. I clutch the woolly material in my fingers and shrug my shoulders up to my chin. I wait for Maggie to finish speaking to Principle Williamson.

"Settling in nicely, Alyssa?" he asks from the doorway.

"Um..." I nod vigorously.

It still seems weird for me to be sitting in a room and expressing my thoughts. When people share secrets with me, I tend to be the best of the best at keeping them. I'm a good listener, and I'm also excellent at making people feel better about things they think have gone wrong. When someone tells me something important that shouldn't ever get out, they walk away knowing nobody else will ever find out. When it comes to me talking to other people—now that's a problem. It's something I'm not very good at. There are not that many people I confide in. Doing these sessions puts me in an awkward position, because all those people who walked away believing I'd never tell their deepest darkest secrets will be disappointed in me, because I was lying to them without even knowing it. I may have to expose their secrets, expose everything if I want to solve this damn puzzle.

"Sorry, Alyssa. Where were we?" Maggie says, making a light thud on her chair.

Maggie appears to be a very laid-back sort of person. She's not your typical teacher, but someone who seems to understand that being a teenager is harder than it looks or even sounds. That's not to say she's not like my mum with the whole 'I was a teenager once you know.' Maggie is more diplomatic about the idea that today's teenagers are all about having sex, drinking alcohol, and doing drugs.

"Ah yes. Do you want to try to talk about that night…" She cocks her head. "Tell me what happened before the party?"

I wearily wave her off. "Same old, same old: Mom went out, and Dad looked after Mia."

"Your little sister?"

"Yep. She's six—cute as a button." I smile.

"Then what happened?"

"Tommy came over for pre-drinks. I say pre-drinks, but it was more of a catch-up and a coin toss to see who the designated driver would be." I place my hands on my lap and cup them tightly. "Ya'see, my father never, ever minds if Tommy wants to come over. Tommy's father passed away when he was five, and since my father came into his life, he's been the closest thing he has to a dad. He's a role model…" I pause. "Better than his deadbeat uncle, who's always throwing punch—" I cup both hands over my mouth.

Too far, Lyss.

"We are not here to talk about Tommy's life, don't worry, but if you do feel something isn't right, please come and speak to the school. I'm sure we'd be happy to help Tommy if he needs it." I look at her shadow—so soft, so kind. "Anyway, back to that night?"

I remember Tommy arriving and my dad shouting from the bottom of the stairs to tell me he was there. I did a quick twirl in the mirror, my bright blue eyes glinting in the glass, and my hair looked silkier than ever. I looked hot in my slinky, sparkly, bodycon dress. Before going downstairs, I saw Mia was hovering outside her bedroom. She waited eagerly and finally said good night…

~

"Hey pretty girl. What d'ya think you're doing still awake?" I asked, hoping she was feeling okay, because I knew I wouldn't be able to leave her if she wasn't. She smiled at me, a beautiful, humongous grin spread across her face. She beamed with affection.

I picked her up and let her legs wrap around my waist.

"I wanted to say good night." She hugged me hard. "I love you, Lyssa."

"I love you too, cutie pie." I kissed her cheek and placed her down. "Come on, little terror, get back into bed before Dad does fee-fi-fo-fum up these stairs."

She giggled.

I started walking away from her.

"Alyssa?"

I glanced back over my shoulder and smiled. "Yeah?"

"Will Mom be home tonight?"

Hurt flashed in her eyes, and I dipped my head. "I don't think so, Mia moo, but if you close your eyes and go to sleep, she'll be here when you wake up." I give her one last kiss and go downstairs to greet Tommy.

~

It's surreal, remembering my sister looking so adorable in her Monsters Inc. pajama set. My father's smile is etched into my brain. He's the one who granted me permission to go to the house party. Mom disapproved, and I think he did too, but he believes in letting me have a little freedom. I remember Tommy's moans and boyish grumbles from the driver's seat, complaining about having to go to "Noelle's stupid party." He grinned at me, sitting openly in clear view as I told him I'd be with him all night. It's unforgettable.

But then, I lied. I lied to him. I wasn't with him all night. I left him to survive a party full of people who weren't his group of friends; they were mine.

I look forward, right at Maggie. "I'm sorry…" I stand up. "C-Can I be excused? C-Can we continue this another time—all these memories, just talking about it…it's wearing me out." I move away from my chair, fidgeting toward the door. There's a long silence.

I think she nods, forgetting I can't see. Two beats later she says, "Yeah, of course."

I shoot out of the door quicker than The Flash himself. I run, clutching at my neck. It feels like a rope is around it, squeezing me tightly and suffocating me. I'm choking, coughing, and spluttering, all my memories closing in around me, pulling the rope tighter and tighter until my head pounds hard against my temples. I run faster, not caring if I can't see where I'm going. I hope and pray people will move out of my way as I sprint toward the front doors of the school.

Before I blink, I'm out of the entrance and brakes start screeching harshly, making me squirm.

Arms come around my waist, forcefully yanking me backward. There's the sound of a horn and it starts to ring in my ears. It's coming from the car, which nearly ran me over. My heart rate doubles in speed and I come to the realization of what just happened. My life flashes before my eyes. I wish they had knocked me down and taken away my pain rather than adding to it. Everyone is standing around, watching me, like a monkey in a zoo. They probably hope it'll hit me next time.

"Are you okay?" asks the guy who just saved me from being splattered on the pavement.

I push him backward, pulling myself out of his grasp, and I press my finger into his chest, trying to catch myself. "I—"

"Just say thanks," Ethan says.

"I—" I feel my head with both my hands and continue to inspect my body, making sure I'm okay.

"Are you all right?" Ethan asks the question again.

Physically, yes, but mentally is a different case. "Ethan?" I mutter.

"Be careful next time!" he says.

I move backward and sit down on the steps that lead up to the school's entrance. "There won't be a next time."

"If you say so, doll face." He laughs tauntingly and walks away from me.

Opposite, standing around the expensive cars bought by their daddy's credit cards, a group of guys and girls laugh loudly in my direction. I dip my head and straighten my hair out. No doubt my skin is looking pinched and red. I cover my face with both palms and groan into them. I'm so embarrassed. I was so stupid to run out like that, to think I'd figure out where to go based on shadows. I want to cry so badly but no more tears form; I'm completely dry. I've cried enough to form a rainfall. If I cried any more, I'd cause floods—I'm empty.

"Darlington: the pretty-eyed girl," Conan comments, walking toward me and away from his friends.

I squint—he can't possibly be talking to me.

"Yo Conan! You coming bro?" Ethan says from the other side of the parking lot.

"I'll catch up with ya," Conan shouts.

"Your loss. Trust me, you aren't gonna get anything out of that slut."

"Get lost, Ethan. Don't call her that." His voice changes, no longer playful but angry. "I said I'll catch you later."

My heart stutters to a halt. I bring my hands down to my knees and try to physically control myself, my legs bouncing. There's no chance of mentally controlling myself at this point, and physically doesn't seem likely either.

"You okay?" He asks the same question Ethan asked, but he places a hand on my shoulder and sits down next to me.

"I'm dandy, fine, completely perfect," I snap. I stand up and straighten my jumper and skirt. I lean against the bumpy hardness of the brick wall, hoping it'll steady my balance. "Are you stalking me?"

Are. You. Stalking. Me? Brilliant, Lyssa.

Musical laughter fills my ears. I'd listen to it all day long. It comes out of his mouth so naturally, I can't help but smile at how beautiful it sounds. "I think you will find Ethan just saved your life. He made sure you didn't end up splattered all over the parking lot."

I glare at him, unable to form any syllables to try to redeem myself.

"I think he deserves a thanks, don't you, Darlington?"

Deep furrows appear in my brow. "Ethan, an apology..." I scoff. "You must be joking. Like, seriously?"

"Wow." He raises his eyebrows at me, the dark lines on his grey shadow appearing to go into the air.

I bring my hair forward, even though most of it is already there, and I wipe underneath my eyes. "I'm not apologizing to him—he just called me a slut." I scowl. "Look, I was only asking if you were stalking me because it's twice now you've bumped into me. Since we were thirteen, we haven't spoken, so you don't have to be a douchebag and start telling me what I should or shouldn't do."

"Why would I stalk you?" I sit on the step below him and he hands me my bag. "You're nothing special. I mean, look at you—you look like you just ran a marathon."

"You—"

"Me?"

"Wow." I pull harshly at my bag and swing it over my shoulder. "You're exactly what people say you are, you know that? You're an obnoxious jackass. Don't soften the blow, will you. How could I ever think *you* would give your attention to someone like *me*! Never mind go out of your way to speak to me." I start walking down the steps steadily. "Joke's on me, eh."

"Wh—wait!" He grabs hold of my elbow, but I snatch it away and keep on walking to the other side of the parking lot. I ring my dad and ask him to pick me up. I don't look back—there's no point. There's nothing for me to see.

Stupidity is something that comes naturally to me. Conan Dwight wanting to speak to me again would have been a dream come true, but it isn't going to happen—not in my reality, anyway. The picture of him burns into my head: his dark, soft hair floating above his eyes, the ringlets on top of his head bouncing delicately, his masculine, toned figure letting every girl know he works out regularly. I admit, I've had a crush on him for years, but after getting more than a few words from him, realization hits me—it's a stupid, pointless crush because he's just like the rest of them: cold and heartless.

Determination.

While my father drives me home, all I have inside of me is determination to find my attacker.

I pick the house phone up off the stand at the bottom of the stairs because, unlike my phone, it's now got braille numbers on it, making it easier for me to use. I dial Noelle's number and ask if I can come over to her place for the night, and without hesitation, our parents agree. I say parents, but I just mean my dad. I take Fusco with me and walk along the path, allowing the breeze to blow dryly around my body. I cuddle my scarf around my neck, tighter to my skin, and I rub my hands together while gripping the leash as we stand outside a big, black metal gate. It probably took me half an hour to get here. I ring the buzzer once, waiting for it open.

"Carlisle household," says a young, male voice, crackling through the speakers.

"Just me, Joe." I smile toward where I remember the camera to be and wave.

"An' who's your friend, Miss Darlington?"

Fusco barks. "My new pet. He's a delight."

Joe lets out a deep chuckle. "Always a pleasure, Miss Darlington. Please make your way up the drive."

The huge gate slowly opens. I head up to Noelle's bedroom, tread upon her grey wooden floor, and sit comfortably next to her on the king-sized bed.

"Oh my God, who's this little fella?" Noelle squeals. Fusco jumps up and starts to wipe his tongue across her face, making her laugh. Hours pass by and we spend our time mind-mapping. On her laptop she opens the camera footage from that night, and since I can't see, Noelle happily explains to me what's going on. With her dad being so wealthy, he has cameras installed in the hallways, on the sides of the garage, and also in the downstairs area, close to where my attack happened. He complied with the sheriff and allowed him to watch the tapes intensively, but they hadn't shown Sheriff Lou any sign of a struggle, therefore nobody had gotten arrested.

We play the first bit of footage, which shows Ashton Marston going into the garage and then coming out again, looking more distressed than he should. I know why the police didn't use this—because he wasn't in there long enough to cause any damage. It was literally in the space of a minute that he went in and came back out again, but I know I asked for his help; the sheriff didn't.

Most of the kids there that night were questioned, and there are no leads that would make one think Ashton did it, or even any of the partygoers. Everyone had access to the garage, and there may have been a lot of people who did enter the garage but didn't see me. I definitely know Ashton saw me, that's for sure, and I can use this tape to prove it.

Tap, tap, tap. Noelle's bedroom door creaks open. "Girls, are you both okay? Do you need anything?" Noelle's dad asks.

"We're fine, Dad."

"Thanks Mr. Carlisle," I say, still holding on to the footage, staring at it.

"Have you found something?" he asks.

I hesitate. "Nothing," Noelle and I say together, and she links her fingers through mine.

"Oh, what a shame." Mr. Carlisle slides his hand up and down the door frame. "I hope you find out who did this to you, Alyssa. It's terrible to think someone hurt you under our roof. You're like family to us. Whoever did this should be behind bars."

"Thank you," I say softly. When Mr. Carlisle smiles at me and leaves the room, I hold up the tape toward Noelle. "Can I have a copy of this?"

"Course..." Noelle perches herself against her headboard. "What are you going to do with it?"

"Maybe get Ashton's tongue tied and heart racing." I smile wickedly at her.

We both laugh as she says, "You're so evil."

Eight

The thing about lies is there are so many of them told throughout a person's life. There are so many different types of lies—white lies, bald-faced lies, fabrications, exaggerations, and even
compulsive lies—but no matter which form you use, it's still a lie, right? People seem to think lying isn't a bad thing to do; you won't have a date with the devil for telling a lie, because if you're good enough, smooth enough, you shouldn't get caught.

Everyone around me lies.

One thing I'd never imagine myself—of all people—doing is telling the biggest lie of all: that there's nothing wrong with me.

Last night, Noelle and I found something I believe could be possible evidence, alongside my own statement and Ashton's confession. I went to the police station, but the sheriff didn't agree and turned me away. When I went home, all I did was toss and turn, unable to sleep after finding out that the flashback I had about Ashton was actually true. To think, somehow, he was involved with what I've become disgusts me.

It's not a bad thing, what I've become—partially blind. I've done my research about all the different cases around the world and how they survive with it with help. It didn't help, though, because I still feel as if this is an unusual situation and I have no idea how to process it all, even weeks down the line.

When Noelle described Ashton to me on that footage and how he walked into the garage but soon came rushing out, my hands clenched into fists. My blood is hot like water on a stove, boiling and bubbling up over the edges of the pan. I'm like a volcano, ready to erupt. How could he leave me lying there after seeing me and hearing me plead for help? How could he pretend I didn't exist? I know he might have been scared, scared of what I might have said considering I woke up in a bedroom after he practically frisked me and dragged me up into it, but surely he has a heart.

The camera only shows us the door. You don't get to see where I was sitting, but to me, the footage tells me a thousand things. It tells me this whole thing is painfully real and I need to unravel the rest of it—*fast*.

Unfortunately for Ashton, even though sheriff Lou isn't taking me seriously, I have this footage in my hands and am ready to take every single bit of it serious.

My knuckles are white. My heart is sinking as fast as a rock forever lost in the deep blue water of the Pacific Ocean. I'm debating whether I should give Ashton the tape, and I shiver. I wonder if ruining his life is the best thing to do, but it's only fair if he's done this to me.

What if he didn't do it? What if he was just as scared as me?

There are a million and one questions I want to ask. I want my attacker to feel remorseful, more than I've ever wanted something before. I want Ashton to regret leaving me as much as I regret going to the party and passing out while having sex with him. I want him to hurt like I do every time I can't see the faces of those I love. I need so badly to make him scared, even if it is just the tiniest bit. That way I can get the answers I'm patiently waiting for.

"Lyss, go on—what are you doing?" Noelle links her arm with mine and places her hand over the top of my shaking one.

Warmth spreads through to my fingertips. "I don't really know."

Surely my plan will work; it has to. He'll be putty in my hands once he watches the tape, I just never thought my stomach would be filled with so much dread—more than usual, more than planned. To know someone who cared for me—or in his case, for my body—could do such a dreadful thing…it starts to feel unbearable to think about. Would I have done the same if the roles were reversed?

Would I heckers.

"Here, you do it." I smile tightly, passing the tape to Noelle.

She slips her hand around the rectangular black tape and starts to fumble with the vent of Ashton's locker. Finally, I hear a slight thud and the tape is gone, securely at the bottom, waiting for him.

"All done."

The hallway starts to fill with students after the sound of an extended ding. We keep our arms linked and walk forward with confidence in our stride.

Today is going to be a good day.

With my disability, Noelle has been placed in as many of my classes as they can manage without affecting her studies or causing suspicion. This makes it easier for me to get around. Senior year was always expected to be amazing. I want to be able to look back at it and remember it plain as day, but so far all I will have to remember is heartache.

This time, I can't blame a boy for causing it.

Even with the slight grey appearing across my eyes and a constant drained expression on my face, nobody has any idea I'm partially blind.

"Good morning, ladies." Mrs. Malone greets us as we enter her classroom. "Miss Darlington, Miss Carlisle." She nods and slightly bows to address us. I see the room so clearly. It's stored in the back of my memory, waiting for me to grasp it. So colorful and bright, it's always been a happy place to be, completely filled with paintings hanging up on the walls and everything you need to create a piece of art available to everyone in the storage cupboard at the back of the room. "Are we both as fresh as a daisy today?"

Mrs. Malone always uses the weirdest of phrases, and that's why she's my favorite teacher. I considered not taking her class anymore due to obviously not being able to see the colors or create a mind-blowing masterpiece, but Mrs. Malone encouraged me to stay—so I did.

I smile at her and offer a small wave. Noelle grunts and shrugs her off, leading me quietly to the back of the room. We sit behind our easels.

"Okay." Mrs. Malone claps her hands. "So, let me begin class with something you should never, ever forget."

Suddenly, there's a bang as the door opens and it echoes around the space, interrupting her. "Sorry," a raspy voice addresses the room.

"Mr. Dwight," Mrs. Malone sings in a voice so cheerful it starts to hurt my ears. "Thank you for joining us—better late than never."

There's a snicker from the rest of the class as Conan heads for his seat.

"Like I said, guys and girls, I'm going to start with something you should never forget: never, ever be late to my class, otherwise it's detention."

Laughter spills from Conan's lips as he says, "Sorry, miss."

My heart starts pounding, exposing itself through my t-shirt, which is grey to go with my grey heart and grey eyesight.

"Is everyone ready?" The chatter gives way to silence. "Awesome. I would like to start by telling you more about art." She starts to slowly walk around as she speaks. "Art is something you yourself have to see. It's a vision of beauty and creativity. Anyone can create a piece of art, but only an artist can feel it with their hands and with their eyes closed." She takes big strides across the room, her presence strong. She's making a statement, and I respect her for that. "Now, everyone please grab a piece of A2 paper and a pen or pencil, whichever you prefer. Once done, set yourself up at your easel and close your eyes."

I listen to scuffles of shoes against the brown vinyl flooring and scraping of stools as they're slid back and forth. Before I can blink, a piece of paper is placed in front of me. "Thanks." I smile.

"No problem, doll face." Ethan chuckles. I hear him high-five someone, probably one of the guys as they all huddle around an easel in their blue letterman jackets.

Lindsey walks past me, hitting my shoulder. "Ugh. Should have made her get it herself—her legs aren't broken."

No, but your face will be in a minute.

"No, but yours will be if you carry on." Noelle stands in front of me. "Keep walking, Montelowe." Noelle places her hand on my shoulder, squeezing it gently, then bends down so her lips are close to my ear. "Ignore her." Noelle sits back behind her easel and everyone waits silently for Mrs. Malone to continue.

"All ready?" Mumbles all blur into one answer—we are set to go. "Everyone please draw what is currently on your mind. Imagery is something artists use every day. It's an expression of imagination that makes your art so beautiful." She sits in her chair at the front of the class. "Please begin."

I hear the pens and pencils scratching quickly against the paper. People are most likely cheating by peeking, making sure it's perfect, but I didn't have that option. I start drawing, letting my hand guide me. I let my imagination take me away, just like she told us to. For some crazy reason, I have a feeling this lesson isn't a coincidence. It isn't about creating an image without your eyes being able to perfect it; she's done it for me, for everyone exactly like me. What none of the others realize is in this moment, while they put pencil to paper, they're just like me.

I respect Mrs. Malone even more for that.

The hour is coming to an end as students place their pencils down. I jump as a hand lands on my shoulder, and I automatically stiffen from the touch. I hear gasps behind me, around me, in front of me, and I suddenly feel claustrophobic as everyone closes in.

"Wow," Noelle starts.

"Amazing, Darlington," Conan finishes.

My cheeks flush pink, filling with embarrassment. I shudder at the touch on my shoulder and grab Noelle's familiar hand, gripping it slightly and hoping she understands that this is my way of pleading with her to get me out of here, away from all the stares and whispers filling the room.

My drawing is of a guy standing with a girl, and that guy is looking at the girl with so much love and care while they are dancing underneath the stars. Coincidentally, the guy's features are similar to those of Conan Dwight. I have completely shafted myself now.

I hear Mrs. Malone's voice in the distance. "Fabulous, Alyssa."

The walk to calculus seems longer than usual. When stepping out of the classroom, I inhale the telltale smells of bleach and lemon zest throughout the hallway. Noelle stays extremely quiet, walking beside me and guiding me. As she leaves to go to her next class, she doesn't even say bye.

Something is wrong.

Mr. Ronald begins the class just like Mrs. Malone did. For the remainder of the hour, he stands at the front by the blackboard and teaches us about equations. I mentally thank him for not asking us to write. I suck away the woody taste of my pencil, which I've just been chewing.

"Please get yourselves into pairs now," he bellows, and the sounds of scraping chairs and constant chatter arise throughout the classroom.

Before I can even think about moving, Tommy sits beside me. "Don't you worry that pretty little head, Lyss. I'm here to save you."

I raise my eyebrows and place my hand under my chin, smiling at him. "Who says I need saving?"

"By the look of that textbook, you definitely need saving." He laughs.

I look down, confused. "Huh?"

"You do know you're reading the equations upside down, right?" He stares at me, amused. The tone of his voice tells me he's playing.

I drop my mouth open while looking at him then back at the book. I quickly snatch it up and turn it around.

This makes him chuckle under his breath. "I know how much you hate calculus. Don't worry, though—you know I always do the work."

He's right. Every year he is there, sitting by my side and making sure I don't fail. Calculus isn't my strongest subject. The only equation I know how to do is guy plus girl equals baby, so use protection, kids, and wrap it up well, guys.

Obviously, this shows I'm doomed. I chuckle along. "My hero."

Noelle is waiting outside in the halls. She loops her arm through mine without saying a single word and we head toward the food hall, just like we do every day.

"Noelle?" I ask cautiously. "What's wrong?" She ignores me and waves at the rest of her friends. "Noelle?"

"Do you remember anything else from that night?" Her question catches me off guard.

I halt quickly and unlink my arm from hers. "Some things." My head debates on what to tell her: *the truth?*

She crosses her arms over her chest. "Like what?"

I can't do it. We start to walk again, heading into the cafeteria. It splits into two lines and we head toward the drool-worthy smell of tasty food from the lengthiest row. We each pick up a tray and saunter to the back.

Surely what I've shared with her is enough?

I stand still in the line, waiting for it to become shorter, for us to get close enough to see the food. For me it's the smell, the aroma of crisp chicken and spices drifting through the air—it smells like an Indian restaurant.

"Well?" Noelle pushes.

"Why do you want to know? Does it matter what else I remember?" I grip my tray tighter. "I've told you everything that's important. You should be more concerned about whether or not I remember who attacked me." I scrunch my face up and start scratching my wrist, balancing the tray over one arm while hiding it.

"Next!" the lunch lady shouts.

We arrive to the front of the line. I place my elbows on the metal counter and lean over to sniff. I hold my tray out, smelling chicken korma as the woman balances my plate on top of my tray, requiring me to stop scratching and grab either end steadily. I start walking toward a table and Noelle follows, grasping my elbow to keep me from falling.

We sit down and I hear Lindsey and Charlotte's voices not far from us, both flirting with Ethan, Conan, Ashton, and Levi—the rest of their gang.

"You lied." Noelle taps the tabletop next to where my food is placed. My attention is on her and her only. "You lied to me. You told me you can't remember anything else."

I gasp. "When?" *I'm starting to lie a lot.* "When did I say that?"

"The day you told me what happened to you, when we were sitting with Maggie—you told me you couldn't remember anything else and I believed you. I assumed if you could, you'd tell me."

"Why the hell does it matter? I told you everything that's important." I squint my eyes. "So, tell me, how did I lie?"

"It matters, Lyss. It matters because you never mentioned you danced with Conan, and I've been waiting for you to remember it."

"Waiting?" I scrunch my whole face up, confused. The room and everything in it stands still. "You're pissed about a little memory I only just recalled…"

She stares at me.

"You're pissed about a little memory that has no significance and that I therefore kept to myself?"

She stands up, slamming her fists down in front of me. "That drawing shows a lot more than just a memory you *just recalled*," she sneers under her breath and leans down closer to me. "If you can remember that, what else do you remember, huh?" Noelle's hands are shaking, shaking the table along with them.

"Am I missing a joke somewhere in this argument? What is your problem!?" I shake my head, disbelieving my ears. "If you really want to know, I was too drunk to even remember if Conan and I exchanged any words with each other, never mind whether we flipping danced! Get a grip—you don't even like Conan."

She's always told me he's too big for his boots.

Noelle pushes her tray into mine harshly, sending chicken korma sauce splashing all over the table. Before I can stop her, she stomps her feet and leaves me sitting alone. By the sounds of squealing and laughter, she's joining Lindsey and her girls.

Two-faced cow.

My mouth pops open. I'm unable to comprehend the point of that argument—why on earth did she just get annoyed with me so suddenly? I don't understand how to conclude that explosion—I don't understand, and I wish I did.

I stand up and walk away from the table, leaving my food untouched. I follow my footsteps back along the way Noelle led me in, concentrating on the grey outline of everyone's feet, hoping I don't fall. I make out the tall lockers as I enter the halls that are familiar to me and I continue to walk, heading toward a safe haven.

Nine

Footsteps tread towards me.

I'm rearranging the books in my locker, hoping the time passes by quickly.

"Darlington!" Conan calls out, and his footsteps begin to stride in a rhythm. His presence makes me weak at the knees, and I don't even have to look at him to instantly know someone swoon-worthy is standing beside me.

I slam my locker door and start to walk off, but he keeps up with my stride. I glance at his shadow and notice a smile upon his lips. Being somewhat blind probably works in my favor because if I could see it clearly, that smile would most likely have me dropping at his feet, passed out.

"Look, about yesterday, you—sort of—um…misunderstood me."

I sigh. I never misunderstand him; his type's predictable. No matter how high I climb up the social ladder, he wouldn't dare be seen with someone like me when it comes to dating.

Three years.

Three years it's taken him to notice me, again.

Three years to remember my name, and it's coincidentally just after the attack.

While we walk, I keep my head facing down to the floor, and he keeps his pace alongside me, showing no sign of leaving. "I didn't mean for you to dislike me. That wasn't the plan."

"Plan?"

"Nah, I didn't mean plan…"

"You said plan."

He glares. "I didn't—"

"What?" I smile.

He shakes his head and sighs. "Has anyone ever told you you're diabolical?"

I laugh. "Nope, but you just did."

He shoves his hands into his pockets and shrugs his shoulders. "So…" He stops and takes one hand out of his pocket, touching my arm gently. "Like I said, I didn't mean for you to dislike me."

My head's facing his and both my eyebrows arch, meeting in the middle. "How so?"

"Well, I know you don't like me, which is cool. I just didn't want you thinking I'm a creepy dude that stalked you."

"Stalked?" I lean my back against the lockers. The hallway is quiet.

His upper arm touches mine as he does the same thing. "Truthfully…" He nudges me playfully, his shadow close to mine, and the smell of peppermint swiftly enters my nostrils. "I didn't want to scare such a pretty girl away, but I'm starting to think that's exactly what I've done." He coughs into his fist. "So…I'm sorry."

I look up at him dreamily, eyes wide, me standing at five foot five and him maybe just at six foot.

"Are you okay after the whole car situation?"

I shrug. "Nearly dying is my specialty."

He turns toward me, his shoulder now touching the locker as he leans on his side. I turn into the same position and we stand facing each other.

"Nearly dying, huh?" Conan says.

I chuckle. "Didn't you know? I love the drama of being involved in an incident."

His musical laughter tumbles out of his mouth, and my heart is drumming so loudly.

He leans back onto the back of heels. "So."

"So," I say, leaning back on my heels. I try so badly to see him, try to see past the dark and imagine his sun-kissed skin so close to mine.

"Hey, your drawing—I just want to tell you, you're an amazing artist. I liked it."

My face is beet red; every time I'm around him, I turn crimson. "Really? Out of everyone, I thought you might have found it a little creepy." I bite my lip to try to keep the smile off my face, though it's trying so hard to surface.

"I liked It. It captures our first dance perfectly." He puts two and two together. "Next time, hopefully it's under the stars."

He places his hand on my elbow and I melt, thinking he's going to pull me in closer, but he just moves us farther along the lockers so a guy can get into his.

"Thanks bro." The guy nods his head while holding an armful of books.

I look at Conan and imagine his handsome lopsided grin. All I want to do is sit and admire it all day. Cutting the moment, an overexcited pig of a guy comes bounding toward us and heavy-handedly slaps Conan's back. Two seconds later, the guy stands in between us and sluggishly hangs his scrawny arms over both our shoulders. His hair is combed over into a high quiff.

"Dwight, my man, come on—you'll miss out standing with this tease here." Levi Foley shakes my shoulder and laughs. "The afternoon game is about to start." He hops a little, clearly excited.

He needs to learn about inside and outside voices, because my eardrum is about to burst open.

Football games are a massive deal in high school; the whole school goes wild. To me, it's an excuse for a party afterward, a reason for the jocks to let their hair down after working so hard on the field. Everyone else raves about the games, drools over the guys, and gives the cheerleaders an excuse to dance in the public eye.

Levi glances to the side and lets his eyes bore into my head. "Hey, I know you—Alyssa Darlington. You're the girl who got—"

Before he finishes, someone slaps my ass, making me tense up. Ethan stands behind me and high-fives Levi, laughing. Ethan wiggles his eyebrows and I grit my teeth harshly, scraping them together. *The blond bombastic fool.* I tug myself out from under Levi's arm.

"Ethan, you—" I go to slap him.

Levi pushes Ethan backward, making me miss, and looks at Conan. "Con, come on, let's go."

"Wait." Conan grabs Ethan's arm and pulls him forward. "Say you're sorry!"

"What?" Ethan laughs.

I fold my arms over my chest and place my back against the locker, not knowing where to look with all three boys surrounding me. Three shadows emerge as the light dims, and I watch as arms grab the guy standing to my left, pulling him in front of me. Conan and Levi laugh in unison.

"Say sorry to Alyssa, Ethan," Conan demands. "You don't treat a girl like that."

Ethan looks at me, a musky smell drifting off him. "Sorry," he mumbles. I barely hear him.

"What's that?" I cup my ear and lean forward.

"Sorry," Ethan says through gritted teeth.

I flash my pearly white teeth. "It's okay."

Levi gets Ethan into a headlock and ruffles his blond waves, making them both laugh.

"Hopefully see ya around?" Conan asks softly. Ethan leans in to kiss me on the cheek but Conan pulls him away. There's a swift motion in the air as the guys wave at me.

"Mm, maybe." My pearly whites are still showing while I grin widely. "Or maybe not. Guess we'll have to wait and find out." My eyes sparkle like stars and my stomach is no longer filling up with dread as it turns into delightful happiness.

"I guess we will." Conan walks away, his back to me.

"Nice meeting ya, Alyssa." Levi smirks. "Don't think we had the chance to make acquaintances at the party."

Levi and Conan push Ethan forward and all three of them start jogging away.

It's nearing the end of lunch as everyone starts filling the halls. I stand there wondering if Noelle will find me. I don't always want to count on her, but recently, it's turning out that way, whether I like it or not.

I think back to this morning and wonder whether my plan will work; I haven't seen Ashton since Noelle and I dropped the footage in his locker, ready for him to watch.

I stand up straight and people pass me by. Everyone heads for the back doors and out toward the football field. Classes were canceled this afternoon for the home game and every student is expected to be there, but I don't want to even attempt to try to make my way into the crowd without Noelle.

The game is still happening and I'm sitting against the lockers, listening to a bit of Jessie J, waiting for it to end. I listen closely to voices around the corner; they're shouting at one another. I slowly take my headphones out of my ears and scramble to stand up. I lean around the lockers and the corner. It takes me a while to realize Ashton's having a breakdown.

He starts to stammer and I hear hushed voices.

"You don't understand—you will never understand," Ashton whispers. "What should I do?" Harsh tones escape his lips and his fist hits the locker door full force. "I swear to God, I'll kick your ass. I am not taking the blame for this."

I place my hand over my mouth and lean back against the lockers, stopping myself from making any sound. I can't believe what I'm hearing. My mind has plummeted sixty miles per hour deep into a world I don't understand.

"That footage will make people ask questions. What if the sheriff brings me back in? I can't handle it." I hear Ashton slam someone's back into the lockers, and I peek around the corner to try to get a better view. "I'm going to be a prime suspect while you walk away hands clean—I don't think so, bro."

My knees give way and I try to balance against the wall, my breathing jagged. I inhale slowly, trying to process everything.

"Me? It wasn't my fault, man!" The guy shoves Ashton backward, making him kick the locker door next to the guy's chest. "Look, I had no idea this would happen, did I? All I did was tell you the plan—it was you who messed it all up," he growls. "You and your druggy ass."

My knees can't handle the impact of the second voice, and before I can do anything about it, I collapse, dropping to the floor from exhaustion, desperation, and maybe even disappointment.

"Did you hear that?" Ashton asks, probably looking around to make sure he's safe.

"You're so extremely paranoid."

My ears are buzzing, they're ringing so badly. I think I'm floating in a nightmare, a paranormal nightmare, unable to escape. I must be sleeping.

"How dare you! All that has happened—it is *not* my fault." Ashton's fist hits the locker again.

"Whatever helps you sleep at night." The second voice returns for me to hear, causing my heart to break piece by piece.

"Your girl makes me sleep at night," Ashton retorts. I cringe.

The guy rams him into the lockers and sucker-punches him. "You wish."

"Dude, I don't need to wish, I've had her," Ashton growls, spitting out the blood, caused from the blow to the face.

Standing ten feet away from me and fighting so casually with Ashton Marston is someone I know—someone I know *very* well. In fact, the voice belongs to a person I not only know, but a person I care for dearly. In a million years, I'd never put these two guys together in one picture, two complete opposites from totally different ends of the social spectrum—but here they are, standing, talking, conversing.

Ashton Marston and Tommy Henderson.

I feel sick.

Ten

Tommy and Alyssa.

Alyssa and Tommy.

We've been best friends for nine years and counting.

We've always spent most of our nights in front of the television and having movie marathons, which always led to me crashing next to him on my bed. By the following morning, I'd be curled up in his arms.

He's such a pain to sleep next to.

If people hadn't known we were friends, they'd probably mistake us for a loved-up couple—which, of course, is absolutely stupid considering he's like the overprotective brother I never had. I've seen more bare skin on him than what you'd see if we were starting out our relationship for the very first time.

After I hear his voice standing there in the hallway, listening to him with Ashton, the thought of us ever—and I mean *ever*—being in a relationship makes me queasy.

What hurts the most is he's normally my savior; at all the parties we've attended, he's always been there to rescue me. I get too drunk, and he drags me away before I make a fool of myself. He's my sidekick, my Ron Stoppable, and I'm his Kim Possible. In fact, we're like a younger, less notorious Bonnie and Clyde.

Tommy Henderson and Ashton Marston—now that doesn't fit. It's like having marmite with chocolate. They've never been in the same social circle, and they've never shared the same interests. Tommy's into books, Ashton's into drugs—like I said, *complete* opposites.

Everyone loves Tommy for the sweet, innocent soul he's got. If I ever told anyone he's the one who attacked me, I doubt they'd ever believe me. *Hell, I don't even think I believe it.* It just doesn't add up. Of all the people, why would Ashton be questioning Tommy, and why would Tommy be involved? I don't—*can't*—understand anything anymore.

I pick myself up from off the floor and lean against the beige wall. I steady myself and stand, frozen in place. I want to run, as fast and far away as I can possibly manage, but only cowards run, and I'm no coward. I try to hold back the tears, but it doesn't take long before I start to tremble. My hands start to shake, my legs follow, and then my whole body ends up quivering. I'm melting down, bit by bit, like a candle. I'm trying to replay the conversation the guys just had.

I hear the cheers and laughter spill into the hallway as the doors to the football field open. Here, in America, football is a massive popularity thing in high schools, especially Valley View High. To me, I find it very similar to rugby. I prefer soccer to football, but then again, my dad never sat me down and explained it.

Joyous squeals and happy chatter fill my ears, telling me we're winning the game. All the happiness suffocating me is everything I felt once upon a time. I used to be amongst the crowds, fangirling over the boys in uniform, squealing and laughing.

Everyone out there is doing exactly that. So, when I hear his voice next to me, it's unexpected.

I push against the wall and start to run as fast as my legs can take me.

"Alyssa! Alyssa, wait! Please, stop." Muscly arms catch me just as I nearly collapse to the floor once more. "What's happening?" I stay curled over with Conan's arms wrapped tightly around my waist, and my head buries into his chest.

"You remember my name?" I ask stupidly. I clutch his t-shirt, letting my fingers curl themselves around the soft fabric.

Of course he remembers your name, you idiot.

My name sounds angelic when it crosses Conan's lips. It's weird to hear him say it again. Conan slides us both down the wall gently, never letting go and positioning himself beside me. I lean into him, snuggling my body into his and allowing the comfort to calm me.

"Yeah, ha. I remember your name." He chuckles. "Why wouldn't I? I've been in the same school as you for years." He stares at me, and I so wish I could see into those beautiful eyes. "Are you going to explain to me why you're sobbing so hard against my chest and drenching my shirt in the process?"

I move my head to rest on his hard, warm shoulder, trying to cherish the moment. The last thing I want is for him to vanish, to go *poof* and be gone.

"I..." I sniff. "I can't really explain." Tears are rolling down my cheeks, dripping off onto my cotton skirt. His finger hesitates by my cheek and slowly reaches to gently wipe the tears away, one at a time on either side. His other hand rubs my arm, and all that crosses my mind is the feel of his body against mine. I sniff, trying to stop the snot dripping out of my nose, and I get a whiff of his aftershave. It's so sweet and light, with a hint of a rich smell. The smell of changing seasons overpowers me—that, and how safe I am.

"No pressure..." His voice is deep and seductive. "But if you ever want to talk about it, Mr. Dwight's ears are open for business." He drags his hand through his dark curls. "You can pay me in favors."

I turn to look at him, really look at him, and try to take him seriously, but his eyebrows start wiggling. He used to do it when we were younger, and it always told me he was in a playful mood.

"Pfft. You sound like an escort." I bring my hair to the front, letting it hang down over my shoulder. I start to play with an auburn strand.

"Only for you, malady." He squeezes my leg gently and tilts his head, grinning ear to ear.

"Malady?" I laugh and snort. My hand shoots up to my mouth, covering it, and my eyes widen.

He laughs. "Well you are British, after all."

"So, I am." I start braiding the strand. "Aren't you missing the football game?"

Conan plays basketball, not football, making him even more dreamy. "Funny thing about that—I came back inside to get Ashton." He looks around. "We were supposed to sit together but he never showed." He nudges my side. "You could always come sit with me."

I'm about to accept Conan's offer then the sound of Ashton's name escaping from his lips catches me, making me go stiff. Then, I burst into tears—*again*.

"Woah!" Conan pulls me closer, allowing my head to bury itself farther into his neck, where I smell all kinds of goodness. "I never thought asking a girl to sit with me would make them cry. Guess there's a first time for everything, huh."

I want to tell him about Ashton so he knows it's not what he's said, but would he believe me? Believe me over one of his *boys*? I doubt it. I stay quiet, knowing it's for the best.

"Are you okay, Darlington?" I hear the vibrations in his neck from where the sound of worry emerges.

"Sorry, I'm hormonal," I choke out. *Hormonal?*

He lets out a belly laugh. "I really, really wanted to know that."

What the hell did I just say?

"I-I'm sure you hear it all the time…" I try to save myself and glance up from under my long, thick eyelashes. "You have what, three sisters?"

"Someone's been doing their research."

I cock my head to the side and stare at the shadow of his face, dreaming of the reality. "I've been in the same school as you for years—we were even friends, once upon a time."

He chuckles. "I guess we were. Tina is five, Ellie is ten, and Lola is twenty-one. It's like home of the Dwight women—we could make our own TV commercial." Conan moves his arm away from me and starts to play with his sneaker. One leg is drawn in, the other stretched out. He balances his arm on the bent one and stares at me.

"Must be tough, being the only boy," I ask, praying I haven't crossed a line.

"It is—well, there was me and my dad. I think even he got sick of the house being overrun by women. Probably why he left us for another family."

"That's awful. Sounds like my mom—she's never at home. I swear she loves her job more than her family—or maybe just more than me." I sit up, grabbing a hair tie from around my wrist. I scrape my hair up high, tying it back into a messy bun.

Conan touches my hair gently. "I like it."

Butterflies form in my stomach and my cheeks turn pink, making it look like I've dipped my head in blush. When I tell Conan things, it feels so natural. My thoughts just fluently release themselves. There's no hesitation, and I'm sure he isn't the sort of person to judge. It's so surreal sitting here with him.

Two girls interrupt the moment and start giggling as they walk past us. They sound like children as they say, "Hey Conan," wiggling their fingers.

"Hey girls," he says, so kindly. Their giggles become louder and more childish until finally fading out in the distance.

"*Hey girls!*" I mimic in a deep, rough voice.

Now who's being childish, Alyssa.

Conan laughs and pinches his nose, his laugh sounding so vocally beautiful.

"Seriously, admit it—you love girls worshipping at your feet."

He runs his hand back through his tight curls. "I'm just being nice."

"Please!" I snicker and we both stare at each other. I can't see much of him, only that he's fuzzy, but his image is gentle and lightly toned. I remind myself to pray tonight that I'll see his face again. It's not an impossible wish, surely.

He cocks his head, "Can I ask you something?"

"I think you're going to ask me anyway, so go on." I place my knees under my chin.

"Do you remember much from...you know, that night?"

I force an unnatural smile out. "Not really." I shuffle my feet beneath me and start playing with the shoelaces of my white Converse. "All I remember is being cold and alone. Anything before that appears as a blur."

Another lie.

"Noelle said you don't tend to act that way, and from what I remember, you were a sweet, innocent thirteen-year-old."

"Noelle?" *Damn you, Noelle.* I stretch my legs out in his direction.

"Yeah, that night I was asked to speak to you, something about you having a *ma-hoo-sive* crush on me." He nudges my side playfully.

"Um, nah." I flap my hand down, pushing him away. "Crush on you? Don't flatter yourself, big boy." My neck turns a darker shade of red that quickly travels up to my cheeks, replacing the pink color. I dip my face toward my lap and laugh.

Conan's eyebrows ride up, meeting his creases. "So, it's not true?"

I stare. "Nope." I pronounce the p with a *pop*.

"Not even a teeny-weeny bit?"

"Not even a teeny-weeny-tiny bit." We both smile and Conan groans, gently hitting his head against the wall, and I can't help but laugh.

He gets to his feet and offers a hand out toward me. I ignore it accidentally and stand up with the help of the wall behind me. I begin to feel better but don't want him to leave. I don't tell him that, though, due to him needing to get his inflated ego to fit through the door frame.

"Well, I'm going to see if I can go home. I'm exhausted," I say.

Conan grabs hold of my hand, entwining our fingers. His touch is electrifying and wonderful all at the same time. I look down to where our fingers fit together perfectly, and I try to wipe the surprised shock off my face.

He leads me toward the administration office. "I'm going to walk with you for a bit—is that okay?" He towers over me, and I think about how every girl in our school appreciates how tall and lean he is.

I nod, very quickly, and I mentally tell myself to stop.

"Are you okay, pretty? You seem a bit rosy in the cheeks."

My free hand flies up to my face and pats. My hands are cold and my skin flushes at the contact, allowing me to become refreshed, and I whisper, "I'm good."

We stand outside the office and Conan keeps hold of my hand, which is a bonus.

He tilts his head to the side and tucks a strand of my hair behind my ear. He seems to like doing that. "There's a party coming up, this Friday." My eyes widen, waiting for him to continue. "I'm wondering...if you would like...I mean, only if you want to, no pressure—"

My insides start to squeal with excitement.

"Alyssa!" Noelle shouts, stumbling forward. "There you are." Her arm slides through mine.

Conan steps backward, as if she's contagious. He nods his head. "All right."

"Dwight." Noelle turns to face me, clearly ignoring everything around us, including Conan. "So about earlier, I was being a bit extreme. You know me, a magnet for drama. Don't worry, though—I'll make it up to you, pinky swear."

I'm not sure where to look. The atmosphere's been cut with a blunt knife. Noelle throws question after question at me and we both end up ignoring Conan as he stands in front of us, which I never wanted to happen.

"Are you ready for your appointment?" she asks me.

"I'll see ya later, Darlington." Conan starts walking away but smiles in my direction—even being blind won't let me miss that. "Hope you feel better soon."

I long for his touch, like a lovesick puppy. Noelle pulls me away in the opposite direction and my mind races back to earlier. I don't feel confident telling her about Tommy and Ashton with her playing hot and cold. I know she'd never purposely hurt me, but then again, I'd say the same for Tommy, and look how that's ended up. Noelle's unpredictable—I mean, she just barged in on me and Conan right when he was about to ask me to the party on Friday. She's just broken all sorts of friendship honor. Not cool. I try to face her calmly but can't help being irritated and flustered.

"What did Conan want?" Noelle pouts.

I snap, "Nothing." I don't want to walk with Noelle, and I definitely don't want to talk to her. Why she's taking me to go see Maggie, I have no idea. I just want to go home.

Noelle guides me to a small confined corridor close to Maggie's office and waits with me. My escape mission is a no-go. I'm stuck here with silence awkwardly dividing us.

"What did he mean, 'Hope you feel better soon?'" Noelle continues to bug me.

I curl my hands into fists. "Exactly that."

She pulls at my arm, forcing me to look at her. Curry lingers on her breath. "Don't be a smartass." Her grip tightens around my arm. "What does he mean? Did he tell you something?"

"Doesn't matter," I say, barely a whisper.

"You're angry at me, aren't you? Has he told you something? Is this about earlier? Come on, just tell me what he meant." She glares, but I don't open my mouth. She flaps the side of her arm and tugs on mine. "Jeez, you're being a bitch, Alyssa. I said I'm sorry."

I stand tall, my mouth dropping to the floor, not understanding why she's behaving this way. How dare she kick off with me and demand I tell her about Conan? We both know it has nothing to do with her.

"I'm not angry. Like, seriously, I just want to go home." I sigh, trying to pull my arm out of her grasp, but she keeps hold of me. "Let go—you're hurting me."

Noelle drops her hand and moves from in front of me to sit on the floor. "I know there's something up, Lyssa."

I sigh heavily and rub my hands over my eyes as my eyelids droop from sleep deprivation. "Look, I'll tell ya what's up if you tell me why you're flipping out so much." I sit down beside her and let our legs touch. I find her hand, place it on top of my knee, and cup it gently.

Her hand becomes clammy. "I was being OTT, way overdramatic—you know me."

I can always tell when Noelle lies because her little finger twitches. She stands up quickly, dropping my hand from hers.

"Liar." I clench my fists and practically spit at her. I stand up and start to walk away, fed up by her outbursts. Before I'm able to take my second step, she grabs my arm—always my arm—to stop me. "Get. Off. Me. Now."

I look around, trying to see If I recognize my bearings before setting off, because one thing I don't want to do is start heading the wrong way. I look left then right, but I'm still not sure which way is the exit. I hate not knowing.

"If I let go, you're going to run off."

I let my eyebrows touch in the middle. "And?"

Noelle throws her hands into the air, defeated, and continues to wave them about, giving me a chance to make my exit. "Please don't go. These sessions with Maggie will help you, and we both want to know what happened. I want you to be happy."

I have my back to her, and I stop dead in the middle of the hallway. "Tell me, why do you even care?"

She collapses against the wall with a light thud. I concentrate on her shadow as she rubs her face with her hands and stomps her foot like a spoiled child. "I don't care about Conan-flipping-macho-mucho-Dwight."

"I never—"

"Don't be stupid—stupidity doesn't suit you." I hear her walk toward me, and she gently brings me to sit next to her against the wall. "You can't leave, Lyssa. You need these sessions so badly, like badly doesn't even cover it. I'm going to wait here until Maggie comes and then I'll leave. We can talk about all this nonsense another day."

"No, Noelle." I look at her sternly. "We will talk about this now."

She laughs, and it's squeaky, high, and fake. "Look, I don't care about square-faced Conan. That's your job."

"As you keep saying."

The pipes in the walls creak like a drill against metal.

Noelle whispers, "You'll hate me."

"Don't be silly—I could never hate you." *Stupid girl.*

"You will. You will really, really hate me. There's no coming back from this. I know you; I know how you think, and I know how you're going to react. If I tell you, you'll really, extremely, wholeheartedly despise me."

I tap her kneecap and chuckle. "Did anyone ever tell you that you should join the drama club?"

She's silent. I hear doors squeak as they're opened and closed and the scuffle of feet far in the distant hall.

"Conan and I…w-we slept together." Barely a whisper comes out of her mouth, but I swear she just said she slept with Conan.

My jaw drops to the ground and my chest tightens. I try to breath, try to take in the words and understand them.

She was right, but I don't just wholeheartedly hate her.

I despise her.

Very flipping much.

"You bitch!"

Eleven

In the space of fifteen minutes, I have a hundred and one missed calls, and even now, the phone keeps ringing. Eager doesn't even cover it, nor does desperation. Noelle calling me endlessly is a sign of guilt, and let's face it, that's what she is—guilty.

After telling me she slept with Conan, her words just kept on coming out, faster and faster to the point where I couldn't even understand her. Honestly, I didn't even *want* to understand what she had to say. I could tell her chin had dipped and her eyes were pointing to the ground. I could also see her hands being stuffed into her coat pockets, buried deep, until she couldn't stretch any farther. All these actions showed she's ashamed, and she didn't even have to say the words: *I'm sorry.*

I didn't want to stick around or hear her voice, so I flew out of the school as fast as a blind girl was able to. My feet stumbled over one another as they moved quickly, and tears rolled down my face, the cold air making icicles appear on my skin. I didn't want to believe my own best friend could jump into bed with the guy she knows I have a crush on. This guy's the same person she supposedly can't stand because he is an 'obnoxious jock.'

Two words come to mind: two-faced.

I lie on my bed and listen as the ringtone on my phone plays again. "You've Got a Friend in Me" sounds throughout the room, filling it and making me want to scream.

"Will you answer that bloody phone before I throw it out the window?" Mom slides her British accent across her tongue, so easily, so effortlessly. She's standing out on the landing, just outside my bedroom, and her words are spoken through gritted teeth and forced restraint.

"Don't you think I would if I could see, mother dearest?" I roll my eyes up into my head. "I'd block the number, wouldn't I? But, oh wait—that's not going to happen because I. Can't. See."

I carefully listen and she stops what she's doing. She stomps toward me, and it can only mean one thing: I've pissed her off. "Whose number?"

She stands in the doorway and places her arms across her chest.

I snap, "None of your business."

Fusco curls himself up into a ball at the bottom of my bed. His little chest expands and contracts, and soft snores emanate from him. He rests peacefully, minding his own business—just like my mother should.

"Excuse me young lady, you're living in my house, under *my* roof. Therefore, your business is my business."

I lower my brow at the petite shadowed figure leaning against the door frame. "Dad's roof, actually."

She starts to brew, like a coffee machine, grinding, stirring, pouring, and steam is letting loose. "That's it!" My mom storms toward me. "I'm sick to death of your flipping cheek." She grabs my arm and starts to drag me off my bed. "Get your ass out of this bedroom now."

My grey long-sleeved top pulls tightly against my shoulders, squeezing them as she scrunches my sleeves in her hands. Fusco jumps off the bed and starts growling, followed by a bark, warning her to let me go. She pulls me onto the landing, and he follows, baring his teeth. Every time I finally get used to my surroundings, she yanks me, sending my mind into a daze.

"Get off me!" I pull away from her, making her grab more roughly, catching my delicate strands of hair in her grasp. Bruises start to form underneath her fingertips, and the tender sensation travels throughout as I start to ache with pain. She doesn't mean to hurt me…I don't think she does, anyway.

There's just me and Mom home, and I'm glad Mia doesn't have to see this. It pleases me more than you know. In Mia's eyes, Mom is golden, the best thing since sliced bread. To me, she's a disappointing, moldy piece of crust with an ugly personality.

My mom's face comes close to mine, nearly touching it. Her mouth is opposite my nose, and distilled alcohol mixed with this morning's coffee enters my body. Normally, coffee is a magical substance that turns my mom from *I can't stand you* to *good morning, my lovely child.* Today, with the mix of alcohol, she's on a different planet, the lady-with-an-alcohol-problem planet.

"You, my child, need to stop feeling sorry for yourself. Stop hating everyone around you. Everyone is trying to help you. Start acting like an adult."

I trip over the clothes on the upstairs hallway, and if not for my mother's very tight grip, I'd be faceplanting on the floor. The dogs start going crazy; Charlie is at the bottom of the stairs, letting out deep, robust barks, and Fusco is still baring his teeth. They are both trying to protect me.

I hate this woman who calls herself a mother. I want the old version of her back. "You're insane."

A mother, she isn't.

Her long, soft hair and electrifying green eyes are the only things that make her beautiful; the rest of her, she needs to work on. Over the past two years, she's learned to ignore us and treats us like dirt on the bottom of her shoes. The only word that comes to mind when trying to describe the woman who's clutching at me is disgusting.

I attempt to pull away from her, hoping she'll loosen her grip. I struggle, trying to see where I am. I keep tugging in the opposite direction, but she doesn't let go. I don't understand the reason for this—what is it achieving?

The sound of the front door opening bounces off the walls and around the house. The dogs start barking toward the entrance, and just as my dad walks in, she lets go of me. I fall backward, not expecting it. I try to steady myself and get my balance, but it's too late. When I bounce back, I hit my head against the wall behind me. Fusco runs over, curling himself up onto my lap and licking my face like I'm made of ice cream.

"Ouch," I curse, more to myself than anyone else. My head throbs, pounding against my skull. I place both hands on the back of it and push down, hoping the pressure will relieve the constant sharp jabs coming through to my forehead.

My father grabs hold of Charlie's collar. "What the hell is going on?"

He raises his voice, shocking me. My eyes fly open and the color drains from my face. I bring my hands from behind my head and start to stroke Fusco's back.

Before my mom opens her mouth, I try to explain quickly. "Mom started it! Grabbing me and dragging me across my bedroom. When I tried to pull away, she wouldn't let go of me."

She stands next to me, silently, not even trying to defend herself.

When I glance around, I struggle to see her shadow, but I imagine the tension between my parents as they look one another in the eyes. I know my dad loves the bones of that woman. Can I say the same for her, or that the same feelings are returned? Two years ago, I may have.

"Where are you going?" Dad asks Mom. "We need to talk about this, as a family."

I watch as the grey image of my mother places a dark, long, probably green coat around her shoulders. It's the same coat my dad bought her for their anniversary last year. He always said it made her eyes sparkle. She buttons herself up and begins to slip her black Chelsea boots on her feet. All I care about in that moment is Dad. Will he be okay? Because he doesn't deserve any of this.

My mom's index finger starts waving back and forth. "We"—her finger points to herself then to Dad—"don't need to discuss anything, but I—I need to go to work," she says, as if nothing even happened.

Behind her, the door shuts gently, and Dad and I both look at each other, knowing we won't see her until the morning. I'm hurting, and in this moment, something comes over me. Whether it's the attack flooding back, the thought of Tommy being the attacker, the fact that my best friend betrayed me, or the desperate feeling of wanting my mother to love me, I don't know, but I break down, good and proper. My whole body crumbles, and Dad scurries up the stairs, taking two at a time, and sits beside me, hugging me tightly and rocking us gently from side to side. He's trying his best to take away all my pain.

Something wet, gritty, and slobbery starts attacking my skin and I laugh, making Fusco and Charlie lick me even more.

"There, there, kiddo," he says soothingly. "Everything will be okay, I promise. I will never let anyone hurt you again."

In this moment, I believe him. He's always right. He's got the patience of a saint and a heart bigger than the world—bigger than the entire universe—and made of gold. If I'm to have anyone in my corner, fighting my battles, someone who will never, ever hurt or betray me, I now know it's my father. Piece by piece, I'm going to become stronger than I ever thought I could be.

We both sit still, his arm around me. "Are you still okay to pick Mia up, or do you want me to do it?" he asks softly.

It's nearly time for me to pick my sister up from her afterschool dance class, because apparently girls her age wants to be famous dancers. I've done the trip so many times before, I don't even have to think about it.

I sniff. "I'll do it. I like doing it. I'll be fine."

My dad always acts like he has loads to do, to show us he's a proactive parent, but trust me, my mom does most of it. She leaves him to feed and look after us. The reason he acts *proactive* is probably so he isn't wallowing on the couch and thinking about the fact that Mom continuously walks out and never discusses anything with him. He's petrified of losing her. He doesn't even need to tell me; it's written all over his face.

Two years ago, they had the worst argument in history. I'd snuck out of the house to attend a party and my mom found me trying to sneak back in at three a.m. the following morning, drunk as they come. Mom slapped me across the face as she'd had enough of my behavior, and Dad stood in front of me, defending me. I stood there silently, shocked and shaken from the sting her slap had caused. I couldn't even bite out a sarcastic remark because for once, I didn't have any. Then Dad told me to go upstairs and stay there. So, I did, but I listened of course, like most kids do. I listened to them arguing, and it carried on into the next day. They never went to bed. I tried to sleep, but it was impossible with the screeching. I'm not quite sure what was said, but ever since, they haven't been the same.

I walk along the lane.

Fusco is in front of me, his tail wagging and hitting my leg. We head toward Mia's elementary school. I put my faith in Fusco and allow him to pull me in the right direction. He always makes sure I don't walk into anything along the way, and I always manage to dodge the hyperactive children running toward me, the three drains you're supposed to detour around if you don't want bad luck (definitely a superstition I brought with me from England), and the bicycles riding on the path instead of the road.

We stand against the school fence and wait for Mia. Fusco sits when asked to and I pat him, telling him he's a good boy. I hear someone chuckle to themselves as they stand next to me.

"Fancy seeing you here."

I wish I could see the clock to know how many more minutes I have to endure. I smell the seasons changing and next to me, Conan has one foot on the ground and the other against the fence. I recognize his voice instantly; it's the one that fills my stomach with a sensation of butterflies jittering around. My pulse quickens to the point that it seems my heart is going to burst.

I try not to speak to him, and more importantly, I shouldn't speak to him, not after what Noelle told me. But, my mouth caves before my head can stop it. "Funny, I've stood here basically *every day* for the last year. I guess you've never paid attention."

"I...um..."

I raise my eyebrows and my lips curl upward. "No biggie."

Conan's never tried to spend time with me or even speak to me. I might have gotten a quick hello or a nod of the head while he walked on by, but normally, I don't exist to him. So, the question is: what's changed?

"I always did think American boys were rude and inconsiderate." I let my fingers curl around Fusco's ear, scratching him gently and making him push his body into me.

"American boys, huh?"

Hurry up, Mia.

"Yep."

"And I've always known you British girls are stuck up."

"Brain box over here."

He starts laughing, tipping his head back slightly. "Feisty." I relax onto the fence and glare at him. "On a serious note—"

I widen my eyes. "You do serious?"

"I thought you English girls loved the American guys," he says.

"I never said anything about *not* loving the guys, just the boys. In fact, let me change that…" I flutter my eyelashes and continue to smile. "Just a boy."

"Well, you can't mean me then, because firstly, I'm a man—a real man, in all areas." He wiggles his eyebrows. "Secondly, I don't normally do pick-me-ups, so no, I wouldn't have seen you." In that moment, I sense the most remarkable lopsided grin across his face.

Ever since my first day of middle school, I practically drooled over Conan, like every other girl in our school; it was normal. The moment he showed he cared for my welfare at school today is the moment I fell hard, harder than I ever thought possible. But there's always been a code between friends, and that code is to never sleep with the guy your best friend is crushing on, and Noelle went and did just that.

Meaning: Conan Dwight is now a no-go on so many levels.

It's not his fault—he wasn't to know—but just maybe if he had used his head instead of his dick, he'd have taken more time to notice me and this wouldn't have happened to begin with. I really want to confront him and say exactly what I'm feeling, maybe even ask why he stopped talking to me and hasn't spoken to me sooner.

Conan places his foot onto the hard pavement and leans down with me to stroke Fusco. "Cute dog. What's her name?"

"*He's* called Fusco."

"Fusco?" He chuckles. "As in Fusco, fish and chips in town?" I nod. "Hello, boy." He starts massaging the back of his ears and Fusco falls hard in love—just like me.

Conan straightens his body and places his hand over mine, holding the leash with me. "So about earlier, about that party on Friday—I wanted to ask…"

His hand drops suddenly as the outside bell rings and the cheering elementary children run toward us.

"Alyssa!" Mia's arms wrap around my waist and Fusco jumps up, demanding attention from her. Standing next to Mia is a small shadow, a little taller than her. Mia lets go of me and my hands become sweaty against the leash, so I wipe them on my blue cotton skirt.

I push Mia forward slightly. "Come on then, squirt, Dad will be waiting."

"Bye Tina!" Mia chirps.

Tina folds her hand into Conan's and swings his arm back and forth; Tina is Conan's little sister and Mia's best friend. She waves. "Bye Mia."

"See you next week." Mia slides her hand into mine.

"Wait…" Conan shouts. "Alyssa."

I don't look back. Mia squeezes my hand and pulls on my arm. I look down at her.

"Does he know you're—"

"Nope, keep walking."

I listen as he turns his attention to his sister. "Me, a slob? Who sits and binges on potato chips every day after school? I think we both know that's you, sweet sister of mine." Conan's joyful laughter echoes in the distance, along with Tina's squeals.

We're closer to our house.

The breeze is soft against my skin and the leaves crunch underneath our feet, lying in a long strip beneath us. If I had my eyesight, I'd admire how beautiful it looks, but for now, I have my imagination to help with that. I shiver and tighten my scarf around my neck, pulling it farther into my black fur bomber jacket. I imagine Conan's beautiful, glistening eyes and his full lips, allowing them to be so perfect. I wish I could go back and speak to him. My heart starts to ache, knowing I walked away. *Awesome.* Now he'll think I don't care, but I do. I care so much. The only thing that puts me off is knowing he's played Twister with my best friend, and I admit it's not leaving my head easily.

Gross.

Mia looks up and scrunches my sleeve in her small hand. "Is Mom home?" She lets go and opens our white front door. "What's for dinner?"

"No, she isn't." We both step through into the hallway. "I'm not sure—ask Dad."

In reality, the whole world is weighing upon my shoulders, and not only do I have the weight of the world, I have the weight of my sister, too. I know she sees me more as a mother than a sister, and I don't want that. To be a mom at seventeen when your mom is actually fine and healthy, well, it doesn't really work for me.

Mia and Fusco bounce farther into the hallway. I place Fusco's leash on the holder on the right and follow them slowly into the kitchen.

The radio is loud, louder than Margo's (our next door neighbor) weekly Saturday karaoke night, which is saying something, because it sounds like a rave once she and her husband, John, get going.

David Bowie's voice fills the whole house. "Let's Dance" comes on, and my dad starts to torture us with a *one-night-only* Mark Darlington performance. Mia giggles at him and slides herself onto the chair at our kitchen table.

"You know it's my favorite song, girls." Dad grabs a spatula, and my eyes may be deceiving me, but I swear he's using it as a microphone. "Let's dance…" Dad sings. I see his outline wiggling his hips side to side, and I smirk, trying to keep myself from laughing.

"Let's dance…" Mia joins in, tapping her hand against the table, the rhythm in sync with the melody.

My dad points at me with the spatula, which he just used to flip the juicy, rich steak sitting in the frying pan. I sniff, taking in the intoxicating strong aroma of fresh meat. As my dad dances around the kitchen, swinging the spatula, it smells as though he's just massaged a well-seasoned cow with it. "Come on, Lyss, let's dance!" I picture his wide grin and his sparkling white teeth (which run in the family) glistening.

"To the song they're playing on the radio…" Mia carries on the song for me, now standing high on her chair with her arms waving in the air, swaying them like a crazy groupie. Well, she's my dad's groupie.

I let go. "Let's sway," I sing, giggling at the sound of my high-pitched, nearly on point Celine Dion voice. I can't help myself.

My dad cheers, turning around, and flips the juicy freshness cooking away in the pan. "While color lights up your eyes…"

I dip my head. The words sting, but my dad doesn't notice as he wiggles his bum and continues to butcher the beef.

"Let's sway, sway through the crowd to an empty space." Dad taps his foot to the beat and Mia jumps down from the chair, laughing at our father's hilarious antics.

I stay quiet, hoping the song will end soon. Light taps on our front door interrupt my dad's musical and I quickly shoot up out of my seat, stumbling over my feet. I get myself out of earshot as I've had enough and shout back to them, "I'll get it!"

I steady myself and open the front door. I recognize his shadow straight away, his tall silhouette and full hips spreading out in the doorway, his brown wavy hair messy and wild. He holds his hand up in a slight wave, just like he normally does, and I slam the door shut right in his face. Shock and horror spread throughout me after realizing what I've done. I cautiously reopen the door.

"Um, hey?" Tommy shakes his hand at me. "Are you going to let me in? It's a little cold out here."

I stand to one side and drop my eyes to the floor. I no longer want to look at him. *He did this to me.* "What are you doing here?"

"Your dad invited me. Problems at home, you know how it is…" Tommy shrugs his shoulders. "I'm staying the night."

My mouth pops open and my legs feel like jelly. Dad comes toward us, still singing and laughing, and slaps Tommy on the back. "Come get some grub—you look starving." Dad pats Tommy's belly. "Doesn't your mother feed you, boy?"

Tommy lets out an awkward laugh. "Only when my uncle isn't there."

"So, your mom decides to put out the trash and makes sure you go with it and now you're here."

Tommy's eyes widen and my dad scolds me. "Alyssa!"

"Forget it," I say then run up the stairs, slamming my door like an overdramatic teenager. *Imagine that.*

The cheek of him coming here, the cheek of him still being my friend, still trying to act like he cares for me. I can't stand the sight of him, and I can't even realistically see him. He disgusts me, and so does Ashton. If my dad wants to dine with him, he can go ahead, but my heart has been through enough for one day.

In fact, I don't think my heart can handle any more pressure; it might just actually break completely, scarring my body and soul.

I'm broken.

Twelve

There's always something about the sun rising, an orange beam glistening through my window; it's calming and grounding. It allows your thoughts to be processed and your eyes to dance with the moment. I used to love seeing the sun set and rise, and it's something I miss dearly. My eyes open automatically at the familiar moment. The alarm never has to be set because I always wake before the dancing bells jingle.

The sunlight doesn't make a difference anymore; now my body relies on the scent of fresh cotton being sprayed across the landing, outside my bedroom door, nearly leading me to have not just difficulty with my sight but with breathing.

When I open my eyes, I always open them to nothing, and nothing is coming to be peaceful for me.

"Can we talk now?" Tommy asks from the armchair at the side of my bed.

I pull my duvet farther up to my neck and freeze. I try to make sure it's covering my bare skin. My breathing becomes shallow,

"Come on, Alyssa. Let's talk." Tommy lets out a thick, heavy sigh.

Today, the scent of fresh cotton isn't coming from the landing like I thought. The fresh cotton is coming from Tommy's freshly washed clothes.

"Damn," I curse. "You…" I throw my pillow at him and sit myself up. "You dumbass!" I pretend to look at him. "Are you trying to put me in an early grave? What are you doing in here? Get out, you creep!" *Huh, early grave…ironic.*

Tommy stays quiet. I have no more words for him, because he did try to put me into an early grave. All I think about is telling him the truth—exactly what he's done to me.

"Spit it out, Lyssa. Say what you want to say. There's something going on with you. You've been acting weird for weeks! You won't even really look at me, always avoiding eye contact."

Because you made me blind you son of a bitch.

"Nothing," I whisper. "You need to leave…" I start scratching my wrist, waiting for the cutting of the skin. "Now."

"I am not leaving until you spit out what your problem is. I've known you, what, nine years? You're my best friend—you're my family." Tommy slams his hand against my bedside table and I flinch, scrunching my nose up tightly. "Is it because Noelle slept with Conan?" He laughs. "God, Lyss, you can do better than Dwight anyway."

I squint my eyes, ready to close them. "How do you know about that?"

"Are you for real? Everyone knows about it. Everyone at that party saw them all over each other. It was disgusting."

I try to look at him to figure out what he's thinking. I'm wondering whether he's the same Tommy I played footsie with when we were ten. Is he still the same guy who demolished ice cream with me at Pablo's parlor until the contents of my stomach finally decided to show themselves again down the toilet? Would he still hold my hair behind my head after it all? Is he still Tommy Henderson, the cute, dimpled cheeky chap I had my first kiss with (which we agreed to never be do again or even speak about)? I know deep down there is an explanation; I just have to trust him.

So, I take the plunge. "Where were you the night I got attacked?" I ask, not even realizing the meaning of the words being released until it's too late.

"I...I was around." He sounds confused, stuttering and slow, as if he has a speech problem.

"You were *around*? That doesn't even make sense." I throw my arms up in the air, exasperated, letting the duvet drop to my waist, my black lace camisole now visible. "Tell me more."

I watch his profile steadily, taking in his shape. The morning sun dims, casting his shadow onto the armchair's lower cushion. He shrugs.

"Bullshit." I throw another pillow at him. "I heard you yesterday in the hall with Ashton. I heard what you two did—"

"Alyssa, let me explain."

"You both said you didn't realize this would happen—what does that even mean, Tommy?" Tears start to slide down my face and I quickly use my fingers to wipe underneath my eyes, catching them. "You both passed the blame onto each other."

"But it wasn't my fault!"

I scoff. "So that makes it better, does it?"

"Yes! It wasn't my fault." He stands up and sits on the bed beside me, and I squirm out of his reach. If he touches me, I know the sick brewing in my stomach will erupt. "I swear, Lyssa. I swear it wasn't my fault. I'm so sorry."

"Are you here to finish me off? Did you not do the 'job' properly?" I explode, nearly screaming. If I could see, the only thing I would be seeing is red.

"Wait…what!?" Tommy touches my cheek with the backs of his fingers. "You're ice cold, Lyss."

My eyes become wide as his fingers make contact with my skin, and before I know it, my legs scramble off the bed and I'm down on my hands and knees. I scurry forward, heading toward the toilet, and puke shoots up, down into the basin. Tommy walks over slowly and pulls my hair away from my mouth.

"Guess you have an effect on me," I mumble between rounds of spewing my guts up. "Please answer the Goddamn question, Tommy."

He keeps hold of my hair as I relax against the toilet seat. "I don't understand what you're asking me. You think I attacked you?"

I nod slowly. "Prove me wrong!" I'm sobbing hard against the toilet, letting all the tears go down the ceramic base.

He lets go of my hair, struck by the words coming out of my mouth. I see it in his posture—he's shaken. "You're crazy. You're my best friend, Alyssa!" He lands on all fours at my side, and we're nearly nose to nose as he whispers, "I love you."

I vomit again, and he catches my hair swiftly.

"Alyssa, I wasn't talking to Ashton about the attack. I was talking to him about drugs."

I groggily reply, "Drugs?" I wipe my mouth with some tissue and sit with my back against the cold tiles.

"Yes. I was involved with a deal. Charlotte asked and I stupidly helped. I was supposed to meet Ashton in the garage where you were, but he came running out, telling me to go upstairs so nobody saw. He never mentioned seeing you until the other day. He's been going on about a tape he received."

I flinch. "That was from me."

"He keeps telling me it's my fault he was even near the garage, never mind running out of it." Tommy reaches for both my hands and squeezes lovingly. My hands are still ice cold, and he cups them tightly and blows into them to help warm them up.

My brain's finding it hard to understand and process everything; it starts to pound against my temples. "So, Ashton attacked me?" I ask. "And you knew?" My brows knit together, and my nose scrunches up. There's a bitter metallic taste in my mouth, and the sour contents of my stomach sit on my tongue.

"No way!" He squeezes my hand tighter. "Ashton found you but didn't say anything. He carried on with the drug transaction, like planned."

"You hate drugs."

He shrugs his shoulders, letting go of my hands. "I like Charlotte."

I know a smile will be on his face; he's liked Charlotte since her boobs magically appeared. *Go figure.* She makes my blood boil.

"What sort of drugs?" I say.

"He was selling her weed, but she couldn't be seen buying otherwise her parents would flip."

As long as Charlotte's okay. Poor Charlotte. I raise my eyebrows. *I wonder...?* "Did he sell her anything else? Something that could have made me drowsy?"

"I'm not sure if he sold her anything else. Honestly, whatever she spiked your drink with, I didn't know about it until recently."

Silence.

"He still left me there, to bleed...alone. Who does that?" Tears start rolling again and my eyes become sore and puffy. Tommy moves to the side and scoops me up, placing me on his lap. I let my head fall against his chest and allow his arms to wrap around me.

"He did. He knows that, but it doesn't make it right. That's why we were arguing." He strokes my forehead, making a soft circling motion along my skin, soothing me. "Is there anything else you want to tell me?"

I hesitate, looking away from him. I wonder if he knows I'm blind.

I decide not to tell him.

"I can't believe you thought it was me who attacked you!" He places the palm of his hand over my heart. "Silly, silly Alyssa. I love you."

I cry as we sit hugging each other for what feels like forever.

"I'm sorry," I whisper. "I'm sorry I got it wrong. I missed you."

Tommy gently kisses my forehead, making a small amount of me better. "I missed you too."

I spend the rest of my Saturday morning lounging about in bed. When it finally becomes time to sort myself out, I jump in the shower and make sure any smell of puke is fully and completely gone. It's time for my lunch date with Tommy. We decided to go later than twelve p.m. and make it more of an early dinner. The revelation of Tommy not being my attacker feels like a tiny weight being lifted off my shoulders, but unfortunately the rest remains.

Short and sweet knocks echo around my bedroom, once, twice, three times, and Tommy lets himself in. "Benjamin Franklin isn't going to spend himself." He stops dead in his tracks and lifts his gaze across my body. I stand in burgundy lace underwear, rummaging through the pile of clothes on my bed. I become agitated, picking them up then throwing them back down again, and this continues for a good minute. "Woah, Lyss—what's wrong?"

Tommy finally lets his eyes drop from my half-naked body and strides over to where I'm now sitting with my head in my hands.

"I don't know what anything looks like. I don't know if I look okay in it. I just…I don't know anything anymore."

"What do you mean you don't know what anything looks like? I don't understand."

I realize what I just said and freeze. "I think I'm ugly in everything I wear." I try to save myself.

Tommy rubs my bare back, up and down, catching my bra strap a couple of times. "It's fine babe. Here…" He takes away the sweater scrunched up in my hands. "I'll pick something out for you. I don't mind."

I sit up and watch his outline going through the big pile of clothes. He glances back at me several times while stifling awkward laughs. I try to cover myself up with the purple blanket that's on my bed, tightly wrapping it around my curvy body.

Tommy smiles. "By the way, you're beautiful no matter what, Lyss."

He's a savior.

My savior.

Lexi's Diner—as we get close to the little all-night, quirky diner, raindrops that have just fallen cling like jewels on the sign above. The busy hustlers around us are passing by, not giving it a moment's notice, never mind a thought. Our feet shuffle along the uneven pavement that bears the cracks of age.

A bell chimes as we open the light, black-framed door. Spread out across the small space are square tables with glass tops and menus lying underneath. Each table has a small white vase of yellow carnation flowers, and the servers are all wearing matching uniforms with *Lexi's Diner* written in white print across their aprons. Our feet take us over to the glass-fronted counter where the aroma of fresh bread makes our mouths water, and an array of cream cakes and pastries are visible for us to drool over. *Well, they're visible for Tommy.*

We stand behind Mrs. Robinson, a small, elderly woman who comes into the diner every day at two p.m. to get buttery scones to take home to her husband. Each time, the barista has tired eyes but a glimmer of a golden heart as she answers Mrs. Robinson's questions patiently and politely. The diner sells all different types of scones that are to die for. It's located five miles down the road, just on the outskirts of town. Tommy and I started coming here when we were juniors, which is how I know what it looks like. It's our spot, and it's refreshing to be back.

I bite into a delicious piece of Italian and herb bread. I continue to sink my teeth into it, bite after bite, allowing my mouth to salivate all over my late lunch and mix the soft texture around, chewy but soft. Once my mouth works through the gooey bread, I devour the pleasantly acidic but slightly sweet cheese inside, making sure I demolish every last inch.

Tommy laughs at me. "You enjoying that?"

"It's good!" I murmur through my mouthful. I keep my eyes shut and concentrate on the food leaving my tongue and traveling into my belly. I pop the last piece into my mouth, open my eyes, and shake the remaining breadcrumbs off my fingers.

"Looks like it."

I wipe a napkin across my plump red lips then place it on the plate. "Best bread in town—that's why we picked this café."

"That and the cute wooden chairs you love so much."

I chuckle. "That is true." I sit on my hands, palms spread underneath my ass cheeks. "So…"

"Sorry about crashing last night. With everything you may have thought was true, I can understand the trauma of having me around."

"No, it's fine. I should have just come straight to you."

I hear his wooden chair squeak before I smell his sweet body aroma coming closer. He leans over the table toward me. "Who do you think did this to you?" he whispers.

I lean closer and squint my eyes. "Why are you whispering?" He lets out a belly laugh, and I squirm. *Maybe I lack humor.* I heave a colossal sigh. "I don't know. If you're saying it's not Ashton or you…and I'm guessing you have an alibi for Charlotte…"

"Actually, I can't say I—"

"What?" I gasp, bringing my hands from underneath me and placing them on the table with a light thud. "You're telling me you did a drug exchange for the girl you like, but the girl you like didn't bother showing?" I lean back into my chair. "Not cool, Tommy." I let out an evil grin. "She's a bitch anyway."

Tommy has been crushing on Charlotte for a year now. She's got him wrapped around her finger, and he comes running whenever she calls. She's so self-centered and a complete boy-hugging tramp. Every time I'm around Tommy, I swear she's there watching. I wouldn't be surprised if she were hiding behind a menu somewhere in this diner.

I look around out of habit, forgetting I can't see. "What happened anyway? At home."

Tommy's voice strains. "You mean with my uncle?" I nod. "When I arrived home from school, my mom was passed out on the floor with an empty vodka bottle next to her. The guy was undoing his belt! His belt, Lyssa. You know what that means. Her dress was high up around her waist, and I went psycho."

"Oh, Tommy." I place my hand over my lips, hiding my gaping mouth.

"If my dad were around, he would have gone after him. I know it." The shadow of Tommy's fist tightens into a little ball. "I stopped him, went for him with the lampshade, and hit him in the back of the head. I carried Mom over to a neighbor's before he woke up and then called your dad. He told me to go to the police, but Mom told me not to." I study his shadow carefully, watching how his head dips down with sadness. "I have to listen to her, Lyssa."

"I know. I know you do, Tommy."

He stands. I do the same, and he pays the bill with a charming smile, making the server's heart flutter a few times. Tommy is handsome; he just doesn't have the confidence like the other guys at school.

I embrace him from the side while walking back out onto the cracked pavement, and I look up to see his jaw harden and set. His hand tightly wraps around my waist and he burrows his face into my hair, giving my head a kiss.

"Everything will be okay, Tommy." I squeeze him. "You have us."

Sundays have always been lazy days.

Mom's actually home, but she's sitting in her study away from beady eyes and loose tongues. Dad's in front of the television, shouting about the football game and shaking his fist at the screen, unhappy about how the ball is being thrown. Mia's in her bedroom, pretending to be Elsa from *Frozen* and singing at the top of her lungs. We never spend Sundays together. We are all in the house but never interact or dig out a board game and play it until one of us loses our rag. We used to, once upon a time.

Fusco sits next to me, licking my hand excessively. I glance down at him, and although I can't see his shiny fur coat or his little button eyes, I know a walk is what he wants.

Fusco, Charlie, and I head for the park, and I silently cherish the sound of cars passing us by and the chirping birds singing a melody. I let my boots sink into the green grass and I inhale the earthy scent. Slowly I exhale, a small smile playing on my lips. The clouds are hanging low and thick. As I make my way over to the middle of the green space, I relish the scent of freshly cut grass, and the dead leaves crunch under my feet. The tension of Charlie's leash as he lunges forward causes a burn in my grip. I let Fusco and Charlie go off to run then I sit on a wooden bench. They sprint away, barking, growling, and nipping at each other.

I stuff my hands deep into my long black coat and let the soft breeze swirl around my face, taking my auburn strands with it.

The aroma of crisp, earthy leaves drifts steadily around my nostrils, but the change soon shifts as a diffused blend of tangerine, lavender, lime, and spearmint is so close, so beautiful. Before I realize *whose* smell I'm letting my nose take in, I hear Tina's high squeals as she bounces around with the dogs.

Rough and rugged, he asks, "Can I sit?"

I hesitate; I shift along the bench and nod. Heat radiates off him. He's sitting so close that if I took my hand out of my pocket and let it hang by my side, I'd be touching him.

I can't do it; I don't have the guts.

He lifts his cap up and runs his hand through his bed of curls. "I'm glad I'm seeing you before school." It's like my lips have been sewn together; I keep quiet, hoping he'll continue. "I want to finish asking my question: I was wondering if you wanted to go to the party with me on Friday."

I laugh. I'm not sure why I laugh, but I continue to do so. "I'm busy, but I've heard Noelle is going."

Smooth.

"Oh." If I had ten bucks, I'd bet his face is crimson. He shifts on the bench. "So, you heard?"

"By the sound of it, I was the last to know. Did it happen while I was being attacked or after Noelle found me?"

"I didn't even really know you then, Alyssa. It's been, what, four years since we used to hang? A lot of things have changed." His hand is moving around his neck, scratching it, rubbing it. "Let's face it, you were too enthralled with Ashton's glistening teeth and romantic eyes. Was it the little bit of facial hair that did it for you?"

I scrunch my face up. "Don't even go there, Dwight."

He laughs and nudges my shoulder. "How about it: you, me, and this party. I'll even hold your hand." He wiggles his brows. I know it's because he's playing with me.

"And what do I get out of it all?"

"What do you get?" He places his hands over his chest, surprised, hurt. "Isn't my hand good enough for you?" He leans in closer, and I inhale peppermint, my head becoming fuzzy. "Watch..." He grabs my arm and removes it from my pocket, entwining our fingers together. "You'd have the touch of me, all night. That's more than Noelle had—she only had me for ten minutes."

I snatch my hand out of his grasp. "Blowing your own trumpet, there."

He holds his hands up in the air in defeat. His musical laughter swirls around me again, and I can't think straight.

"Noelle was nothing to me. We were just being reckless at a party. If I remember correctly, so were you. Look, for reasons I'm unaware of, I've always wanted to talk to you, but you're always around Tommy. If you'll let me, I'd really like to get to know you again." If I could see, I'd see the hotness of his eyes gazing into my soul. "Please?"

"Fine, but you're meant to take a girl on a date before heading into a socially awkward scenario—with the outcast."

"Date." He draws the word out, as if he doesn't understand it.

"Yes. Food, drink, chat..." I cock my head to the side. "Date."

"I can do that," he says slowly.

I laugh. "I hope so."

"I mean, how hard can a date be?" He laughs.

"Wait? You haven't been on a date before?" My eyes pop.

"Well, let's just say, you can be my first." Conan nudges my side playfully. "Seven thirty, Wednesday." Tina runs up to us and tugs on his arms. He keeps his eyes on mine. I wish I could see them. "Pablo's?"

"Conan, let's go," Tina says.

I smile.

Tina's voice becomes high-pitched. "Conan, pleeease can we go."

"Yeah, tiny Tina." He stands up, holding her small hand in his. He looks down at me. "I'll see you then?"

Conan Dwight needs reassurance from *me*? I nearly choke on my answer. "Yes. See you then."

He leans in and kisses my forehead. His soft lips touch my skin, sending electricity all throughout my body, jumpstarting my heart.

I have a date. Me, Alyssa Darlington, the blind, socially awkward girl has a date with Conan Dwight.

Conan Dwight, the most popular guy in school.

How the hell did this happen?

Thirteen

I pick up the pencil and twirl it between my fingers.

I keep twirling until it finally loses balance and collapses onto the desk.

"How are you feeling today?"

I cross my right leg over my left and sigh. "Fabulous, like every other day." I shake my foot in circular movements, just like I have in all the other sessions. "Did you know children as young as two weeks of age can distinguish the color red? Red has the longest wavelength among colors, making it the easiest color to process by the developing receptors and nerves in the child's eyes." I bite my index fingernail. "It would have to be red, wouldn't it—the doom and gloom color, the color of human flesh and blood."

"That's..." Maggie hesitates, not sure how to respond. "Interesting, Alyssa."

"I was covered in blood that night."

"You were? How do you feel about it now?"

I huff, "Well, I'm not covered in blood now, am I?"

I want to crawl up in a corner and pretend none of this ever happened. It's like I'm telling the same story all over again. I'm Alyssa Darlington. I went to a party. I got as drunk as a sailor. I was drugged. I slept with a boy—well, I *think* I did. I was attacked. *The End.*

If only.

"In three words, describe how you felt in the garage."

"Lost," I whisper.

"Go on…"

"Cold." I start scratching my wrist, forcefully digging my nails into the pale skin, a habit I can't stop. "Alone."

She keeps pushing me. "Now, use those three words and talk me through it."

"It's like when a person meets someone for the very first time…it's daunting and petrifying. I met the garage for the very first time that night. I had never been in it before. I didn't even know it existed since their house is so huge."

"So, you were a stranger to a room which was, in your eyes, non-existent."

"Exactly." I prick my skin and the blood starts to trickle down my wrist, tiny dots, tiny specks, nothing that will cause suspicion. I lick my finger and rub the blood away swiftly. I flinch at the sting. "I was lost."

"Now talk me through being cold."

"The temperature had dropped dramatically. All throughout the night it was like any other summer night, a cool breeze with a slight twinge of heat that's not quite disappeared. But that garage…it's as if I was in a different universe. It was freezing, unless it was just my body coming down off the drugs that had been put in my drink."

"Drugs?"

~

I walk down a hallway and pass several people who ignore me. I see a red cup floating between two heads. Lindsey Montelowe is standing on one side and Charlotte Summers is on the other. The hand holding it out toward me is manicured—soft, pale, well-groomed. My eyesight becomes blurred and I stumble to the side, steadying my balance by holding both arms out as if walking a tightrope. I smile to myself, pleased. I look back over at the floating cup and grab it.

I stare at Lindsey's pointy, beady face. "What you looking at?"

"Something that's just crawled out of a bush." She turns her head to the side to look at Charlotte and they both snicker.

"Whatever." I wave my hand at her and stumble slightly backward. I catch myself and in just one gulp, the liquor from the red floating cup trickles down from my tongue and into my stomach. It makes me remember why I love parties so much.

I turn around and walk away.

"How much did you put in it?" Lindsey says.

"Enough for her to regret everything," Charlotte snipes.

~

"Alyssa," Maggie snaps her fingers in front of my face, the sound echoing between my ears. "Tell me about the drugs."

"I knew it! What a stupid cow."

"Excuse me!"

"Not you." I glance up quickly at Mrs. Hall and my eyes widen. "Definitely not you."

"Then who?"

"I-I..." I stand up slowly, keeping hold of the arms of the chair. "M-My mom. Yes! My mom, she...stole my toast this morning. I'm so sorry. Please excuse me."

Without any more explanation, I shoot out of the door like a bullet ready to puncture.

Fuming doesn't even cover it.

I'm *absolutely* foaming at the mouth. If steam could come out of my ears, it would be billowing right now. I'd be like a kettle, boiling and ready to use.

I push through the glass doors leading to the gymnasium, and as I step in, I scan the shadows of the room. I hear a cackling laugh and see a tiny-framed shadow at the far side. Standing with her are Ethan, Levi, and Conan as they all laugh along. I hear her voice and know it's Charlotte, so I charge. I run at her shadow and knock her to the ground. She's screaming now, kicking and scratching at me. I grab a lump of her over-sprayed hair within my palm and pull. I try to get myself on my feet.

"You spineless…" I spit. "Stupid—"

"What are you doing, Alyssa?" Her face is close enough for me to hear her teeth grinding. She's holding on to my hand, which is still clutching her wavy hair. "Let go of me, you psycho."

I stare at her tiny shadow bending over, trying to stop the pain I'm happily inflicting. "I'm a what, you say?"

"Psycho." She spits in my face. "Psycho whore."

I use my free arm to wipe away the slimy phlegm dripping off my chin.

A large, rough hand comes over mine, trying to pry my fingers off one by one. "Come on, Alyssa—let her go," Ethan says woodenly.

"There, there, little pup, do as you're told," Charlotte continues to taunt. You would think she'd be a bit more careful about what she says considering I could yank her hair so hard.

Lindsey squeals and tries to grab me. "Stop it, Alyssa!"

Noelle stands in between Lindsey and me, blocking her. "Don't you dare," she growls.

I pull harder.

Charlotte screams, "You're hurting me, Alyssa."

"Good." I glare at her. "So, what did you call me?"

"Well you do sleep around, and you are very much psycho right now," she says.

I pull her face closer to mine, our noses inches apart. Everyone's watching. Everyone stops their chatter, drops their basketballs, and freezes mid-stretch. I have their attention. "I wouldn't have slept around if I hadn't been drugged by you."

Everyone gasps, and whispers fill the gym as everyone starts talking amongst themselves.

"You were drugged?" Conan repeats behind me.

"You did what, Charlotte!?" Noelle flips at my side. "You're a nasty piece of work!"

"Holy—" Ethan lets go of my hand and nods his head at me. "She's all yours."

Charlotte gasps at Ethan and her hands are still grasping at the air.

Then she's saved by the bell.

The doors bang loudly.

"Alyssa Darlington, please release Charlotte's hair this instant." The police dogs have arrived. It didn't take Mrs. Hall long to find me. It didn't take her long at all. "Everyone, please get back to what you were doing."

I turn Charlotte around to face my guidance counselor and smile politely. "But miss, I'm only showing her how people were disciplined in the good old days."

"Alyssa, now!" She isn't asking; she's telling me.

"Fine." I untangle my hand from around Charlotte's brown strands of hair and I glare at her, not really seeing her. "This isn't over. It's because of you I don't remember if I slept with Ashton."

I start to walk away, treading carefully toward Mrs. Hall's shadow standing in front of the entrance.

"Alyssa." Conan's hand touches my arm and I flinch.

I let my feet trail slowly across the floor. The air is sweet—dead flower sweet. "Yes?"

"I'll still see you Wednesday. Pablo's?"

Lindsey gasps. I glance at her outline, which is dark just like her soul, hiding behind Conan's broad shoulders, probably hoping he'll protect her. I look back at Conan's head just as he runs his fingers through his curls.

"For sure, Conan." I smile.

"That psycho needs locking up!" Charlotte lets out a shrill wail like a siren at Mrs. Hall and me.

Maggie turns her body around after opening the door, encouraging me to let it all go. "That's enough, Miss Summers," she says sternly, with authority, shutting Charlotte's siren mouth up instantly.

Lindsey and Charlotte want to play games? Well, it's about time someone popped them down a peg or two.

I'm back in Mrs. Hall's office.

"Are you comfortable?" Maggie asks. "Would you like some water?" It's the first time she's ever asked me if I want a drink. Out of the three sessions we've had, she's never once considered it. *Why Mrs. Hall? Why now?*

"I'm fine, thank you." I take the seat I always do in front of her desk, and I let my body slump into it. I'm aching from top to bottom, and my face is the same shade as the blood pulsing through my veins. My pulse is hopping, thumping hard against my neck and wrists; the adrenaline flowing around my body is traveling fast, faster than the speed of light.

"What you did to Charlotte is unacceptable."

There's a knock. Then another knock.

Maggie wheels her chair backward, her feet move toward the door, and she opens it slowly. I sit still, stay silent. Small, hushed whispers bounce around the room, and finally, Principle Williamson addresses me.

"Alyssa..." He coughs, clearing his throat. "I'm afraid I've been told what happened in the gym and it's made me very disappointed in you. Given the circumstances, you are only going to be suspended for two days. I will call and inform your parents, and you may come back to school on Thursday."

"That's fair, isn't it, Alyssa?" Maggie says.

"Fair?" I echo. The outlines of their heads nod, both at the same time. Their eyes are upon me, and I feel like a juvenile princess. "Fine, it's fair."

What isn't fair is the fact that Charlotte gets to walk her fragile little body around these halls and the drugs are being unanswered for. Did nobody hear me when I shouted out that she drugged me? She drugged me and got away with it and I'm the one paying for it, in more ways than one.

Principle Williamson bids us goodbye and Maggie returns to the black swivel chair. "Well, Alyssa, we will finish the session we started, and then you may leave the premises."

"Yeah," I whisper, so quietly it sounds like a murmur.

"What would you like to talk about?"

I turn my fingers over. "I don't know, everything?"

"I don't think we can talk about everything, but we can start somewhere."

There's a long pause. I rub my thumb in a circle against my index and middle finger, the touch of my soft skin and the feel of the friction comforting me.

"Let's start with Charlotte—isn't she your friend?"

"You need to define 'friend' if you want to start with her."

Maggie laughs. "Right." The clock on the wall clicks—*tick tock, tick tock*—like someone is using their tongue on the roof of their mouth. "I've seen you in the halls before, talking to each other...don't tell me you aren't friends."

"We aren't friends. Never have been, never will be."

"Never say never."

I glare. "*Never.*"

I'd rather poke my eyes out than become friends with that gremlin.

"Let's go back to the garage—we'll try to jog your memory to see if you can remember anything else significant. You told me before that you saw *two* people walking away." Maggie tilts her head to the side. "Are you sure about this?"

"I'm positive." *I think...*

I mean, I was out of it, for sure. My eyesight wasn't the best to begin with—better than now, but still not great—but I'm positive there were two figures walking away from me. Why would I make that up? If anything, I wish it were just the one person; then I wouldn't have to try to track down two people. I know it only takes one person to hit me over the head and the second person was just a spectator, enjoying the show, but they (whoever they were) never said a word to me.

~

My head sways to one side; it's heavy on my neck, feeling like a boulder hanging from a chain. I step one foot forward on the hard concrete floor. I look around with a passing glance, but the light is dim, making it impossible to see clearly.

Silence...complete silence all around me.

I place my hand on the hood of the black car. I lean on both elbows and slowly slump my head into my hands. My legs are like jelly, wobbly and shaky. I slam the palm of my hand against the metal and scream. I pace my feet slowly around the side of the black Mercedes and I glance at the windows, which are covered with condensation. A flicker of movement catches my eye, but I shake my head. It's just the alcohol.

I allow my body to rest all its weight against the passenger side, and I use all my energy to try keep myself upright.

My body collapses to the cold floor and I lean my head against the aluminum door. I hear hushed whispers and I close my eyes; they're coming from the Mercedes...they're arguing.

Laughter interrupts it, coming from two girls on the other side of the garage.

They don't notice me.

I turn my head to the side to try to concentrate on the hushed whispers, but before I know it, my stomach turns, and I violently curl over and throw up. Vomit is everywhere, all over my dress, my right hand, and the concrete floor.

~

My body is still in the chair opposite Maggie's, and my eyes are wide.

She puts a hand on my shoulder. "Alyssa, are you okay?"

I nod slowly.

Condensation? Why were the windows covered in condensation? Hushed whispers? Who was it and why were they arguing? The two girls? They could have been anyone, but did they see something?

I stand up and hold on to Maggie's arm. "Two people were arguing before I was attacked. I'm not sure what they said because their voices were hushed and I was dazed, but I'm sure I wasn't alone moments before it all happened, and I think they could be my attacker."

"Okay, okay, Lyss—slow down. So, you remember voices arguing..." Maggie pulls a chair toward me and sits in front of me with her hands cupping mine. "Try to concentrate on that, or moments before it—what do you see?"

"The windows are covered in condensation. I'm walking by the side of the car and I'm looking into the windows..." I think back to the memory, so clear at the front of my brain. "I-I can see something...inside the car. There's movement. I thought I was imagining it, but I can remember it clearly now. Yes!"

"Movement, Alyssa? You see them?"

"Not clearly." I take my hands out of hers and lean back in my seat. I start scratching my wrist, trying to open the old wound. "They were kissing. There's a handprint on the window. They pull apart as I glance in, then they're still—that's why I thought I was imagining it. I can't see them…the condensation is blocking their images…th-they're just shadows."

It just keeps on getting worse: *who are they?*

After the session, my dad picks me up out front. I'm happy I don't have to see the scowl on his face and only have to listen to his patronizing voice—like he didn't get suspended all the time when he was in high school.

Humph.

"Oh Alyssa, fighting, really?"

Oh Alyssa, did you really have to stoop so low?

Puh-lease, she deserved it.

Like the coward I am, I mumble, "Sorry, Dad. It won't happen again."

Fourteen

The days I'm suspended are draining and long.

Wednesday makes an appearance quite quickly, making a wave of sickness come over me. I'm so nervous about my date with Conan, I even start spluttering at the kitchen table.

"You're not going—you're suspended," my mom lectures from the counter as she prepares dinner.

I groan, "But Mom!"

"You think fighting with a girl, getting suspended, and then lounging about doing nothing is going to change my mind?" She turns to my dad. "Mark?"

"She was only—"

"Don't bring Dad into this. You know he'd let me, it's only you who won't. Don't you understand..." I lean over the kitchen table and sprawl my arms out over my head. I place my jaw against the hard surface and beg my mom with my dull grey eyes. "I really like him, Mom. Please!"

"Nope," she says coldly. "Now come chop some carrots."

"I'd rather starve," I bite out.

"That can be arranged." There's no remorse. Cold. *Heartless.*

I gasp.

"Melissa!" Dad scolds.

I push my chair back harshly. "Ugh!" I walk away, waving my hand at my mom and slamming the kitchen door behind me.

I curl up on the sofa next to Mia and she snuggles her head onto my lap. "You okay?"

"I'm fine, Mia moo. You know me."

She does know me, and she knows I'm lying. I'm not okay. I've now caused my date to be jeopardized, so not only does Charlotte get away with drugging me, she ruins my night too. The little witch—

"Conan will understand." Mia cuddles me.

I kiss the top of her head. She's so adorable, so vulnerable.

Tension and anger build up in the kitchen, and we hear Mom and Dad shouting. I cover Mia's ears with my hands. Mom's shrieking at the top of her voice again, telling him how useless he is and saying he never takes her side. Dad's trying to explain that there isn't any side to take and I deserve to be happy after what happened to me. *Dad the martyr.* We hear banging and slamming and before I know it, the front door shakes the house and Dad mutters under his breath, "What do you expect when you're never here?" But Mom doesn't hear, and by the sound of it, she's long gone for the night.

Like always.

Dad opens the living room door. "Sorry, kids." He places his hand on the top of my hair and strokes it.

"You best get ready, kiddo, otherwise you'll be late for your date."

I squeal and both Mia and I jump up. I wrap my arms around him and squeeze. "Really?"

He chortles. "Really! Go have fun."

Mia starts jumping up and down on the couch, cheering for me. I laugh lightly, playfully pushing her backward so that she falls onto the spongey cushions. "Geek!"

Dad bellows the time up the stairs.

It's already 6:30 p.m., and instead of bouncing down ready to get dropped off at Pablo's, I'm sitting on my bedroom floor in front of a mirror I can't see. I always thought one day It would sink in that I can no longer see what I look like. I'm so used to checking myself in the mirror before leaving for a party, so used to the satisfaction of knowing I look okay, more for my own self-esteem than anything. Since being partially blind, I haven't tried that hard with my appearance. The only make-up I wear is a bit of lip liner, lipstick, and blush—nothing else matters. Before, I'd have been carefully applying a full face of makeup, including using my contour palette and fluttering my fake eyelashes. Beauty was magical for me; applying makeup and transforming yourself is something incredibly satisfying.

"Alyssa, Conan's at the door for you," Mia shouts, halfway up the staircase as if it's no big deal.

My head snaps up out of thought and I quickly scramble to my feet to grab my black leather handbag off the bed. "One second!" *He's come for me, like a proper-proper date,* like a formal *'I'll introduce myself to your dad' date.* And he acted like he didn't understand the concept. *Pft.*

I use the palms of both hands and straighten out my royal blue dress. I bring my soft, freshly straightened hair forward and run my fingers through my bangs. I inhale deeply and hold my breath, letting the air rush to my head, as if I just inhaled gas and air. I exhale slowly then head for the front door.

I hold on to the banister rail and carefully take one step at a time. I see three shadows and instantly recognize Conan's sharp, outlined, hard silhouette. I smile broadly, flashing my pearly white teeth—the only good thing going for me.

It's hard to explain the feeling I get when I know someone is staring at me, because normally I'd be able to tell by seeing their eyes boring into me, but I can't do that. Still, I know, I *know* his eyes are gazing upon me affectionately. He's looking at me with those big crystal blue irises, trying to find words to explain what his mind is thinking. His outline doesn't move once; he's still while watching me make my way down the stairs.

I hear a sharp intake from my father. "You look lovely, Alyssa." He pecks me on my forehead after I step down into the hallway.

"You're beautiful," Conan whispers then coughs awkwardly, giving my dad a guarded look.

Crimson travels around the base of my neck, but I manage to steady my beating heart, which is fluttering within my ribcage, and I stop myself from turning the same color as my painted nails: red.

Conan gets under my skin in a way I can't explain, but in a good way. My senses are drowning in him, and I'm happy to be drowning in something other than dread.

My dad's holding my hand and he places it into Conan's with one swift motion. Conan's soft, large hand electrifies my senses, jolting the sensation of pins and needles throughout my body, stopping at my heart.

"No drugs, drinking, or sex." My dad raises his eyebrows. "Understand, son?"

"Yes, sir." Conan nods his head quickly.

I gently squeeze Conan's hand and giggle, holding my hand over my mouth. I lean in close to his ear and whisper, "He's only trying to scare you."

"I'm being deadly serious, young lady," my dad says sternly, cutting my giggles short.

"Don't worry, sir. I understand." Conan leans in closer to my ear and whispers, "I'm a gentleman." He wiggles his eyebrows so close to my own.

Dad claps his hands. "Right, scoot. Go on, get outta here." He flicks his hand toward the door with a finger-shuffling motion and we comply. "Have fun!"

"Bye, Alyssa," Mia says, happily waving us off. "Bye, Conan," she shouts flirtatiously.

"Good night, Mia moo." I wave and blow her a loving kiss, and Conan chuckles.

Her tiny shadow catches it and places it over her heart, holding it there until we drive away.

"Your sister's cute."

I smile. "Thanks." I dip my head and entwine my fingers, trying to keep the nervous laughter from crossing my lips.

I stay quiet throughout the car journey, letting him concentrate on the road ahead. Finally, he puts his blinker on and reverses into the bay outside Pablo's parlor. He jumps out of his red Camaro and jogs around to open my door. He holds my hand, helping me out of the car like the gentleman he said he was.

I smile at him and he brings my hand up to his soft, plump lips, the lips I'm starting to long to feel on my own. "Thank you."

"Like I said, I'm a gentleman." He wiggles his eyebrows and lets out a deep, masculine laugh.

"My dad would be proud."

He laughs boyishly. I link my arm with his and he guides me to the entrance.

When walking into Pablo's, it's like falling into the sixties. The red stools sit high around the Formica countertops. The servers all wear matching dresses and aprons, and they tread upon black and white square vinyl. Red leather two-seaters are spread around the parlor, ten booths in total for kids and families to pile into. One waitress is always carrying a fresh brew of coffee around with her, and the others have always got a thin notepad, ready to take orders.

I open a heavy glass door and we're greeted by Pablo and his grandson, Lucas.

"Alyssa, my girl!" Lucas hugs me tightly.

He is tall and has black, messy hair that sits tightly on the top of his head. He's got golden brown eyes and his arms are toned and muscly, allowing him to pick me up off my feet with just one arm around me. He's just turned the big twenty-one.

Conan's body stiffens at my side and his jaw clenches. I untangle myself from Lucas's hug and place my hand on Conan's upper arm, my touch softening his stance. "This is Conan, my date."

"About time, girlfriend." Lucas holds his hand out to Conan. "I'm Lucas." They shake hands, and Lucas leans in close to my ear. "He's cute."

Conan stiffens again, and I burst out laughing. "Y-You're gay?" Conan asks, looking back and forth between us.

"Why? Would you turn for me, darling?" Lucas flutters his eyelashes and I laugh even harder, my cheeks sore.

"I thought I had some competition, bro." Conan slaps Lucas's back in an honorable way.

"Darling, you do, just not me." Lucas smirks. "Have you seen our girl here? She's a bombshell!"

"Lucas, leave them be. Do you have to annoy all my customers?" Pablo's grandfatherly voice echoes around the diner, comforting me. He smiles at Conan. "Go take a seat in the first booth. I'll be with you shortly."

We nod, I kiss Lucas's cheek, and Conan entwines my fingers with his, walking us over to the red leather seats. We sit opposite each other and I straighten the bottom of my dress with my hands, making sure it's not too short. A feeling of contentment washes over me and I sit quietly. If I had my eyesight, I'd be happily staring at Conan's handsome features. Instead, I'm daydreaming about them.

"You really do look beautiful tonight." I imagine Conan's lopsided grin as he speaks. "Thanks for coming. I thought maybe you'd get cold feet."

In the last week or so, Conan's exceeded the reputation he's maintained in the past. He's sweet and sincere, and he really is a gentleman. There's no disguise. Maybe having different girls on his arms all those years was just an image, the norm of popularity.

I drop my eyes to the shadow of the tabletop. Two sodas are placed in front of us, and I sip mine slowly. I pause. "Why do you like me?"

He chokes and spits the carbonated liquid into his palm, his other hand grabbing a napkin to wipe it away. "W-What? Why wouldn't I like you?"

"It's taken you years to even look in my direction." I glance at him.

"I-I guess." Conan finds my hand and squeezes. "It's not that I didn't like you, honestly. I've changed as a person. If you'd gotten to know me last year, you wouldn't have liked me." He drops my hand and shifts in his seat.

I look at him intently. "I get it…I think."

He sighs. "I don't think you do." His right hand picks mine back up and he uses his thumb to stroke over my knuckles. The heat radiates off him, making my skin prickle. "You…" He cups my face, his palm gently warming my cheek. "Your eyes, your laugh, your smile, your presence, everything about you warms my heart. All of it sends a tingling sensation all throughout my body and my heart pounds faster than a lightning bolt striking. It was the same when we were thirteen, but then, you were always around Tommy."

I'm speechless. I smile, turning my head deeper into his palm, and I blush, pink up to my eyeballs.

"There's nothing going on with Tommy and me."

"That's good to know." He smiles and strokes my face one last time and drops his arm. "Let's order?" Conan takes charge and orders our meals, getting himself the wing meal and me the chicken tenders. He pays the bill, helps me out of the booth, and leads us back to the car, the date having been successful in *every* way possible.

I pretend to look out the window, admiring the scenery.

"Why did you go after Charlotte in the gym?"

I huff. "She's a—" I glance next to me, see Conan's shadowed expression, and realize he's surprised at my outburst. I shrug. "Well, as you heard, she drugged me."

Conan hesitates, thinking about his reply. "Yeah, that's not right." He laughs. "I dunno, I just didn't expect you to fight like a cat."

I laugh. "Oh shut it. You're such a guy."

"I always imagined you'd throw a punch. You have that *don't mess with me* stature."

"I do not."

He smirks. He puts his car into drive and turns out of the parking lot. "My parents are away—do you want to come over?"

I raise my eyebrows.

"No funny business, I promise." He reaches his arm over to me, glancing back and forth from the road ahead. He moves a strand of hair behind my ear and drops his hand to hold mine, our fingers interlocking so perfectly, so symmetrically.

I hesitate, but my head nods before I even answer. "Okay."

He squeezes my hand. "Thanks. I don't want to leave you just yet."

I adoringly smile at him. "You came and picked me up—why?"

"I couldn't let my date make her own way there." Conan looks out of his side window and changes lanes. "What sort of guy would that make me?"

"I wouldn't have minded. I sort of pushed this date onto you, didn't I?"

"I don't do anything I don't want to do. So, trust me when I tell you, I'm yours."

I shoot my head in his direction, my heart on fire. "Y-You're m-mine?"

He turns his blinker on to go left, and the journey feels familiar. I don't need to have my eyesight to know we've arrived at his house. He stops the car and places our entwined hands into his lap. "If you want me."

"This is…" I inhale sharply. "Quick."

"It's not a marriage proposal, Alyssa."

I study the outline of his face, the firm jawline and his curly hair hanging slightly over onto his forehead. He pushes it back with his fingers, as if he knows I'm thinking about it. I let my eyes drop.

"Since watching you and getting to know you at school and seeing how fragile you are, I feel the need to protect you. I want to be yours."

I laugh. "You're talking about yourself as if you're an object."

His laughter fills my ears. He gets out of the car and helps me out, just like he did at Pablo's. He keeps hold of my hand and walks us to the front door. He stops us and twirls me so I'm facing him. He leans in, touching his forehead against mine as if it's the most natural thing to do.

It feels right.

We're both breathing heavily, cherishing the moment. I know it is dark outside, the thick clouds covering every shining bright star.

"Darlington..." he whispers.

Butterflies awake in my stomach and the hair on my arms stands up, prickly and hot from his touch. He brings his hand up to curl around the side of my face, and I place my hand over his. I lean my head into it and I groan, not meaning to. It's a good groan, a *please just kiss me* groan.

"Lyssa, I don't think you know what you're doing to me."

His voice, body, fingers, skin—it feels like a burst of sunshine upon a desolate landscape. I'm lost in the moment. I don't want it to end, don't want him to let go. *Am I dreaming?*

His mouth is directly over mine as he whispers, "I want to kiss you." He moves in slowly, and my legs are trembling with anticipation. "Can I kiss you?" The invitation is there, and I don't say no.

Is this really happening? Before I can question myself once again, his lips touch mine and my body hums, an electrifying zap bringing me through to reality. Our tongues become tied and he moves his hand behind my back, bringing me in closer. We're flush against each other and my palms are against his hard chest. I'm absorbing him, all of him, and I have this sensation as if I'm melting away under his touch.

"Darlington..." Every time he whispers my last name, I dissolve. He grabs my bottom lip with his mouth and gently tugs it into his, sliding his tongue across it. My heart thumps loudly against my chest, against his. We breathe heavily, trying to steady ourselves, and his breath is warm as it drifts across my lips. His forehead is touching mine, and the pressure of his fingers has changed as they leave my face and slide into my straight, silky, auburn hair. He tilts my head up to look at him, but I can't see him.

He just doesn't know it.

"So worth the wait." He grins against my lips and starts planting kisses at the side of my mouth, trailing onto both cheeks. He wraps his arms around my back, allowing me to listen to his beating heart. I smile against his chest. He whispers, "I'm yours."

And I know it's true because I'm his.

He has me completely, whether he wanted it or not.

We stand in Conan's bedroom and I try to figure out the interior design. I imagined it being like any other boy's bedroom: messy, smelly, and all over the place. That's how my mom always described it to me when she spoke about her life when she was younger, living with her brother.

Surprisingly, Conan's bedroom is clean, fresh, and tidy.

I inhale and a citrus smell enters my body, making me want to inhale deeper. Conan holds my hands and pulls me farther into his bedroom. "Stay?"

It's a rhetorical question; he doesn't want me to say no. He doesn't even want me to reply; instead he wraps his arms around my waist and walks us backward to sit on the bed.

I drop my bag down at the side of the large bed and shuffle myself farther up so my back is against a feathered cushion. He sits beside me, crossing his legs. I curl myself into him, and he welcomes it.

Eventually, we end up lying upon the firm mattress, our legs entwined and my head on his chest.

His fingers are running along my upper arm, his touch sending fireworks into my stomach.

Conan strokes my hair and kisses the top of my head. "Let's play a game." My eyebrows furrow and I look up; his shadowed face has crinkles at either side of his mouth, and they go darker as they go deeper—he's smirking at me. "It's an activity two or more people can participate in for amusement."

I hit his chest and chuckle. "I know what a game is, you dick."

He laughs, bellowing all the way from his stomach.

"Okay, what shall we play?" I ask.

Conan grins and mumbles against my head. "Two lies and a truth."

I snuggle closer to him, wrapping my arms tighter around his torso. "Go on."

"I'm going to tell you two lies and a truth, and you have to say which is true."

I snicker. "Easy peasy lemon squeezy."

"That's what you think." He smirks, props his head up with his hand, and stares down at me. I wish I could see him so much it hurts. "I'll begin: I have a tattoo of a shark on my ass."

"Can I see?" We both laugh and he shakes his head in disbelief.

"You're on a different level, Darlington."

I blush, hiding my face against his side.

"Second: I can list all the state capitals."

I laugh. "That requires a brain cell."

Conan's hands start tickling me, making me jolt and laugh harder.

He raises his eyebrows. "You're pushing it." I curl in closer and encourage him to continue. "Finally, I struggle to sleep at night." He leans his head back against the headboard. "So, Darlington..." He taps my nose with his finger. "Which is the truth?"

I tap my finger against my chin, thinking carefully about my answer. "I don't think you can list the state capitals, not because I think you're stupid, but just because I don't think it interests you. Hmm, the tattoo on your ass...I'm not too sure. It's between that and struggling to sleep at night." I think about it before I answer. "I'm going to go with struggling to sleep at night."

"Well done. You're right." He curls his hand around mine, which is lying on his chest, and brings it up to his lips to kiss it. He shrugs. "Though maybe now that you're here, things will change."

I smile at the possibilities. "Why do you struggle?"

"I walked in on my grandad dead when I was ten. He'd committed suicide. I'm guessing he couldn't stand the pain anymore." I gasp. "Ever since, I've had night terrors, really hard to get rid of."

"I'm so sorry," I whisper.

"Don't be." He kisses my head. "Your turn."

I sit myself up a little so he can read my face. "Okay. I have never, ever broken a bone." Conan laughs, finding something funny. "What?" I ask.

"If you keep taunting Charlotte there could be a first for everything," he says.

"Har, har." I stare at the darkness around the room and continue. "I love chocolate chip pancakes. They're the best."

"Go on."

"My last one: I've got a brother in England."

"A brother?"

I nod. "We left him there with my auntie and uncle."

Conan sharply inhales. "That's a bit harsh, isn't it?"

I smirk against his chest. *Surely he doesn't think that's the truth.*

Conan wraps his arms around me tighter. "Okay, so I believe it to be the first one, you're too cautious to break a bone."

"Hmm, interesting." I sigh against his chest. "Nope, nah-uh. Wrong."

"Okay, okay." He nuzzles his head into my hair and breathes in. "Surely you don't have a brother?"

"You're really bad at this, aren't you?"

"Thank God it's not the brother. I'd have to get all testosteronal if I met him."

I laugh. "You're so weird." I tap his chest with my palm. "I love chocolate chip pancakes."

"If you're still here in the morning, maybe you'll get lucky and I'll make you some."

I smile into him, making sure he doesn't see me smile too much, making sure he doesn't think he has me completely—but *oh boy*, he does. "Your turn."

I hear him yawn, making me yawn automatically with him. I stretch out, curl my toes, and re-tangle my legs around his.

"I love orange juice," he says.

"Okay."

"I *hate* being popular."

I snort. "You hate being popular—that's definitely not true. You love when girls come swarming around you. You can't get enough of it. Conan Dwight, king of the school."

"Behave." He strokes my hair away from my forehead and places his index finger under my chin, tipping my head up to look at him. "I never slept with Noelle Carlisle."

I stiffen. *He never slept with Noelle Carlisle.* "Did you just—"

"Which one is the truth?"

"This is harsh on so many levels." I sit up and put my back against his headboard, moving out of his embrace. "It's obviously the orange juice."

He smirks at me. "You think?"

"Why would you even bring that up? Noelle is my best friend. You slep—"

"I didn't sleep with her."

"You slept with her." I stop. *Wait, what did he just say?* "You what?"

"I didn't have sex with Noelle."

"But, how? She said…"

Conan places his head in my lap and brings my arm around him, kissing my knuckles. "Lyssa, you weren't the only one who was drunk that night. We were kissing and we made it to the bedroom, but she passed out."

I can't help but laugh. "She passed out?"

"I'm glad, actually, because I know the next time I kiss you, you won't be thinking about how your friend broke a promise." I open my mouth. "Lyssa, I know how girl code works—I have sisters, remember?"

"Oh." I whisper, "I'm glad you didn't have sex with her, Conan."

"So am I."

"Why did you lie?"

He wiggles his eyebrows. "To make you jealous. Did it work?"

I slap his upper arm. "You twat."

Conan laughs, which turns into a large yawn. "Go on, back to the game."

With his head still in my lap, I move farther down onto the bed and lay my head against the pillows. "Okay. I've been to Las Vegas."

"So jealous," he whispers.

"I have a tattoo."

"Mmhmm."

I hesitate. Before I know what I'm doing or even think about it, the words on my lips escape. "I'm partially blind." I clamp my mouth with my hands.

Silence.

He doesn't reply. *Did he already know?* I'm not able to see his face. I lie still, patiently waiting.

Silence.

It lingers around me. It's as though I'm suffocating on air itself.

It's painful.

Fifteen

"I'm partially blind." There's still no answer. "Which one is the truth?"

Silence.

Then I listen carefully, and the slightest snore fills the air. Conan's head is on my stomach and he's drifted soundly to sleep. A part of me is relieved he didn't hear what I said, but there's a fraction of me that wishes he did, wishes he knew, otherwise this whole…whatever it is will be based on a lie.

I yawn one last time before I place my hand on his head and play with his soft, small curls. I stroke until I finally drift off to sleep, expecting the orange beam to appear once more and wake me up in time for school.

My chest tightens, wanting to confine the happiness.

I'm content, and I never want to let that go.

I wake up to my whole body wrapped around Conan's and still fully dressed in last night's clothes. The room is still dark, but I sense the morning arriving. I reluctantly sit up against the headboard, groggily forcing my body to function. Conan turns over and continues to snore lightly.

I'm in Conan's bedroom, in Conan's house—Dad is going to flip.

"Conan." I shake his hard frame and panic arises. "Conan, wake up." He turns over and tries to bring me down to cuddle him, pulling me by my waist, but I struggle and wiggle, wiggle and keep wiggling out of his embrace. "No, Conan, wake up. What time is it?"

He mumbles and groans, but eventually he sits up and checks his phone. "Five a.m.—plenty of time to snuggle." He pulls me onto his lap.

I wrap my arms around his neck. "Conan, please." I pray for forgiveness. "I have to go. I need to get home before school."

Lights flick on somewhere in that brain of his, and I pray I won't be in trouble. "Damn, you're right." He runs his hand through his curls. "C'mon, I'll drive you." He kisses my cheek, and with his famous lopsided grin, whispers, "I like the bed head." He places me back onto the soft sheets and gets up with a chuckle. I try to watch him while he changes shirts, but it isn't the same as actually *seeing* him. It's like I'm a peeping Tom, just without the actual peeping.

"Meany," I grumble, running my hands through my hair, shaking it out around me and sliding my fingers under my eyes to get rid of any excess makeup.

Thursdays.

Thursdays are useless: the day in between Wednesday and Friday that people wish didn't exist. I'd rather jump straight from Wednesday to Friday—the week would be shorter, the weekend would arrive quicker, and there would be fewer days at school: win-win.

Tommy can't pick me up today, something to do with Charlotte wanting a ride from her strapping boyfriend, so as soon as Conan wishes me goodbye and I hear the grumbled remarks from my dad about being disappointed in me, I jump in the shower and get myself ready.

Once done, I dial the only other friend I need—Noelle. I call and she comes, just like always. I can't be angry with Noelle anymore, not since Conan told me they didn't sleep together. She might not know this, but it changes things. She's always been a patch of brightness in my life. She's always been her, just her, never trying to be anyone else. I miss her snide remarks and her headstrong arguments. I miss her.

I have my foot perched on the edge of the passenger seat and I'm trying to tie the laces of my white Converse. I have my mom's voice in the back of my head, explaining to me how to tie a shoelace. "Guess what?" I look at Noelle, holding my hands still. "You didn't sleep with Conan." *Over, under, around, and through.*

Noelle turns her blinker on, looks in her mirror, and starts to drive away. "As much as I wish I didn't, I did, Lyss. I'm sorry."

I'm still tying my shoelace. "Trust me when I say you didn't." *Meet Mr. Bunny, pull and through.* My mom's voice whispers the final line to tying my shoelaces off and I drop my foot to the floor of the car.

Noelle's voice is skeptical. "Oh, were you there?"

I snort. "No, but I had a date with Conan last night." I straighten out my denim skirt, making sure everything is perfect.

"And?"

"He told me you didn't have sex—you passed out." My eyebrows meet in the middle, and I look in her direction. "Maybe we're not so different after all."

She's quiet for a long time, debating it. "He told you that?" she finally says, nodding her head. "That's, that's good."

"Good?" I echo. "It's awesome, Noelle." I grin, super big.

Noelle smiles tightly, her posture stiff as she turns into the school parking lot. "We're good?"

She brakes, making me jolt forward. I place my hands on the dashboard then look in her direction and nod. "Better than good."

Best friends, sisters, family—nothing is going to come between us, though Noelle doesn't appear too pleased about the fact that she didn't sleep with Conan. Whether or not she believes me, I'm not sure, but in this moment, all that matters for us to be okay is that I believe it didn't happen.

I keep a radiant smile on my face as we walk into art class and I sit behind my easel.

Someone drops something into my lap, and I flinch. When I touch it, I feel the paper-thin texture and I look down, realizing it's a note. I'm not able to read it. So, I do the only thing possible: I plunge my hand into my densely packed denim pocket and drop it, deep below, as a keepsake.

The day is passing by quickly, and Lindsey and Charlotte keep their distance. Noelle and I are back to being the terrible two, and Conan has even pulled me aside to tell me what a good time he had last night. Nothing could dampen my parade.

"Alyssa!?"

I'm standing in the library. Behind me, there's the quiet flip of a page. It's awfully warm in here. I quickly put the braille book I'm holding in my hands back on the shelf and turn around, coming face to face with Ashton Marston.

He's much too close for comfort, but I take a deep breath and move slightly to the side. My whole body screams at him, but my mind is telling me to take it easy. All I want to do is kick him where the sun doesn't shine, but I know it wouldn't help. It would make me feel better for a split second and then it would be over, and everything I feel now—the suffocating, like a miniature whirlpool is pulling me deep below the surface—will drown me. My hands are shaking, but it's better than being on the verge of a total nervous collapse, and I thank my body for that.

The air conditioning snaps on and I get a whiff of Ashton's spicy cologne.

I look at the musty carpet and place my hands behind my back. "Ashton," I mutter. "What do you want." It comes out more of a statement than a question.

He cringes. "I…look, at the party…"

"Spit it out." I practically do spit at him, my patience running low.

"I-never-touched-you," Ashton says, way too quickly for me to process. "You keep telling people you're not sure if you slept with me or not. Well, you didn't. It didn't feel right, ya know?"

I give a sinister laugh. "Didn't feel right that you were practically dragging me up the stairs when I kept telling you to stop?" I smile tightly "Well, thanks."

"I'm sorry," he says in a pseudo-sincere tone.

"Don't worry about it," I snap. "Everyone will soon find out *everything*."

"What are you talking about?" he asks, his voice cracking.

I point my finger into his chest, giving me the courage to stop my hand from shaking. "You, leaving me bloody and scared on that garage floor—I remember."

He growls. "You! *You* put that tape in my locker." He steps toward me, and I hear the tap before I see the shadow of his foot. I step back against the wooden bookcase. "You're going to regret threatening me, you little—"

I flinch but before I have anything to be scared of, Tommy interrupts. "Back off, Marston."

Ashton doesn't move. He's still glaring at me, like a bull on its prey. All I need now is a red flag. "Henderson, this has nothing to do with you."

"She's my friend," Tommy replies matter-of-factly.

Ashton laughs loudly, as if he's telling himself an inside joke, and the librarian tells him to be quiet. Tommy stands at my side and holds on to my hand tightly—too tight. Ashton stays quiet for far too long, the silence killing me. I need him to walk away. I need him to leave me be.

I step forward, bravery pulsing through me. "Look, I did put that tape in your locker. What did you expect? You left me lying there and didn't help." I squint. "Who does that?" I hold my hands up in surrender. "I'll stop. I'll leave it alone, but tell me…" I scratch the side of my head. "Why? Why did you just walk away? Did I not mean anything at all? All these years you've known me, spoken to me, even kissed me—did you not even care?"

"I was scared." Ashton doesn't elaborate. He was scared. Just scared.

"Well what about me? I was petrified."

"I'm sorry, Lyss." Ashton touches my arm, and I cringe.

"Right." I nod my head as if I understand, but I don't—far from it.

Ashton exhales loudly, as if he's been holding his breath for a very long time. He thinks it's over. It's not. I lied.

Tommy and I walk away. Confrontation feels good. I'm happy I got the chance to ask him why. Even if I didn't get the answer I wanted, it's enough for now. He made me realize the only thing Ashton Marston is, is a coward, a revolting, sadistic coward who only thinks about one person—himself.

Tommy and I are walking down the hall. "Don't you think he looks really rough, Lyssa?" He leans into me and whispers, "Did you see that fully-grown beard? He used to just have stubble! His dark hair is straggly, and he looks skinnier. It looks like he hasn't showered for days."

"I don't care," I say woodenly. I don't. I couldn't care less whether all this is affecting him. It's affecting me ten times more; *they* just don't know it. "Thanks for interrupting us."

"You're welcome." Tommy doesn't say anything else, just walks with me, letting me keep my arm linked with his until I leave him to go into the girl's bathroom.

I'm supposed to meet Noelle here after grabbing my braille book, which was ordered specifically for me. I left it back in the library not even thinking twice about it while going head to head with Ashton. I'll ask Noelle to go back to get it for me; I'm sure she will. I open the door slowly, pushing it gently. I hear girls whispering and my body halts. *Grow a backbone, Alyssa.* I inhale the damp air and walk deeper into the well-perfumed bathroom.

"Look what the cat dragged in." Lindsey snickers, and I hear the sound of water running over her hands. Her friend Isabelle stands next to her, snickering too. I see Lindsey's shadow so definitely. It's thin and never wavers, not once.

I look back and forth between her and the door. I raise my eyebrows high, as high as they can possibly go. "There's a cat?" I pretend to look under the sink. "Where?"

I straighten up and look at her silhouette with a bored expression on my face.

"You think you're all that. You're not, Alyssa Darlington. You'll get your comeuppance—it's coming your way." Lindsey's disembodied voice is self-righteous, making me want to punch her.

I scowl. "What have I even done for me to get my *comeuppance* for? Please, enlighten me?"

Lindsey wipes her hand on a paper towel. I hear the rough paper scraping across her skin, like a shovel against gravel. "Just remember, Alyssa, the boys at this school belong to me and my girls. The squad owns them, and you need to keep your grubby little fingers off."

The air *whooshes* as she shoots the crumpled paper towel into the bin beside the sink.

The bathroom door bangs hard against the wall. "Do the boys know this?" Noelle interrupts cockily.

Lindsey sweetly smiles. "Of course they do, but it doesn't apply to you. You know you're one of my girls."

Noelle's looking my way. "Lyssa, you should tell Conan before things get serious." Her shadow leans against the first stall. "Aren't you his date for Lindsey's party tomorrow?"

My lips curl at the sides. "Yeah, I guess we're *that* serious. I'll let him know what you said, Lindsey."

"But—" she gasps.

"Guess he prefers his girls with a bit of class," Noelle interjects, challenging Lindsey. "Now leave us be—my patience is running out."

Lindsey huffs, "Come on, Isabelle, let's go." They storm out like spoiled five-year-olds, bouncing their feet off the floor. Lindsey scowls like her life depends on it.

Noelle crosses her arms over her chest. "Where were you?" Her shadow is hard to make out as she quickly moves over to the mirrors. "I came in earlier but you weren't here, so I went looking. When I got to the library, the lady said you'd already left with a boy, and she said you left this as well..." Noelle leans over and places the braille book firmly into my hands.

My eyes widen. "Thank you!" I put it into my bag, which is hanging over my shoulder. "Yeah, I ran into Ashton. Tommy saved me before I got splattered against the bookshelves." I close my bag up and nudge the strap farther onto my shoulder.

Noelle sighs. "I can't believe I'm saying this..." I give her a funny look. "Lyss, you should tell Tommy the truth."

I drop my mouth open. "*What?*"

"He should know," she says tightly.

"Oh yeah, I'll just tell him over a light lunch, shall I? *By the way, Tommy, I'm blind.*"

I hear a gasp and our heads jolt in its direction. Noelle stands up straight and I feel uneasy. Callie McGovern, frizz-bomb and clumsy-klutz, trips over herself (it's like Bambi on ice) and lands on her knees by Noelle's feet. "*Fantastic.*" Noelle says it in a way that makes it obvious it's far from fantastic.

"Oh my God," Callie shrieks. "You're blind!?" She gathers herself up, dumbfounded. Noelle groans, and I drop my head into my hands. Her Hermione-looking hair isn't the only thing we have to watch out for now; we also have her top-notch gossiping to keep contained.

I'm busted.

"You're actually blind!?" She walks toward me. One step, two step, three steps, *four*. She snaps her fingers in front of my face. "Tell me what I'm doing."

"Snapping your fingers. I'm blind, not deaf."

Noelle laughs under her breath. "You idiot." Callie claps her hands and bounces up and down. Noelle's disgusted. "Why are you so happy about her being blind? You sociopath."

Callie grunts. "I'm not, silly. I'm happy that I know a secret." She claps her hands together again and smiles. "*Me*, Callie the loner, knows a secret." She giggles childishly.

I tilt my head backward, looking up at the ceiling, and pray. I've always known she's more than slightly insane. I pray to God, *just end it*. If I died, would it all end? I can only hope.

Save me, please

Sixteen

The morning of the party, Mia comes into my room and bounces on my bed. "Dad said you and Tommy are taking me to school."

I'm sitting on my stool, brushing through my hair. "Tommy isn't picking me up today, so we can't take you."

Mia whines, "So who is?" She lands on her bum, hanging her legs off the side of the bed. "Please, Lyssa, Dad's in a bad mood, plus he said he was leaving early."

"Where's Mom?"

"Work."

Work. I should've guessed she didn't come home last night, probably stayed in a condo near town. "Conan's picking me up." It was agreed yesterday, just before Noelle and I left school, that he would come get me this morning. He wanted to walk through the doors of our school holding my hand. He's trying to be cute, so I let him.

"Conan? Tina's brother? That's great. He can take me to school."

"You're six—you don't get to dictate!" I retort angrily.

"Nearly seven." She points her nose up high. I've taught her well. Her eyes are wide, begging, but they don't work on me.

I scowl. "Right, therefore you're young and Dad should be taking you."

Mia groans and flops backward onto the soft mattress. "Lyssa, I told you!"

I slam my brush on the dresser. "Fine." But it isn't. I'm infuriated to the point of saying anything to shut her up. "Make sure you're ready."

She jumps down off my bed and skips out of my room, practically singing, "I will!"

A few minutes later, Conan pulls up, and I see his shadow—slightly paler than his car—getting out. He waves over to us. My stomach swirls, making me feel sick and anxious, as if something dreadful is going to happen. I try to put it to one side and smile at him. Mia's holding my hand and guiding me down the path without making it noticeable. I hear the engine running and his tailpipe backfiring.

His hand comes around my waist, turning me around so we're both facing Mia. "What's up kiddo?"

"My name is Mia," she scoffs.

I laugh and glare at her. "My dad's gone out—are we able to drop her off at school?"

Conan fidgets at my side and scratches the back of his neck. "I don't see why not."

Mia pushes in between us and opens the door to the back seat. "Thanks," she says cheerfully then hops in.

Conan puts the car in drive and looks out toward the road. "So, you're Tina's friend, right?"

I sit silently in the passenger seat. Mia starts chomping down on her breakfast bar, chewing it like a wild animal. "Close your mouth, Mia," I lecture parentally.

She swallows and smiles. "Sorry." She's probably rolling her eyes at me. "Yeah, I'm Tina's *best friend*. You're her brother, the guy who brings home that really nasty girl all the time."

My mouth hangs open and I look at his silhouette. He's gripping the steering wheel tightly. "I—um—Lindsey Montelowe."

I raise my eyebrows. "Lindsey?"

"Yeah, that's her." Mia's nodding her head. "She locked Tina in a cupboard once."

Conan and I glance at her in the back seat. "She did what!?" We both say it together, absolutely gobsmacked.

"She's a witch," Mia says, her tone serious.

I nod. "I can think of a few uglier words for her."

"Well, I didn't want to say bitch, Lyssa," my sister shoots back, her voice orotund.

"Mia!" I scold her, trying to contain my laughter. Conan's laughter fills the vehicle, making mine escape me too. I've always wondered if she has a filter, but then I guess that's what happens when I become the closest thing to a mother she has, because I certainly don't set a good example. *She's doomed.*

Conan's still laughing when we drop her off at school, waving our goodbyes. "Your little sister cracks me up."

"She's also very truthful," I point out.

He nods and grabs hold of my hand. "Lindsey was a long time ago."

I nod too. "I know." He kisses my knuckles before putting the car back into drive.

Lindsey and Conan dated back in junior year. They were the bee's knees, the best couple in town, the favorites to win king and queen at prom. Everyone believes they'll go off, get married, and have babies after graduation. They didn't last long in a relationship, always on and off, constantly bickering, but when they were good, they looked amazing.

I hear the loud chatter in the school parking lot as I step out of Conan's car. I know everyone's looking at me—well, looking at him, hand in hand with me. I listen to the beeping sounds of car doors locking. There are vehicles crawling past us, and I curl my toes in my shoes at the hard concrete underfoot.

Ethan, Levi, and Ashton all shoulder-bump Conan until finally they're staring my way. "Alyssa," they chime.

"Hey boys." I nod my head and lean against Conan's car, waiting patiently for him and blowing the stinging smell of new tar out of my nose. Conan wraps his arms around me and nuzzles my neck in front of them. I forget all about our audience and lose myself in the moment.

"You guys are...a *thing*?" Ashton burns the question into my mind. He's practically spitting it at us, as if it's the worst possible relationship that could ever happen at Valley View High.

"I—" I start to stutter.

Conan stands in front of me, staring his friend down. "Yes, bro. Is that going to be a problem?"

Ashton dips his head to the ground and mumbles. "No, no problem at all."

"It better not be, Ash." Conan glares at him.

Ashton waves his hand at the guys and walks away. Ethan and Levi both laugh and bounce toward Conan and me. Levi lounges against the car next to me, and Ethan gets Conan into a headlock. I watch as the shadows play out in front of me. Ethan ruffles Conan's hair with his knuckles, and they're both laughing as they try to tackle each other to the ground.

"You've grabbed yourself a right little hottie there, haven't you," Ethan comments in a honeyed tone.

Conan punches his side playfully. "Shut up. Just because you want her..." They continue to play fight in the middle of the road, passersby stopping to watch.

"I think it's cool. I haven't seen Conan smile like that in a long time." Levi's husky voice turns my head.

I jump and let out a nervous laugh. I didn't expect him to be so close, never mind actually speak to me.

"Oh, I'm glad he's happy." I smile to myself.

"He really likes you." Levi points out the obvious in a satisfactory way.

"I really like him," I state matter-of-factly.

Levi straightens out the cuffs at the bottom of his sleeves, of his letterman jacket. "Then tell him."

I freeze. *What?* "T-Tell him what?" I scrunch my eyebrows together. "That I like him? He knows."

"You know what, Alyssa. Callie told me about your condition." His tone is grave.

I gawp. "Why would *Callie* tell *you*?"

He shrugs so I feel it, his shoulder touching mine. "Callie and I are brother and sister." My mouth drops open even wider. "Nobody really knows, and I'd like to keep it that way. I'm adopted."

"Adopted...you and Callie are siblings?" I can't believe what I'm hearing.

He nods. "I promise I won't tell anyone. I'm sorry this happened to you, Alyssa." He places his arm around me and gives me the most awkward hug in history. "I know Conan—he'll still like you. He'll stand by you. You should tell him, otherwise things will come out and he won't forgive you."

"Is that a threat?"

He nudges me. "God no—don't be so stupid."

I cross my arms over my chest. "Levi, tell Callie to keep her mouth shut, and please, please don't say anything. It's my business."

He loops his pinky through mine. "This is what girls do, isn't it?" He holds on tight and shakes my little finger. "Pinky swear."

I giggle and Conan saunters over toward us, wrapping his arms back around my waist and pulling me closer to his lean body. Levi kicks Ethan's ass and drags him away. "See ya' at practice, bro."

"I like Levi," I say.

Conan tips my head up to look at him. "Yeah, he's cool." He leans in and touches his lips to mine. "Not as cool as us though," he mumbles against my mouth. My whole body does backflips and shoots fireworks down into my feet, making me go up on my tiptoes, pushing myself farther into his kiss.

"Hey, did you get my note yesterday?" Conan lingers his lips close to mine.

I slide my hand into my pocket and feel the crumpled piece of paper. "That was you? I didn't have chance to look at it. What did it say?"

He kisses me tenderly, lovingly, and I don't want him to stop.

Noelle interrupts from behind us with a disgusted, "Urgh." Noelle's fingers are most likely in her mouth, gesturing like she's about to bring up her breakfast. "Stop fondling in the parking lot, guys." She moves her hand to her hip, tapping her foot behind us. "Conan, if you don't mind, Lyssa and I have places to be, people to see, etc., etc."

Conan pulls away and groans. "You're like a fly on the wall we can't get rid of."

Noelle flips him off. "Never forget it."

I touch my finger up to my lips and re-imagine all our kisses. Conan molds his hand into mine. "We'll all walk in together. I want people to know she's mine."

Noelle looks bored. "Seriously, I think they do. You haven't put her down, you love machine."

"Noelle!" I laugh and swat her arm. We're walking up the steps to the entrance and she's holding on to my elbow slyly, trying to keep me steady.

"What!?" She laughs too. "I'm just saying, now that I know we didn't sleep together, I don't have to be polite to him."

Conan's eyebrows rise, forming dark lines on his forehead. "When have you ever been polite to me?"

"Ugh." Noelle thumps his ear. "All the time, Dwight."

Principle Williamson is standing with Maggie—Mrs. Hall—when I walk into my counseling session. He isn't normally there, and they're quiet—too quiet. I halt at the door, seeing their shadows hunched together behind her desk. They're whispering about something important, information I shouldn't listen to, so I close myself off as I sit in the chair in front of them.

I hear a cough from behind me, making me jump out of my skin and place both hands on the desk in front of me, steadying myself.

"Miss Darlington, sorry to be visiting you in school, but some new information has come to light." Sheriff Lou pinches the end of his nose and sniffs as if he's trying to get rid of unwanted snot.

"What new information?" I look confused.

"Maggie, please explain it to her." Principle Williamson says her name with so much authority, and the statement is clearly a demand.

My head is beginning to spin. What could this be about? Do they know who did this? Do they know something I don't? Maggie comes around and perches beside me. "Don't be scared, Alyssa. I know this will be worrying for you, but it's about the other day with Charlotte."

I glance around, knowing the shadows won't tell me anything else, but I still do it out of curiosity. "Charlotte?"

"Miss Darlington, you made an allegation in front of the majority of the senior class that Charlotte Summers drugged you, but you didn't come to us?"

"I—"

"You need to be honest. Is this the truth?"

I close my eyes and think about it. Does she deserve to be punished? No, she doesn't. We all make our fair share of mistakes, and I know this was hers.

"Alyssa," Principle Williamson says sternly. There's no kindness in his voice like there was the first day back. It now sounds like his patience is running low, as if he's too old to be doing this job. "We've never had to deal with drugs in our school before. I'd appreciate your cooperation."

I laugh nervously. "Drugs are all over your school, are you blind?" Figuratively speaking.

The statement hits close to home, and I wish I hadn't said it. No, he isn't blind—I am.

"Alyssa, your sessions here have been productive. Each time you've remembered new things, and I think you've remembered more than you share. I think you believe you can solve this on your own. Being drugged is a serious thing, and it may have contributed toward you not being able to defend yourself. We need to know what happened."

I hesitate. I'm petrified to speak and resist forming any words. Instead I place my head into my hands, and I think deeply. Do I tell them? They're adults, teachers, police…do I trust them to help me? Or do I only trust myself? My mom lets me down day in, day out. Noelle's parents couldn't stop what happened at their house, and the police are not doing their jobs to find out what happened. I've given them enough of my time to be able to dig further. They sent me away when I went to them about Ashton. Will they talk to Charlotte and send her on her way too?

I start scratching my wrists, both of them, my palms under and over. My nails are digging hard into the skin. I want to break it, to break the skin and let me feel the sharp pain. *What is wrong with me?* "It wasn't Charlotte." My voice breaks, and with that break comes a flood of tears. "I mean, it was, but it wasn't."

I'm sniffling. I'm squeezing my eyes, willing the water to stop, willing everything to stop.

Maggie grabs my hands, stopping me from hurting myself, and I thank her mentally. "It's okay, Alyssa."

I sob hard. "It's not. I don't want her to get in trouble. She was having a laugh, and I know that now. I was angry—I am angry—but she didn't know this would happen. She doesn't even know *this*"—I point to my eyes—"has happened."

Principle Williamson and Sherriff Lou stay quiet. They watch as I smash, like glass shattering in front of them.

"It's okay, Alyssa. I'm sure she didn't," Maggie says comfortingly.

"It wasn't her. Ashton had the drugs. He's the one who's addicted. She was having a laugh, it just—"

"She shouldn't have done it," Sherriff Lou says matter-of-factly.

"It just got out of hand," I growl at him. What is it with him and Ashton? It's as though he's protecting him. "It was Ashton Marston that started this. How else would she have gotten the drugs?" I snarl. I can't believe I'm trying to protect Charlotte.

"We will search lockers." Principle Williamson looks at Sheriff Lou. "If you will, bring in the drug-sniffing dogs. We will search locker by locker, and we will talk to Charlotte Summers before informing her parents."

"Okay." Sheriff Lou nods his head and agrees. He places his hand on my shoulder in reassurance and walks out of the room, probably to call for backup.

Seventeen

I'm standing by my locker. I'm scratching my arms, my wrists sore from earlier, and I lean quietly against the metal frame. Conan has his arm slung around me, and he's the only source of heat. His locker had already been searched—no drugs. Ethan and Levi are standing by theirs, opposite us, and they both slide across the space between.

"Wonder what it's all about," Ethan says. "Whatever it is, I'm all clear."

"So am I," Levi tells us.

Noelle sneaks up beside me and places her hand in mine. She leans in and whispers, "You okay?"

"What about you, Carlisle? Has daddy's little princess been cleared?" Ethan snickers and high-fives Levi. Conan laughs beside me, his shoulders moving in sync. I nudge him. He places his head into the crook of my neck and apologizes, but I pretend I didn't hear it. I don't want to hear anything.

"For your information, guys, my dad is very proud of me, and I of him. I would never have anything in my locker to jeopardize that."

What does that even mean?

"You been searched yet, doll face?" Ethan brings the attention onto me. I squirm under Conan's arm, wishing I could disappear.

"Um—yeah," I mutter, lying to him and everyone else. They don't need to search my locker; it's because of me they're searching at all.

Conan kisses my cheek, his touch sending shivers down my spine—good shivers. Noelle is still holding my hand. I relax into the comfort of them both and breathe, because that's what my head is telling me to do. *Breathe in.*

"What's going on?" Tommy joins us, asking me directly.

I shrug.

Out.

"You're really pale, Alyssa," Tommy says. All eyes are on me now. "Are you okay?"

"Stop being OTT, Tommy. Lyssa is fine," Noelle barks, like a guard dog. *Breathe in.*

Everyone's bickering, worrying about my physical health, until Callie's voice comes out of nowhere and tells us to be quiet. "Guys, look!"

I didn't even realize she'd joined.

"What the—" Conan's arm drops from around me and he's now intently looking diagonally across from us.

Out.

My stomach sinks like a stone in water. I'm hungry, but I know even if I eat, the hunger will still be there. I hear sobs farther down the corridor; the cries are coming from Charlotte. I hear Maggie's voice asking her to calm down, and then it all happens too quickly. Ashton Marston is slamming his foot against the locker door.

"That's not flipping mine!" he shouts.

In.

"Ashton Marston, you're under arrest for the possession of marijuana." Sheriff Lou places Ashton's front against the locker and I hear the clip of the handcuffs, like a bomb dropping in a silent room. "You have the right to remain silent. You have the right to counsel. Do you wish to enforce your rights, or do you want to say something? Remember anything you do or say may be used against you in a court of law."

Out.

I start pacing, back and forth, little steps. Nobody's watching me, too enthralled with Ashton's arrest. He's kicking, fighting for his release, and I suddenly can't breathe properly. My throat is closing up and I'm struggling for air. I place my palm against the locker and try to catch myself, but I'm gone, and before I realize how far I've actually gone, I'm no longer in my body but floating above myself, as if I never existed, as if I never should have made it to begin with.

I'm not sure how long I'm out for.

I'm not even sure if I pass out, but my shoulders are being tugged on harshly, bringing me back down to the ground. I'm sitting on the cold, hard floor against the lockers, and everyone is crowding me.

Callie, out of everyone, stands in front of me, pushing everyone away and stopping them from coming near me. Noelle and Conan help me stand.

"This is your fault, Alyssa Darlington." Charlotte and Lindsey are being held back by Ethan and Levi. They're trying to get me, to hurt me. I don't blame them. "You'll regret this."

"Leave her alone, Charlotte," Tommy snaps. "Stop being such a vindictive cow."

She screams, scratching at Levi's face. I see her silhouette, black like a witch's cat and angry—so angry. She's pointing her finger at Tommy. "We're *so* over."

"He should be relieved," Noelle interjects. "You're a whiny bitch anyway."

Ethan and Levi laugh. I don't find it funny. I just want to escape, so I do. I run.

Conan shouts after me, "Darlington!" He tries to grasp my arm, but he misses. "Alyssa, wait!"

I don't glance back; it wouldn't make much of a difference in what I would see. I hope he runs after me and catches me. I'm doing what my body wants. It's telling me to run so I'm running—the consequences can come later.

The only place I need to be is home. There's nothing better than taking your shoes off and letting your feet sink into the living room's brown, plush, cushioned carpet.

Conan drives me home and offers to come in for support. He holds my hand tightly and takes the seat on the sofa next to me. My toes curl slowly, cherishing the melting-away feeling. The smell of bacon drifts up my nostrils and I realize my dad's sitting in the arm chair, chewing a large bacon and egg bap. Fusco and Charlie bounce toward us, sniffing and licking our skin, sending endorphins throughout their little furry bodies. I tickle Fusco's ear, and he pushes his head farther into my leg.

"Alyssa, it's not even lunch time yet—what are you doing here?" Dad stops chewing, surprised to see me.

"I can't do it." I beg with my eyes. "Please let me stay home. It's the end of the week anyway." The last thing I want is to be forced to go back to school.

"You can stay home, love." He chews and swallows. "But I can't let Conan—he's not my responsibility."

"Don't worry about me, sir. I'm a straight-A student. Principle Williamson loves me." Conan puts his hand on my knee. "If you don't mind, I'd like to stay and make sure your daughter is okay."

I know my dad appreciates this. I watch his shadow steadily, waiting for him to reply. His dark-outlined, bald head nods at us and gets up to go into the kitchen. I sit and wonder where Mom is, and I ask myself why Dad is doing this on his own.

Conan and I both release a heavy sigh, not having realized we were holding our breaths, and we relax against the sofa's back. I curl my feet up underneath me and lean my body into Conan's. I hug my arms around him, and he strokes my arm, up and down. I place my head on his shoulder and summer fruits drift from his skin, up into the highest point of my nose, sending shivers down my spine. I'm drunk off his smell, drunk off his touch, mesmerized by his kindness.

"Conan?" I try to look at him, try to see his handsome face.

He strokes my cheek, "Yeah, Darlington?"

"What did the note say?"

He kisses the top of my head, "It said: *I could search the star-lit sky, the world, the universe and I would never find anyone as perfect as you.*"

I think I'm in love. Can falling in love get any better than this? I don't think so. In fact, I don't care.

This is my love story.

Eighteen

Lindsey's house party: nothing nearly as chaotic as Noelle's, but still, the air smells like a mélange of everyone's perfume and cologne. Outside in the back yard, sweaty bodies sway and twirl on the dance floor. The undertone of booze tickles my nostrils, making me want to vomit. The charred scent of a barbeque sizzles from the corner of her yard, smoke drifts around my face from the fire pit, and those smoking are mashing their cigarette butts out on the walkway. Couples are in the shadows, making out, and memories of my last party clash together in my brain. I try to separate them one by one, placing them back into chronological order.

Everything will be okay, Lyssa.

Conan left me earlier today to get ready and meet Ethan and Levi. Even after I told him I wasn't coming to the party, he didn't believe me and laughed it off. "You have to come to the party with me. You're my girl. I need you," he said, practically begging me in between sweet, senseless kisses trailing down my neck and along my collarbone. I wanted to stay home. We all remember what happened last time I went to a party. This time, I can't see. Drunk and blind—I imagine that not mixing well.

~

"You're so drunk, Alyssa. It's embarrassing," Noelle tells me with her mom look plastered on her face. It's

the same look my mom has when I've disappointed her. Noelle laughs.

I look at her quizzically. "What are you laughing at?"

"It's just..." Noelle perches on her kitchen counter. "If my dad could see you now, he'd be mortified. You realize he worships you? He thinks you're this goody-too-shoes golden girl. The only reason he's not here now, shutting it down, is because he knows you're here. 'Oh, Alyssa will keep it in order. She's a good girl.' Those were his exact words this morning."

My mouth drops open. "He knows you're throwing this party?"

"Who do you think got us the alcohol? It didn't just magically appear." Noelle takes a sip of her Jack and Coke.

I'm more of a gin and tonic kind of girl.

~

I stumble forward and hold on to Tommy's arm with so much force he flinches at the pain. "Sorry," I mumble. I can't believe I forgot about Noelle's dad knowing about the party; they've kept it so quiet since it happened. Does she have something to hide? Noelle is trailing behind us, tapping her two-inch heels upon the well-put-together patio. I'm dressed in a black and purple dress that flares out at the bottom, making me look like a princess.

Noelle takes over, freeing Tommy's arm. "Go have fun," she orders.

Tommy kisses my forehead and asks me if I'm okay before leaving me be. I do the only thing my body lets me: I nod. I concentrate on the large mass of shadows, all hunched together around a table of food. We zigzag through the crowd and the smell of rum drifts by me, making me waver. Noelle holds me still, and all I can think about is how I was attacked at a party.

How I didn't look after myself.

How it's all my fault.

"Try not think about it, Lyssa," Noelle says, as if she can read my thoughts. I smile tightly at her and shift my eyes down to my shadowed feet.

"It's hard not to. It's like I'm out of place." I shiver as the cool air drifts around me.

She rubs my arm and leads us to a crowd of shadows surrounding a long table: beer pong. "Don't think that. You belong here—you're my best friend."

"Only when you want me to be." I raise my eyebrows.

Noelle laughs, the sound like a lullaby to my ears. "Too true."

I slap her across her upper arm and gawp. "You aren't meant to agree with me."

Noelle lets go of me and leans over a table in front of us, looking for a cup full of alcohol. "Drink?"

"No thanks," I whisper. "Remember, I have my appointment tomorrow."

"Oh, yeah. What's it for again?"

I shake my head and smile. "Just an update."

"Well, one drink and a little gyrating won't do any harm." She shakes her hips.

I push her lightly. "Give over."

"Maybe you and Conan will do a little gyrating tonight," she says suggestively.

I laugh. "You're one of a kind."

"I know." She flips her long blonde hair over her shoulder and smiles broadly, the shadow changing so delicately, so beautifully. I capture the picture and lock it away.

Kids from Vallyeont live by one rule: party hard, make mistakes, and laugh endlessly; after all, you're only young once. What they don't realize is it will all follow them into their futures. They're molding their futures right now, but that's hard to do when you don't let go of the past. I'm doing the same and I know it's not healthy, but how can you get over something so awful? Do you just forget and move on? It sounds so easy when it's put like that.

I hear his laugh, the laugh of a God, before I see his strong, healthy silhouette. I've learned to recognize it out of a swarm of shadows so easily it's second nature. I smile widely, all that worry and pain drifting out of my body, as if he's summoning it all.

Conan's socially smoking, and I don't mean a cigarette. He's playing beer pong, and he's on fire. I try not to interrupt his winning streak. Ethan and Levi are at his side, cheering him on. Every time the ball goes into a cup, they smash their beers together and sing a victory song. Standing at the other end of the table is Tommy. His shadow is curled over, drinking each cup as fast as he can. The beer spills down either side of his mouth. Once he finishes, he holds his hands up in the air and chants loudly.

Noelle and I stand next to him. She pats him on the back. "You're such a loser."

Tommy gives her a pondering look. "What did you just call me?"

"I called you a loser."

"Was that after having the flaming sambuca?" Tommy quips. I try to resist a laugh and high-five him. I chuckle at the smile he's hiding. Noelle's fuming, glaring at him with big, round eyes. I swear she loves it, really.

Tommy leans down and whispers in my ear, close enough for Noelle to hear, "I should learn to behave."

I giggle.

"Amen," Noelle says absently.

"Henderson, are you playing or chatting?" Levi hollers from the corner.

Noelle flicks her hand and turns her nose upward. "Believe me when I say, you can have him."

I glance across the long, shadowy tabletop, and standing next to Conan with her arms draped around him is Lindsey. He's trying to pull out of her grasp as nicely as he possibly can, but she isn't having any of it. I want to open my mouth and tell her to get off him, but it's too much pressure and I'm nervous. I glance down to the floor, pretending I haven't noticed.

"Montelowe! Get your filthy paws of my friend's guy," Noelle shouts, standing behind Tommy, using him for balance as she's up on her tiptoes. I try to hide my smile. I can always count on Noelle to say what I'm thinking. I love her for that.

"Excuse me?" Lindsey's squeaky voice stops the game for a second time.

"Come on, Lindsey—you know I'm not into you like that," Conan says quietly.

"But you're into *her*?!" Lindsey bites like a rabid dog.

"Yeah, I really like Alyssa." Conan grins and I place a hand over my heart for him to see.

Lindsey straightens her body and holds her chin up high. She lets go and brings herself around the table to stand in front of me. I step back automatically, not thinking about how it makes me look. Lindsey's pack grows larger as they all swarm around her. There are more shadows than empty space, and it makes me feel woozy.

"Look at you—you think you're so tough." Lindsey looks back at her girls and laughs.

I shakily laugh with her. "I'm just here for the party. I have no dramas with you."

"No dramas? Funny, considering you're having sex with my boyfriend."

"Last time I checked you'd broken up." I stay strong. "And not that it's anyone's business, but I'm not *having sex* with anybody."

"Leave her alone, Lindsey," Conan shouts, pushing his way through Lindsey's army. "I'm not your boyfriend—you don't own me."

"You're mine!" she whines.

"Back off before I knock you onto your backside, flat on the floor." Noelle stands between us. "Troops or no troops."

The room is quiet. The only voice I hear is Charlotte's, standing in the doorway to Lindsey's kitchen, and she's frothing with revelations. Girls around her are asking her questions, and all anyone hears is, "Ashton has been charged with drug possession. Apparently to shorten his sentence, he's told them a name of the person he works for."

Ethan jerks forward, but Levi holds him back. Conan's jaw tenses, and Lindsey awkwardly coughs.

Charlotte looks around, and like a witch on her broom, she flies toward me. "What the hell, Alyssa? What the hell do you think you're doing here?"

"She's with me," Conan roughly tells her from behind. Charlotte halts, not sure how to respond. I dip my head to the floor. *Please be over soon. Please be over.*

"And me," Noelle says in a threatening manner.

"Yeah, me too," Tommy whispers, his balls obviously dropping.

"Oh, what the hell—she's with all of us. You going to kick us all out, babe?" Ethan shouts, placing his cup on the edge of the table. "If so, party at my place?" Cheers fill the back yard.

All I need now is tequila, super lemon, and a sidekick whiz kid (where's Callie when you need her?) and I'd be on my way to verbally, maybe even physically assaulting these bitches. My mouth waters for the alcohol, for the encouragement.

Charlotte looks at Lindsey, waiting for Lindsey's approval, before telling everyone coldly, "She can stay." Her eyes are daggering me. "Stay out of my way."

Before I know it, my mouth reacts. "Considering you hate me, it's pretty strange that you're stalking me like this."

Everyone laughs.

She glares at me, and I imagine the hatred radiating off her face, her eyes squinting as if she's got something in them and her mouth in a tight line. "I'll do what I want." She lets out a menacing smile. She hands me a drink and I hold the cool beer cup against my palm, close to my chest. "Be careful—you never know what's in these drinks nowadays."

"You—" I shoot my arms out at her, chucking the cup and the substance in it in her direction. My hands are aiming for her neck, but Tommy grabs me by the waist, stopping me. Charlotte laughs and walks away, swaying her hips with so much attitude. *Yeah, you better walk away, you bitch.* Tommy drops me to my feet.

Conan's by my side after finally getting through the crowd of girls. He's staring at me, his expression wry. My face is flushed. Charlotte's just played me like a dealer at a poker table, and I didn't even realize. My breath is like scraping metal and before I can stop myself, a rainfall of tears bursts out of me like a collapsing bridge dropping into a river.

Conan holds me close, his lean torso firm against my tiny frame. We fit together perfectly.

I stay at the party. I don't leave; if I did, I would be giving the chuckle sisters the satisfaction they crave to be able to get through life. I keep my distance and keep a smile upon my face for everyone to see. Conan's bouncing on the soles of his feet along to Tom Walker,

"Leave a Light On". Everyone's singing as high as their voices allow and I smile, happy because he's happy.

The air is dry, flavored with the skunky odor of pot. Where there's a party, there's a dealer, and where there's pot, there are brainless bodies. *Let's all get high.*

I look for the toilet and bump my shoulder into many drunken kids. I apologize softly and then fumble with a smooth doorknob I saw pushed open earlier in the night. I walk in and instantly realize it's not the bathroom. It's *definitely* not the bathroom. I hear light moans and breathless murmurs. I concentrate hard, trying to get my eyes to process the distilled image, the sharpness, the brightness, the clarity—all of it.

"Oh, Tommy," the girl whispers breathlessly. With it, the scent of sweet almond with a hint of cherry follows.

Tommy. Wait—I know that voice. I place my hand over my mouth, trying to stop from exploding into a giggling fit. I never, ever imagined this—*ever*.

"Oh my God." I swallow hard and stay standing there, unable to move my feet. They both stop what they're doing, untangle themselves, and jump apart.

"Alyssa!" Noelle says my name, shocked to see me. "It's-not-what-it-looks-like."

Tommy stutters. "N-Not at all."

I laugh into my hand. "What does it look like?" I can't help myself. The room is small, and it starts to feel clammy and claustrophobic. I stifle another giggle with my palm.

"I-I don't like him," she states boldly.

He's putting on his shirt. "Well, I don't like you either."

"You both need to just admit it." I raise my eyebrows and lean against the closed door.

"This is just..." Noelle is standing in her underwear, as I see the lined shadows of her bra, nothing I haven't seen before. "Weird."

I snort. "You're telling me!?"

"Okay, Miss Bombastic." Noelle places her hands on her hips. "Get out." She extends her arm and points to the door.

"Okay, sorry..." I laugh and open the door, about to slip out. "Lovebirds." I snort again and a shoe flies at me, narrowly missing my head. "You missed!" I taunt. I shut the door slowly and gently, still listening in on the final moments of their sailing love ship.

"Ugh," I hear her say, exasperated. "Just get over here and kiss me before I change my mind."

Tommy chuckles. "I'm game."

Like I said, they have a love-hate relationship. They love to hate, hate to admit it, love to play on it, and hate to show it, but let's just say it: they're in love with each other.

Nineteen

We're walking along the cracked pavement, the moon high in the sky, shining brightly down upon us. It's radiating a soothing white light onto Conan's handsome shadow, and I admire it intensely. He's grasping my hand with his and slowly rubbing his thumb across my alabaster skin. I cherish the moment, not wanting it to end. His black leather jacket is slung over my shoulders, keeping me warm.

We open the glass door of Lexi's diner and take a seat in the window. The open-24-hours-a-day diner is quiet, only one other customer inside. Conan orders us two hot chocolates with the works—marshmallows, cream, and chocolate sprinkles. My stomach grumbles at the smell of cocoa. He spoons me a mouthful and I groan at the sweet sensation.

"I'm glad we left the party. I felt like I couldn't spend much time with you." My hair is tied up in a neatly formed bun, and Conan pushes back a strand of my auburn hair that has come loose. "Perfect."

"Far from it," I whisper. I look at him through my eyelashes. "Are you okay?"

He scrunches his face up. "What do you mean?"

I have to ask about Ashton. "I know you and Ashton are practically like brothers."

"Oh." He holds my hand across the table. "*That.* I'm cool. He's stupid, isn't he—he shouldn't have gotten himself caught up with all that."

I nod.

Or caught up with me.

"Don't you worry, though, because I'm not," he says.

I smile broadly. "I won't."

He picks out a yellow carnation from the small vase on the table and hands it to me. "For you." I take it and continue to smile. "Seven billion smiles in this world, and yours is my favorite."

My cheeks turn a rosy pink and I look away, embarrassed. He leans over the table, turns my head, and pecks my lips. Electric waves travel down into the soles of my feet. I always believed love to be the meeting of two souls fully accepting one another, accepting the dark and the light within…together, bound for eternity to grow through struggles and adapt into sweet bliss. Looking at Conan and the way he is with me, I know I'll have that. Maybe I've already got it, but I don't want to scare him away with the three little words begging to come off my lips. When I look at him, he awakens my soul.

"Conan?" I whisper. *I love you.* "I really, really like you."

"I really, really like you too, Alyssa."

I come around the table and slide myself into his lap. I close the distance between us by placing my arms around his neck and leaning in. I hold my lips above his and feel the need in his body. I smile and close the small gap by sliding my tongue across his bottom lip, tasting him and parting his lips so we're dancing together. My body tingles magically, and I never want it to end. His hand is at the crook of my neck and he's holding me delicately, like I'm an ornament that could break.

"What time do you need to be back?" he mumbles against my lips.

"I don't," I say, trailing kisses down his neck.

"Won't your mom be mad?"

I shrug my shoulders. "Yeah, but only if she's actually at home."

If. It's a big if, a never-going-to-happen if. *If only*...if only she cared, if only she loved us, if only my life was different.

Conan pays the bill and I head for the toilet to freshen myself up. I place a light shade of mauve lipstick on my fingertip and dab it on, plumping my lips by smacking them together. I run my hands through the top of my hair, making sure it's perfectly arranged, and then I wash my hands. I practically skip back out to the front of the diner.

Not looking where I'm going, my shoulder hits a woman's side. She steadies us both. "Oh gosh I'm so—" my mother mumbles.

I stand still, stunned. "Mom!?"

"Alyssa?" Mom says my name is if she didn't choose it. "You should be at home."

"Shouldn't you?" I retort. "You do have a six-year-old, or have you forgotten?"

She doesn't say a word and fidgets in place. She appears uncomfortable. *What is she even doing here?* A little diner, off the grid, not really an adult zone. Why is she by herself at one in the morning?

I don't have to ask the question aloud as it's promptly answered for me.

"Come on, babe. You said you were just going to the restroom." The man slides his arm around my mother's waist and pulls her snug into his side. He bends his head down into her neck, still not noticing me, and kisses her jawline. "The sooner you go, the quicker we can get back to the hotel."

"Hotel?" I choke. I choke at his voice, at his musky, whiskey scent, at his *lies*. "Mr. Carlisle!?"

He swears under his breath and mutters into my mother's ear. "You should've told me." He tightens his grip on her.

Conan's voice interjects. "Is everything okay?" He's never met my mom, and he's never going to. I barge through, making sure I separate them, and I head straight for Conan.

"Love! It's not what it looks like," my mom calls out, trying to save herself.

Low blow.

Mr. Carlisle grabs my wrist, halting me. "Wait, sweetheart—"

"Dude, get off her!" Conan shoves him backward, rubbing my wrist with his hands.

"This has nothing to do with you, son," Mr. Carlisle growls.

I stand in front of him, blocking Mr. Carlisle's gaze from Conan's. Noelle is going to flip. Her poor mom…my poor dad.

Disgusting.

"You walk out of here and you don't say a word," Mr. Carlisle demands. "You never saw your mother—"

"Your mother!?" Conan asks quizzically.

"Later," I mouth at him. I stare back at my mom and her bit on the side. "Which one is it? 'It's not what it looks like' or 'It is what it looks like, so don't say a word'?"

"Quit the cheek, girl," my mother warns.

"Once you come clean to Dad, then you can go back to telling me what to do, but for now, I'd say I can speak to you how I like."

"I'm still your mother!"

"Then act like it!" I scream before running out of the little diner, pieces of me breaking, my family collapsing. I just thought she hated being a mother, not that she hated Dad enough to do this. Conan's running after me and I finally collapse to the pavement, a mile from the diner, far away from their lies, far away from them completely.

My mom is having an affair with my best friend's dad, and it feels somewhat familiar to me, as if I've dreamt it before. One thing I'm sure on is that it's disgusting.

Absolutely disgusting.

Twenty

Conan's bedroom is dim, the lighting just perfect enough for me to see his long torso. He's lying on his bed next to me, his bare chest visible, allowing me to feel along his hard abs. He's defined in so many ways, and it sends shivers down my spine, exciting me. I lean my head against his chest and sigh. He's given me an old t-shirt, large enough to come down to just above my knees. We lie there silently, him stroking my hair and me staring into the distant darkness.

"She's your mom?"

I nod. He turns onto his side, holding his head up with his arm. My head drops to sit against his pillow, and I stare at the shadow of his face.

"Conan." I choke back the tears. "I don't want to speak about my mom."

"That's okay, pretty." He strokes my cheek and kisses my nose. "We can just lie here."

I can't think about the lies my mom's been telling. It makes me hate her, but it makes me hate myself more.

"Conan? I need to tell you something." I look away.

He moves his face closer to mine, looking directly into the depths of my eyes. "Yeah?"

"You might not like me anymore after I tell you."

"Not possible," he whispers.

I sit up farther against the headboard. I wrap my arms around my legs, pulling myself tighter into a ball. *It's time.* I'm going to tell him, tell him everything. He realizes I'm being serious and slides his body farther up the bed as well.

"The night of the party…" I rub my chicken legs, the friction forming heat burns. "The night of the party, when I was attacked, they poured something over me…"

"But you're okay."

"Wait. Just listen. I'm not okay—far from it. The police…they're looking for my attacker, because…" I stare blankly, trying to find the courage to tell him. "Because what they did to me…it had an effect."

"What kind of effect? Like anxiety?"

"No. Worse." I rub my face with the palms of my hands and groan. "I'm blind, Conan. I'm blind. I see shadows and that's it. I can't even see you now to see what you're thinking. I'm blind and I don't think I'm going to be anything different, so I understand if you don't want to be mine anymore." I cry hard into my hands. "I understand."

He sits up completely. He's shocked. "You're b-blind?"

"Yes," I whisper, my voice barely audible.

He's silent for what feels like forever, and then finally he wraps his arms around me and places me in his lap. I cry even harder than before into his tanned skin. The smell of dried rose petals mingles with my thoughts, and I breathe steadily against him.

"Oh, Darlington." He's trailing kisses down my face, along my neck, and then one kiss per eyelid. He lays me down on my back and moves above me, holding his weight up with his arms. His mouth captures mine. He kisses me fiercely, lovingly, cherishingly. I give it back to him. I trail my hands into his hair, tugging at his curls. I move them down and start tickling the back of his neck with my fingers. He groans against my lips and pushes harder against my tiny frame. I embrace it.

He's taking away all my pain, all my worries, my hatred, my dread, and he's saving me.

"I love you," he whispers into my ear, kissing my temple. "I fell in love with you. I don't know how, I don't know when, but I just did." He flips onto his back and pulls me into a cuddle. "I love you, Darlington. I don't care if you're blind. You're mine. We'll get through this. I'll do anything I can to get you through this. I promise."

If it didn't feel real, I'd pinch myself to make sure I wasn't dreaming.

There's nothing left to say as we lie in each other's arm and drift off to sweet slumber. When I cry, he dries my eyes. When I laugh, he laughs with me, not at me. When I smile, he smiles lovingly upon me. When I need him, he makes sure to comfort me. He's everything I asked for and more.

The homey smell of frying butter brings my body out of sleep. I roll over to touch Conan's body, but my hand is met with thin air. I pat the bed repeatedly until I conclude that he *definitely* isn't here. The rich buttery smell gets closer and it seeps up into my nostrils, making my mouth water and my mind daydream about fluffy, warm goodness.

"Rise and shine, Darlington."

I push myself up against the headboard and cross my legs underneath the duvet.

"Don't say I never treat you." Conan leans down and kisses my forehead. I flutter my eyelashes and my heart starts beating as fast as a racehorse. He places a plate in my lap and steam floats up into the air above my chocolate chip pancakes, making me crave the warm, gooey sensation in my mouth.

"Did you make them?" My face lights up like a light bulb.

He scratches the back of his neck and laughs nervously. "With a little help from my mom."

I giggle. *Mommy's boy.* I like that. "They're perfect." I drop my head down and take one last whiff before demolishing them all. I look back up at Conan's outline where he's perching on the bed. "Is your mom okay with me being here?"

"Yeah, she's more than fine. She told me to tell you you're welcome any time."

I stab my fork into the soft brown piece of heaven and cut. I lift it toward my mouth. *Pure delight.* I let the first bite sit on my tongue, allowing the chocolate chips to melt away. I relish the sugary taste and the way my taste buds tingle. I swallow, allowing the warmth to leave a trail down my throat.

I moan in delight. "Best thing since sliced bread."

"You're so British." He laughs, shaking his head at me.

"You love it."

"Do I say it like *love* it, like you do, or is it just love it," Conan torments, mocking me playfully.

"Love it." I nod, smiling. He laughs harder, holding his sides.

"Christ, I love it when you talk dirty."

"So, let me get this straight…" I smirk. "Me talking in a British accent is me talking dirty to you?" I splutter, "How is that—"

"Oh yes, it's very sexy."

I gape. "Has anyone ever told you you're diabolical?"

He smirks. "No, but you just did." He stabs his fork into one of my pancakes and places it in his mouth.

He keeps his mouth shut while chewing and cheekily grins, showing dark lines around his perfectly formed lips.

I slap his shoulder. "That's mine!"

"Do you want it?" he says with a mouthful of chewed-up pancake.

"Nuh-uh." I laugh. "Keep it."

He wiggles his eyebrows playfully. "Thanks. It's mine now, Darlington." He watches me eat. "How does it work?"

"How does what work?"

"Your eyesight."

I finish chewing the last piece and place the plate on the bedside table. "I see shadows. I see either bold outlines or light shadows, dark shadows. I see contrast in light if, let's say, you smile or wink or even crease your forehead."

"So, you can still see some part of me? It's not like you're completely dark."

"You mean it's not like the lights are completely out?"

"Exactly."

"No." I perch myself beside him, our shoulders nearly touching, my tiptoes touching the wooden flooring. "I have an update today, about whether it'll get worse." I grab hold of his hand. "Conan, I've always been warned that it'll get worse. I'll go from partially to completely blind, and I understand if you're not ready for that."

"You're not getting rid of me that easily. Do you want me to come with you?"

"I—" Conan's ringtone cuts the conversation short, making my body jump. He scrambles over to his desk and picks his phone up.

"Hello?" He paces the room. "Yeah, she's here." He's nodding his head. "Yes, sir. I know about her being blind." He keeps nodding. "Yeah, I understand."

Sir...blind—my father.

I hold my arm out, demanding the phone. Within seconds, Conan places it in my hands. "Your dad," he whispers.

"Alyssa, love." His hoarse voice crackles through the speaker.

"What's wrong?" I say.

"It's Tommy." Dad hesitates. "He's been arrested."

"*What*!?" I stand up and squeeze the phone. "Arrested for what?"

"Your attack, Alyssa."

I drop the phone and Conan quickly reaches out to catch it. My eyes are wide, and my jaw is dropping to the floor; I have no idea what to do. I exhale, trying to comprehend what my life has become.

Twenty One

My hands are placed under my thighs and I'm rocking back and forth in my chair. Sweat trickles down the side of my head and I begin to bounce one foot up and down.

"Alyssa, how are you doing?" Dr. Loveday asks. Her office smells like pure hand sanitizer.

"I'm good," I say quietly. My dad and Mia are sitting beside me, each in their own seat.

"Good." She fiddles with a stack of papers and starts shuffling them. "I understand you have offered to do more tests, but it won't be necessary."

Dad coughs. "Won't be necessary, why?"

"Is Lyssa going to be fixed?" Mia says loudly, overly excited.

"I—" Dr. Loveday dips her head down. After a few seconds, she looks up. "I'm sorry. We know everything we need to know. In three weeks, there will be no shadows, Alyssa."

I stare forward, admiring the shadows, because in three weeks, they'll no longer exist. She's just told me everything I already thought would happen, everything I've been patiently waiting for. If pain existed other than the way I feel it, I might appreciate it more, but right now, all I am is numb: numb from the exhaustion and concentration.

I want it to end.

This isn't real.

My feet trip beneath me, dragging along the ground. Dark, blurry shapes cross my line of sight, and the sound of the cars parking in the school lot roars in my ears. It's Monday morning, and Tommy is still being held down at the station. There's no sign of Mom, and Dad has been going crazy trying to find out where she is. I stayed quiet, not wanting to be the bearer of bad news. How do you tell your father your mother is worth no more than the t-shirt on his back? In fact, she's worth less—less than him, less than this family. How do you tell him she's cheating on him?

Noelle comes up beside me and links our arms, her steps as light as a ballerina. I stiffen. *Does she know about our parents?*

"How's your weekend been, Lyss?" Noelle yawns.

Could've gone better. "Good, yours?" I say, my voice monotone.

"Well, about Friday night, please don't think anything of it." Noelle speaks in mouthfuls at a time, too fast for me to understand. "Tommy and me"—she shakes my arm— "he's just a one-night stand, nothing more."

I guess she doesn't know about our parents. "Um, yeah, if you say so." She and Tommy have always been at each other's throats, but that's what makes them tick. "Noelle..." I sigh. "Tommy has been arrested, for my attack."

She stands still, making me halt. "What?"

"Yeah, and Conan knows I'm blind. I told him."

"That's good, but Alyssa, Tommy didn't do it!" Noelle says adamantly.

"That's what I believed, but there must be evidence. Apparently, there's a witness."

Noelle shakes her head vigorously, side to side. "No, I know he didn't do it."

"I know you have a soft spot for him, Noelle, but he must have."

"No, that's not why."

"How d'ya know then?" I ask.

"Because..." Noelle's light skin goes a shade darker. If color existed in my world, she'd be bright red. "Because he was with me."

"How? I don't understand."

Noelle shifts from one foot to the other and coughs. "When I thought I slept with Conan, I remembered waking up, but Conan had gone downstairs. I heard whispers and arguing. It was Tommy and Charlotte, and they were arguing about drugs. Tommy left her standing at the top of the stairs and came into my bedroom. I started throwing up, so he held my hair back for me. I told him if he told anyone I'd kill him."

I laugh.

Can anything else possibly surprise me?

We start walking, pushing the entrance doors wide open. "But there's a witness."

Noelle and I look at each other, raising our defined eyebrows, and speak in unison. "*Charlotte.*"

This is low even for her standards, though bitchiness is woven into her core. There's no changing her; she's definitely a sly little birdie. Noelle leaves me outside the library, having to run to calculus, the only class we don't share. "Don't worry, Alyssa, I'm going to see if my dad can help in some way. He's good friends with the Sheriff."

I nod.

Let's hope and pray.

Tommy doesn't deserve this, and neither does our friendship.

Before my next class, I head for the girl's bathroom. I push the door open and find none other than Charlotte Summers standing by the sink, and she's sobbing like her life depends on creating a small lake in the ceramic base. I shift uncomfortably.

"Charlotte…" I tread toward her carefully, just in case she goes for me. "Are you, um, okay?" There are so many sobs, so much hiccupping, one after another. Uncomfortable doesn't even cover it; I'm incommodious, the air squeezing in around me. Of all people, I never would have thought Charlotte to be the type of girl who breaks down in the school bathroom. I thought she had more class than that. *Okay, that was harsh.* "Charlotte…" I touch her back gently. "Do you want to talk?"

Her voice is high-pitched, and her body starts trembling under my touch. "It's all my fault."

"Oh, love." I rub her back. "What's all your fault?" *Tommy, that's what.*

"H-He told me to lie. He told me nobody can know where the drugs came from."

I try to search her; if I had my eyesight, it would be easier. "Who? Who did, Charlotte?"

She turns around, and we're both leaning against the hard surface of the sink. "I-I can't say. He threatened my family." Charlotte is looking at me, completely unaware of the fact that I can't see her. "I-I'm scared, Alyssa."

My mind is searching for answers. All I want is answers. Nothing is making any sense. "Charlotte, what did you lie about?"

She shakes her head. "I-I'm sorry Alyssa."

"Why are you sorry?"

"It's all my fault…"

"What is!?"

"I lied about you. I told Sheriff Lou Tommy was the one who hurt you." I move away from her and she tries to grab my arm, pleading with me. "He didn't, Alyssa. He wouldn't, not sweet Tommy. I hated him.

When I ended it, he didn't care. Then my family was threatened, and I couldn't see a way out."

"Who threatened your family?" I ask bluntly.

"I-I can't tell you." Charlotte wipes her face with a paper towel. "All I can tell you is they told me to lie and say Tommy attacked you and supplied the drugs to the party. They wanted me to tell Sheriff Lou Ashton and Tommy were in it together."

"This is crazy," I mutter.

Charlotte cuddles me. "Please forgive me."

I push her back. "Get off me." I point my finger at her. "Go to the police right now and tell them it wasn't Tommy."

"I-I can't."

"You can, Charlotte. It's the only thing that's going to make you feel better. Tell them someone is threatening you, and they'll help you."

She looks down at the floor, no doubt, a distant look on her face. "Nobody can help me."

I have to find Conan. I walk out of the bathroom, leaving Charlotte to break down on her own. I can't comfort her when she won't tell me the truth. Someone's behind all of this, from the drugs to my attack and straight through to all the events that have followed—but who is that someone? Why can't I remember? I'm sure I saw my attacker that night, but my mind has blocked it out, as if it's something I really don't want to remember.

Ethan and Levi are standing by the bleachers, stretching their legs, ready to run the school marathon. There's no sign of Conan anywhere and I know he should be standing with them, ready to participate.

"Levi." I nod my head at him. "Have you seen Conan?"

"Has he finally gotten fed up of you, doll face?" Ethan slaps my ass. "I'm free."

"Slap my ass again and the word free is what you'll wish for while behind bars for sexual harassment," I growl. I've had enough.

Ethan holds his hands up in the air in surrender. "Jeez, I'm only joking."

I look at Levi. "Conan," I demand. "Have you seen him?"

"He didn't show today, sorry Lyss." Levi holds on to my shoulder, showing me some sign of affection. "I don't know anything."

I exhale, not having realized I was holding my breath. I walk away. Where is he? I should have known as soon as I told him I'm blind he would do a runner, getting as far away from me as possible. He doesn't owe me anything. I'm not even sure if we're official. The word girlfriend hasn't even come into it, but then, the three little words that mean everything to me have. My gut is sinking so low, I'm not sure how to alleviate it. I don't think I'm ready to have my heart broken so soon. I thought at least a year would pass before this happened, but perhaps I'm thinking too highly of myself.

I meet Noelle in the cafeteria and tell her everything I've found out. We sit with a tray in front of us, the burnt crisp smell of tikka chicken making my stomach growl. I start pulling at it with my fingers, putting small pieces in my mouth at a time.

"Someone threatened Charlotte," I whisper.

"Who?" Noelle puts her fork down on the table.

"I'm not sure. She wouldn't say. The only thing she told me was Tommy didn't do it and she lied to the police because someone told her to frame him."

"Who would do that?"

I grimace. "The person who did this to me."

"Jesus."

"I know."

Lindsey is cackling with the cheerleaders at a table in the middle of the large room, and there's no sign of Charlotte…or Conan, for that matter.

I glance back at Noelle. "There's one more thing."

She pushes her tray away from her, hardly touching her food. "Go on."

"The person who went to Charlotte wanted to set Tommy and Ashton up for the drugs too." I blink three times. "It's all connected, Noelle."

There's a pause and then Noelle stands up suddenly. "I have to go."

"What? What's going on?" I ask quickly.

"I'll talk to you later." Before I can ask her anything else, Noelle runs out the door as if her feet are on fire. I do know one thing: my brain is burning away slowly, and I need to hurry up and put out the flame before I mentally turn to ash.

Twenty Two

I'm sitting at the kitchen table and Mom still hasn't come home. She's been gone for days, this being the third, and Dad's become frail and exhausted from trying to find her. Mia keeps asking where she is, but nobody has the answer. How do you tell your six-year-old little sister that Mommy's gone?

I still haven't heard from Conan, and normally he's in touch every night before going to sleep.

The sound of Velcro tearing apart interrupts my thoughts. Mia slides her feet into her school shoes and places one up on the side of my chair so she's able to push the Velcro fastening back down. Finally, she drops her foot to the floor. She stands beside me and glares. "It's all your fault."

"Excuse me?" I turn in my chair, her shadows hard to see, but I want to make sure she knows I'm all ears.

"You." She's choking back her tears, and Mom's voice enters my head: *big girls don't cry.* That's what she says to Mia all the time. "If you were nicer to Mommy and didn't get yourself blind, she would be here, having breakfast with us."

I don't want to argue. She's young, and she doesn't understand. "If you say so."

"I wish you had gone, not Mommy," Mia shouts, storming off to sit in front of the television. Her words are sharp, on point and hurtful. They're stabbing me, not completely getting my heart, but definitely grazing the side. I know she's missing her mom and, in the meantime, she's trying to find someone to blame for her disappearance. Someone other than our actual mother.

I go through to the living area and sit next to Mia. I grab her hand. "Mia moo, I'm so sorry Mommy isn't here. I really am, but you don't mean that." Tears start to well up behind my eyelids.

"I do," she says.

"Mia—" I begin.

The doorbell rings and my dad shouts to say he's going to answer it. There's hope in his tone; he probably thinks it's Mom at the door and she's forgotten her keys. It's just wishful thinking, though, because it's actually Sheriff Lou.

My throat tightens. I hear them whispering until Dad finally lets the Sheriff come through to confront me.

"Alyssa."

"Sheriff." I nod my head.

He sits down on the armchair opposite. "I know you can't see my face..." He coughs as if something is lodged in his throat. "But please be aware that I'm going to tell you this with so much sincerity."

"Tell me what?" I don't care; he can shove his sincerity where the sun doesn't shine.

"Earlier this morning we received a phone call from somebody who spotted a crowbar, the same crowbar used to attack you."

"No." I shake my head. I know what's coming.

No phone calls, no signs of him... *But he said he loves me.*

"I'm sorry to say this crowbar was in the possession of Conan Dwight. It was found deep in the trunk of his car. The tipoff was correct, and we have now arrested him."

"But Conan wouldn't hurt Alyssa," Mia's sweet voice, whispers.

I slide off my seat and onto the floor, holding my hand over my mouth. I tremble. My dad crouches down next to me and places his arms around my shoulders, radiating warmth and safety. My breathing is shallow and I'm trying to stop the tears from coming down my face by squeezing my eyes tightly.

Don't open them.
Don't open them.
Don't open them.

I open them wide and try to speak, but my voice breaks. Water wells up behind my eyelids and finally it appears on my cheeks, soaking my pale blue t-shirt. My hands are in my wavy auburn hair, pulling at the strands, trying but failing to take away the pain in my heart.

I want to scream. I want physical pain. I want to curl up and never fall in love again. First, though, I need to fall out of love. He lied to me, lied to everyone. He pretended to care—he told me he loved me, oh no, *he declared his love for me!*

"I-I don't understand..." I hold on to my dad for dear life. Mia's standing next to me, watching us. "Dad, h-he loved me."

Sheriff Lou interjects, "He's pleading not guilty, saying he didn't do it, but I'm afraid everything links to him—the weapon, the time frame, no alibi. We're positive it's him."

"Like you were positive it was Tommy?" My dad asks beside me, asking the question I was thinking.

"Tommy wasn't in possession of the weapon, which has put your daughter into this state. I know this must be frustrating for you all, but by the looks of it, he's your attacker."

That is not what I wanted to hear.

What seems like hours passes, and Noelle picks me up to take me to school. Dad told me I could stay home if I wanted to, but I need normality. I need faith. Noelle's checking her mirrors and moving in and out of lanes. When she's driving along a straight stretch of road, she finally speaks to me. "Tommy should be out—I heard he got released last night."

I murmur. "I'm glad."

"I'm—I'm sorry about Conan Lyss," she whispers.

I let a tear slide down my face.

"Do you mind if we go back to my place? I forgot my English book."

I nod and stare out into the grey, blurry distance. I picture the shining sun beaming down onto my face. I cherish the dry warmth covering my cheeks and the tingling, light specks of hot rays catching my skin, all the way down my neck and onto my chest. I had to change my top into a green camisole, all because I drenched my pale blue t-shirt. I never realized I had that many tears to spill. For him, I'd let my heart spill out into the open. He's broken me.

We pull up into her large, fancy driveway and I hop out of the car, using the aluminum to keep me steady. Mr. Carlisle comes out of the house. *Great, that's all I need.*

"Hey, Daddy." Noelle greets him. She looks over her shoulder and shouts, "I'll just run in for it, Lyssa, won't be long." She bounces into her house after kissing her dad on the cheek.

"Alyssa, how are you?" David walks closer toward me. I wish he'd stayed where he was.

He's revolting.

"I'm good. Can't say the same about my little sister." I stare at his tall silhouette. "How's my mom? I'm guessing you've seen her."

"I don't know what you're talking about."

I sigh. "Of course you don't."

He leans against a massive post that's part of the façade of his house. "I've just heard the news. Isn't it great that Tommy is no longer being held?" He searches my face for answers. "Noelle told me about him, how he didn't do it because he was with her. I spoke to the sheriff myself, tried to get him out for you both."

"That's nice of you. Why don't you try to get my mother to come back to her family?" I reply sternly. "While you're at it, why don't you leave her alone and disappear?"

"I know you hate me."

"Hate you?" I raise my eyebrows. "I could use harsher words."

"Alyssa..." He closes the space between us, and I step away from him. "Please, you don't understand."

"She doesn't understand what, Daddy?" Noelle says from the front door. She prances down the stairs, a spring in her step. She's happy—who am I to destroy that?

"Oh nothing, sweetheart." He grabs the back of his daughter's neck and kisses her forehead. "See you after school. You girls be good and be safe."

"We will, Daddy." Noelle places her hand on my back and helps me into the car.

I hope he chokes.

I knock.

I knock again. *Tap, tap, tap.* There's still no answer. I know its lunch time, so maybe she's out of the office. She's not normally out of the office, but it's fine. I just need to get rid of this awful feeling squeezing in my stomach, the feeling of being a failure and being alone. I need her.

As if she hears my prayers, she opens the door. "Sorry Alyssa, I was just tidying up." She steps to one side, opening the door wide enough for me to step in. "I'm glad you could make it today." Her voice is gentle and friendly. She takes her normal seat behind her desk and waits for me to talk. I shuffle my feet a little bit at a time until I'm touching the arm of the chair, and I sit down.

"How can I help you, Alyssa?"

"I need answers," I say. "Proper answers."

"Okay." Mrs. Hall nods her head skeptically. "Tell me how I can help."

"It's just... everything—everything is so hard."

"Tell me about it." Maggie's drumming her fingers together. "Tell me what's so hard."

I scratch my wrists, just like I'm used to doing. It's a habit for me, a coping mechanism. "Conan's been arrested. Everyone is saying he did it."

Maggie separates her hands, picks up a pen (or pencil—I can't actually tell), and taps it against her desk, like normal. "Do you believe he did it?"

"The evidence says he did."

Maggie sighs loud enough to surprise me. "I know, Alyssa, but do you believe it?"

"No." I shake my head side to side. "He's too kind, too gentle." Maggie purses her lips. "I don't believe Conan attacked me," I repeat.

"Then who do you believe did?" Maggie encourages me to remember. "Why did they do this to you? Did you hear something, see something?"

~

My eyes hurt. My arms hurt. My legs hurt. Everywhere hurts. I didn't mean to see them together. I never wanted to see them. It's scarring me. I can't get the image out of my head. They're panting. She's sweaty. He is too.

"I can't let you tell anyone, Alyssa."

That voice…I know that voice. I've heard it so many times before—before tea, before bed, before he kisses us good night. He's looked after me when I've been sick. He's treated me well, given me birthday gifts. He's treated me like a princess…

~

"Alyssa, have you remembered something?" Maggie's next to me and holding my hand. She's kneeling down on the floor, holding on to me tightly to try to stop me from hurting myself. I run my fingers over the slick warmth of the blood across my wrists, just like that night.

~

He's walking toward me, telling me he's sorry for everything, saying he loved me, cared for me. Saw me as a daughter. I find it hard to believe. He tells me I'll be missed.

~

"I feel sick," I choke out. "I'm going to throw up." I place my head between my knees. She's rubbing my back gently and holds out a glass of water. I take small sips, a bit at a time, and try to compose my thoughts. The memory is so vivid, I remember that voice. "Mrs. Hall, I need to go home."

"I'll try to get you a pass." Maggie nods and taps my leg while taking the glass from my grasp. "Alyssa, have you remembered something?"

I scrunch my face up, trying to forget. "I think so, but I need to go home to be sure." *I want to be wrong.* "Please, Mrs. Hall."

There's a loud crack against the wall as the door to her office swings open. Standing in the doorway are Tommy and Noelle. Noelle's trying to hold him back. "I'm so sorry, Ms. Hall. He wouldn't listen!" Noelle squeals. "Alyssa, he knows everything! I had to tell him—please forgive me."

"Alyssa! I didn't hurt you. I didn't hurt you. I would never hurt a hair on your head." Tommy begs me to believe him.

I'm already on my feet and I run into his arms. "I know, Tommy, don't worry." We're embracing one another and he's crying, crying real tears, and it's awkward. "Tommy." I hold his head in my hands. I fight to lift it up so he's looking at me. "Why are you crying? Please don't cry."

"You're b-blind." His head dips low and I lean my forehead against his. "I left you at that party and now you're blind. It's all my fault."

Noelle is rubbing his broad, defined back and I'm kissing his forehead, one after another. *Silly, silly boy.* "Tommy, I love you—you stupid idiot. This is not your fault"—I look at Noelle's well-shadowed porcelain face and my heart sinks low in my stomach—"but I need to go home. I think I know whose fault it is."

Twenty Three

Tommy and Noelle are holding my hands as we walk up the porch toward the front of my house.

"Your front door is open," Noelle points out, and she's right; I don't see the shadow of a closed door. The light is shining through, and I notice the slimmer lines of the banister rail.

I walk in first and then Noelle follows, Tommy entering last. Mia is at school and the kitchen door is closed. That's where Fusco and Charlie are locked in, and they're barking loudly. Tommy goes into the living area while I stand at the bottom of the stairs, trying to process everything.

Where's my dad?

"Alyssa, you need to come here," Tommy bellows. Noelle holds my hand tightly and leads me into the room where my father is sitting in the armchair, rocking back and forth.

I run over to him and curl my arms around his broad shoulders. He seems broken, more broken than I've ever seen him before. "Dad! Dad, are you okay?" I grab his face with my palms and try to lift his head up but he's pulling against me, trying to drop it back down again. He's too strong. "Dad, please, you're scaring me. What's happened?"

I hear a light bang from above me. *Mom and Dad's bedroom...have we been burgled?*

My dad lifts his head suddenly and leans it against my chest while my arms wrap around him. "Your mother..." He chokes. "She's leaving." Tears leave wet trails down his face. "She's leaving me."

"Leaving?"

The tears are raw, real, and heartbreakingly sad to see. "She's going back to England."

I stand up and find my balance on the balls of my feet. "Stay with my dad, Tommy. Make sure he's okay." I bark the command before using my hands to guide me across the walls and make my way upstairs.

Standing over her bed and packing her belongings into her small brown suitcase is my mom. Her back is toward me, and she looks like she's ready to do a runner. I take a deep breath and head toward her a little shakily.

"Mom?"

"Hmm?" She doesn't turn around. It's as if I'm non-existent.

I swallow all the phlegm sitting in my mouth and pluck up the courage to confront her. "Mama?" I use the name I called her when I was younger. Whether it's because I used the nostalgic term or because something in my voice made her care, she shows she has some sort of maternal instinct and turns around.

"I'm sorry, baby," she begins, and then every word I thought she might say to me freezes on her lips. "I had to."

My heart is hurting more than ever. "I know you were there."

"Where, baby? What are you talking about?" She tries to walk past me, suitcase in hand. I grab it out of her grasp and throw it across the bedroom, letting it hit the dresser.

"Just explain it to me!" I scream. "Tell me why!"

"Baby—"

"Stop 'babying' me!" I say coldly. "You lost the right to say that when you shacked up with that horrible man!"

I hear footsteps running up the stairs and Noelle's by the bedroom door, panting hard. "Alyssa, is everything okay?"

"No!" I shout. "Everything isn't okay." I glare hard at my mom's skinny shadow. "I want answers *now*."

"I'll just—" Noelle starts.

"Stay, Noelle. You'll want to hear this." She turns her body to face us. I know she's confused, and I know she only stays for me. "Come on, Mom, tell us— how long have you been sleeping with Mr. Carlisle?"

Noelle gasps. "My dad? No...I don't believe it."

"I caught them, at Lexi's diner." I move closer toward my mom, who's now perching on the side of her bed. "How long?"

"T-Two years."

"Two whole years," I mock.

"You're lying." Noelle spits from the doorway, missing my mom's legs by a couple of inches.

She's looking past me now and straight at Noelle. "I'm sorry. Y-Your mom…she knows."

"And Dad?" I ask.

She dips her head—in what, shame? Her shadow moves slowly and changes shape as the top of her head lifts up to face us. "He knows too. I just told him."

"You're disgusting." She drops her head to the ground and I close the gap between us, lift her head up with my finger, "Now, tell me the rest. What happened the night I was attacked? Why were you there?"

Noelle drops her phone to the ground; most likely she was about to call her dad. I hold tightly on to my mother's arm and start to pull her to the top of the stairs. I keep pulling and she's trying to get my hand off her, but she doesn't hurt me.

"In fact, come on, Noelle—my disgusting excuse of a mother can tell us all." With that, I take her to the living area. I push her onto the sofa, and Dad's now standing behind me.

"What's going on?" he asks.

"I'm sorry, Dad. I know about the affair. I've known for days." I try to hold back the tears. The last thing I want is to hurt my dad. "But…there's more. You'll want to hear it."

Dad raises his eyebrows and wipes the tears away from under his eyes. Mom's got her head in the palm of her hands. Her legs are shaking, and Noelle's looking at her for answers. "Go on."

"I'm s-s-so sorry. I didn't want it to happen. You're my little girl…" Mom cries. "But it did. I tried to stop him, tried to get him to leave you alone, but he wouldn't listen. All he wanted was for you to forget, to never be able to say a word to anyone."

"I-I don't understand, Melissa," Dad chokes out. "What are you saying?"

"I'll tell you exactly what she's saying: Mommy dearest was there the night of Noelle's party, in a car…naked…kissing Mr. Carlisle. I didn't actually see it at the time, not properly." I glare at her. "I could have quite easily forgotten it with me being drugged, but I guess my brain thought it to be important for me to remember."

"Stop, Alyssa. Your dad and Noelle don't need to hear this."

"Oh, I think they do." I walk toward Noelle and embrace her. "I'm sorry, but you need to know." I look at everyone, keeping my hand entwined with my best friend's hand. "Noelle's dad is the person who attacked me."

"You really are a psychopath!" Noelle harshly pushes me back. "Why are you saying this!"

I don't even have to open my mouth to respond, because my mother does it for me. "It's the truth."

"You can't be serious," my dad interjects.

"Deadly," I say. "I saw them that night and Mr. Carlisle didn't want me to tell anyone, so he attacked me, and Mama over here let it all happen."

"It's not like that!" she squeals. "Noelle, you know how dangerous he is." I look at Noelle's tiny shadow standing next to me, looking at us quizzically. "He's the one behind the drugs. He's the supplier—all of it, Alyssa. Ashton has been running the drugs for him. He needed to keep you quiet. He told me nobody can know about me and him because it would destroy him and I didn't want that, because…" She keeps her voice as even as she possibly can and looks my dad deadpan in the face. "I love him."

"You make me sick," Dad growls. He tries to grab her, but Tommy holds him back.

"You're my mother!" I shout. "I was lying there bloody and broken, pleading, and you let him hurt me."

"He…He didn't expect you to survive," she whispers.

I choke and splutter but manage to get out, "And that's okay? You were happy to let me die!?"

"M-My dad…h-he wouldn't," Noelle cries.

"I'm sorry," Mom repeats. "I pleaded with him to let you live, Alyssa. I didn't want him to hurt you as badly as he did, and when you survived and couldn't remember, my prayers were answered."

I bray, "You mean you were pleased you and your little dirty secret hadn't been caught."

Dad walks toward her and grabs her upper arm, lifting her off the sofa. "You're no longer welcome in this house. You disgust me, d'ya hear? You can tell your lover he's not getting away with this. I'm ringing the police." Dad pushes her close to the doorway of the living room. "Get out." He places his phone to his ear. "Yes." Mom stays still, most likely not sure what to do. "Sherriff, please, I know who attacked my daughter…"

My dad's voice drifts off, making him background noise. Noelle is on the ground now, crying hard, her arms up to her chest and her head bent forward from exhaustion. Tommy runs to her and scoops her up into his arms, cradling her like a baby, like they've just gotten married and they're walking over the threshold. I let him comfort her; I just want it to be over.

My mom suddenly runs out of the house, leaving everything behind. The siren of sheriff Lou's police car is in the air, getting closer. I struggle to see around the room as the blue and white of their vehicles flash past the window, leaving the brightness blocking my view and switching any remaining image off. I could get used to seeing only complete darkness; maybe it's not going to be so bad.

All that's on my mind now is Conan alone in that holding cell, wondering if I hate him. I'm counting down the minutes, all the way down to the seconds until I see him again.

Everything is going to be okay.

In the distance, I hear a shrill scream, and it confirms that my mom has been found running along the road away from our house.

I'm empty inside. I don't hate her or love her—she's nothing to me.

Twenty Four

Mrs. Halls office is filling with teenagers.

Sitting and standing, we're all looking at her to start. I'm sitting in my normal chair next to Noelle. Standing in the corner is Tommy, and next to him is Ashton, who is out on bail. In the chair beside me is Charlotte Summers, and we're all sitting patiently, waiting for our group session to begin.

It's been two days, twenty-four minutes, and three seconds since Noelle's dad and my mom were arrested. There's still no sign of Conan, and the Sheriff refuses to tell me anything about what's happened. We have all given statements, all of us who were involved in one way or another. We were then invited to this group session to talk about it all, to ease us back into school.

"So, we'll go around, one after another, and please explain your story." Maggie claps her hands. "Alyssa?"

"You all know my story. In fact, the whole school knows now due to my story published in the newspapers. I'm blind. I was attacked by Mr. Carlisle, Noelle's father, at her end-of-summer party. My mom stood and watched. All because they thought I caught them having an affair. How twisted is that." I shrug. "That's it."

Maggie nods and gives me an encouraging smile, the dark lines curling up around the corners of her mouth. "Noelle?"

"It's my dad who attacked Lyssa, but he was always kind to me. It was only a few days before Alyssa confronted her mom when I found out my dad's a drug lord. He supplies the drugs to the Bellevue Gang. I wanted him to stop because my best friend had been drugged, but he didn't listen—he *never* listens. He told me he was going bankrupt and needed the money to keep our house. I didn't know how to tell you, Alyssa, because I know how much being drugged destroyed you."

"Okay." Maggie nods her head. "Ashton, it's your turn."

He coughs. "You thought I hurt you, Alyssa, but I'm telling you now, I would never hurt you. I was scared I'd be found out about selling the drugs. Mr. Carlisle asked me to make sure I got the shipment to the Bellevue Gang without anyone knowing. I'm only a drug runner, but I'm also an addict, and I didn't know how to stop. I'm sorry."

I nod my head. "It's fine, Ashton. It's over now." Saying the words aloud seems surreal.

"Charlotte?" Maggie turns to her, and her frame is shaking at my side. "Tell your story."

"I—"

I looked at the other side of me and reached out to her. "Don't be scared," I say, holding her hand.

"I was threatened by Mr. Carlisle. He told me if I didn't tell the Sheriff Tommy attacked Alyssa, my whole family would die, and it would look like an accident. I didn't know what to do. I'm sorry, Tommy." He closes the space between them and places his hand on her shoulder. "I couldn't tell you, Alyssa, but he knew I drugged you, so he was threatening to tell the police, but I guess the police had already found out, from you, which I understand. My family, though...that's a whole other ballgame." Charlottes scans the room. "I know I can be a bitch sometimes, but I do care. I care more than you think."

The door creaks open and my nostrils flare at the scent of summer fruits drifting in. I know that smell a mile off—Conan Dwight. I lift my head up and smile widely. My heart is fluttering, and my mouth is dry. I want to run into his arms, but I try to stop myself. I tell myself to wait. He leans against the wall, next to the door, and crosses his arms over his chest.

"What I don't understand is how that crowbar got into my car," Conan says, his voice low and deep as he looks at everyone in the room. "Someone here must know."

Noelle coughs. "I know how." We all stare at her. "I went to my dad for help. I needed him to get Tommy out. Once Alyssa and I knew he didn't do it, my dad told me he would work it out. I didn't think anything of it." Noelle hesitates. "Yesterday I visited him." Everyone gasps and Maggie hushes us. "I asked him why Conan was arrested. He told me he had to keep his family safe, and if I loved Tommy, Tommy was his family. He knew you were seeing Alyssa because he told me he had seen you together at the diner. So, he placed the crowbar in the trunk of your car and told the sheriff he had seen you put it there after the party, when you left. He told them he hadn't thought anything of it until now."

"The son of a bitch," Conan growls.

Everyone starts talking over one another and the room fills with noise.

Maggie slams her hand against her desk. "Everyone, please." We all quiet down. "You all know the truth now and justice will be served but use the rest of your senior year to help each other. Don't push each other away, and my door is always open." Maggie waves her hand toward the door. "If there's nothing left to say, you're all dismissed."

I hear the scraping of chairs and the mumbles of my classmates. Ashton and Conan hug each other and I hear the slap against Ashton's back, letting me know they're okay. Tommy kisses me on the cheek and walks out of the office hand in hand with Noelle. I'm happy, and a sensation of warmth spreads through me at knowing they have each other. I patiently wait outside the office door for Conan to appear, and before I get a good look at his shadow, he's lifting me up and letting my legs wrap around his waist. I bury my head into the side of his neck, leaning it against his shoulder, and he's grasping me tightly, his hand in my hair, his head pressing into the side of my face, kissing me where he can.

"I'm so happy you're here." I squeeze, holding on for dear life.

"So am I, Alyssa," Conan whispers sweetly. "So am I."

"I thought I'd lost you." I smile. "I knew you didn't do it."

Conan places his lips upon mine, holding us there in that moment, and finally says, "Every time I see you, I fall in love all over again. You could never lose me. I'll always be yours."

Twenty Five

I'm curled up on the couch with Mia.

Conan's sitting in Dad's armchair, and Dad is in the kitchen, making dinner.

"Alyssa, I didn't mean what I said," Mia whispers, her soft, short bob covering her face. Her head is laid against my legs, and I'm running my hand through her beautiful strands. "You're my mommy, more of a mommy than *her*."

"No, little one, I'm your sister, and I'll always be here to look after you." Mia has taken Mom's arrest very well. She's more mature than we give her credit for. She understands Mom has done something bad, and although Dad says you can see the pain in her eyes, she's staying strong. I lean down and kiss her head. "I love you Mia moo."

"I love you too, Alyssa."

Three loud bangs on the front door interrupt our night. Conan gets up and answers it, Dad is still standing over the cooker, frying, the aroma of a faintly sweet meaty dish, drifting through the house.

"Can I come in?"

"Of course, sir," Conan replies. "Alyssa, Mr. Darlington! It's the sheriff." Sheriff Lou takes off his hat and places it against his chest. I hear him scrape his feet against the shoe matt and tread his way toward the kitchen. I follow behind and take the nearest seat next to him.

My dad turns the cooker off and sits down opposite. Last time we were here, my world was ripped apart.

"I've just come to give you an update—"

"Daddy—" Mia interrupts from the door.

"Go upstairs, Mia. I'll be up in a second," Dad tells her softly. I hear her tiny feet take one step at a time up the staircase.

"Sorry," Dad mumbles.

"It's fine." Sheriff Lou nods his head. "Mr. Darlington, your wife has told us everything. She's given a witness statement, and now there's more news: Mr. Carlisle has pleaded guilty and will plead guilty on the stand. You won't have to give any account, Alyssa. It's over." He shakes my shoulder kindly.

I smile, trying to hold back the river of tears forming behind my eyelids. Conan comes over to my side and rubs between my shoulder blades.

"Thank you, Sheriff Lou. I will walk you out," Dad says. The officer scrapes his chair backward and shakes my hand. I smile, thankful for his update. I lay my head against the smooth, cold surface of our dining room table and let out a large exhale.

It's all over.

Conan and I decide to put Fusco's luminous vest on. Now that everyone knows about me being partially blind, there's nothing to hide. We take Fusco and Charlie out for a walk. We walk along the streets of Vallyeont, listening to the busy traffic and the crunchy leaves blowing across the hard road. We sit down on the bench where he asked me out (well, technically, I asked him out) and I gently lean into his side. Fusco and Charlie are barking in front of us, running off into the distance to fetch sticks, and I smile.

It's all over.

"Are you okay?" Conan asks me for what seems like the forty-five-millionth time these past two months, and I nod.

"Better than I've ever been." I sit up and turn to look at his lean, defined physique. "I thought my mom and dad had it all. I thought that was what love is, but you…you made me realize." I hold his hand. "I know what love is because of you."

Without his love, I can do nothing. With his love, there's nothing I cannot do.

"Alyssa, your dad will get through all this. He'll find someone who loves him, someone who will never want to hurt him." Conan cups my face. "It might not feel like it, but this will all be a distant nightmare. You will graduate and travel the world, because I'll help you. You will experience all the things you thought you couldn't, because we'll do it together." Conan kisses my nose. "Remember, you may only hold my hands for a short while at a time, but you hold my heart forever."

"Oh Conan, I love you," I say breathlessly, my forehead leaning against his and my heart beating so fast I'm breathing quicker to keep up.

"Always and forever, Darlington."

I know in that moment I don't need my sight, not really. How do we describe someone's sight? Something that's regarded as worth seeing? It's the process, power, or function of seeing. It's an ability people depend on to be able to look beyond, to observe and to determine direction or position. If people around you are willing to help, you don't really need your sight, and I know that now. I was so petrified of letting people in, of letting them know I'm blind that I forgot how special it makes me. Yes, Mr. Carlisle took away my vision, but he didn't take away my view of life. I'm now unique. I'm finally happy in my skin, and I have the love I need to push me through the hardest times.

It's over now, and I'm fine with that. This is my life played out before me, as it should be. This is how it *should* be written: with love, hope, friendships, and even betrayal, and if this is how it's supposed to end, I'm fine with that too.

But life is not always black and white, sometimes it's a thousand shades of grey and when it all became my twisted reality, it made it easy for the shadows to overtake…

Twenty Six

That Night…

I open my eyes painfully and look around to see I'm in a bedroom—walnut everywhere with the contrast of lavender walls.

I'm still at Noelle's end-of-summer house party.

I stand up and pull my black bodycon dress down from above my waist. I'm disgusted with myself. The room is spinning, and every step seems difficult to take. My head is in a haze as I make my way downstairs, ignoring all the stares and whispers. I stumble against the front door. Hands and elbows from several teenagers are shoving me, trying to get past me, pushing me hard into the wall.

"Alyssa?" Conan slides across the room and holds me up.

I stare into his crystal blue eyes, which are sparkling like stars, and admire his bouncy curls, sitting perfectly on his beautiful head. "You're so handsome."

He laughs at me. "You're not bad yourself, Darlington." I place my hands around his neck and sway my body with his. "Fix You" by Coldplay is playing through the sound system, and he's staring at me like I'm the only girl in the world.

He starts to lean in slowly and my heart is beating at twice the rate it was ten seconds ago. My hands are clammy behind his neck, and I'm starting to have heart palpitations. He's so close to me, so close to kissing me—but then a large crash pulls his gaze from mine.

"Shit," Conan whispers, so close to my lips. "I'm sorry." He glances toward the kitchen where the crash came from. "I have to go, Darlington." He holds on to me, giving me one last look. "Wait here." Before I register his words, he's disappeared into the crowd.

My body feels like I'm full of brittle bones. I stumble through the nearest door and try to get my bearings.

Distantly in the dark I see two cars: a red GT and a black Mercedes. I place my hand on the black hood of the Mercedes. I lean both elbows onto the car and slowly slump my head into my hands. My legs are like jelly, wobbly and shaky. I slam the palm of my hand against the surface and scream. I tread slowly around the side and I glance at the condensation on the windows. A flicker of movement registers in my gaze but I shake my head, thinking it's just the alcohol.

But then I see it. I see the handprint on the steamed window, and hazily through the glass I see two people, naked, kissing. I look away quickly. I allow my body to lay all its weight against the passenger side of the vehicle, and I use all my energy to try to keep myself upright.

I collapses to the hard, cold floor and I lean my head against the door. I hear hushed whispers and I close my eyes; they're coming from behind the Mercedes—they're arguing.

"We can't carry on this way. We should tell people," I hear a woman whisper.

"No," the man sternly replies. "Why ruin everything we've got? What they don't know won't harm them. We need to deal with her."

"You love me, right?" the woman's voice whispers again.

"Of course," he replies.

Laughter interrupts from two girls on the other side of the garage.

They don't notice me.

I turn my head to the side to try to concentrate on the hushed whispers, but before I know it, my stomach turns, and I violently curl over and throw up. Vomit is everywhere, all over my dress, my right hand, and the concrete floor.

I try to keep my eyes focused on the blurry lights shining into the garage from the outside window. I have the need to drift soundly off to sleep, but I fight it, like the warrior I am.

I hear the footsteps first—one step, two step, three steps. I have company. *I'm going to be okay.* I use my last bit of energy and see him: tall and ruggedly handsome. He's smiling at me, and I know I'm in good hands.

"Help me." My voice breaks, my body weak, as if I've been drugged. "Help me, please. I can't feel my legs."

He stands, towering over me, not making any movement to help. I know he will, though; his daughter is my best friend. This is his house. He's Mr. Carlisle. He has to.

He stands very still.

"What are you doing?" I whisper.

"I can't let you tell anyone," he states. "I can't let you go."

"Tell anyone about what?" I choke. I don't understand.

"You know what you've seen. I can't let you talk," he repeats.

"I don't understand."

"Your mom understands, don't you darling." I hear a sob from the side of the Mercedes.

I murmur, "Mama?"

She looks away from us both. "I'm sorry, baby girl."

"I don't understand," I repeat again.

"David, please don't do this. I'm sick to death of being told no. You always have some pathetic, ridiculous answer as to why we can't just be together.

You either sort this out or whatever *this* is, it's over," my mom shouts.

Suddenly, not only is he the devil in disguise, he's death, rancid and vile. He picks up a large bottle: laundry detergent from the shelf beside him. He brings it toward me. Before I can catch my breath, it's soaking me head to toe. It's slimy and slippery and smells like soap, fresh and clean.

I try to look around. I try my hardest to catch my breath. I turn my head side to side, trying to make it stop, but it keeps on coming. I'm too weak to scream, to tell him to stop. Through the drowning, I hear my mother doing it for me. Her screams wail through my body, making the hairs on my neck stand up. My eyes burn, so I squeeze them tightly, hoping it will go away. I grab his leg, tugging at him, pleading with him. He kicks me backward. I try to move, to crawl away, but evil just keeps on following. He keeps pouring, keeps laughing, deep and malicious—a laugh I could never forget.

"My answer is final, Melissa. You won't be ending this, and you definitely, most certainly will accept it," David Carlisle sneers.

My mother is scratching and clawing at him to stop. "She's my daughter!" He slaps her in the face, leaving her curled up on the floor beside me. She scrambles to the corner, getting away. She covers her eyes—out of sight, out of mind.

He throws the empty bottle behind him with a hollow thud. I pray it's over and squeeze my eyes shut. He walks away from me and I sigh with relief.

Mr. Carlisle…David Carlisle…Noelle's dad walks back toward me and my heart jumps. I hear a loud screech, like a nail on a chalkboard. In his hands, he swings a crowbar back and forth.

"David, if you love me, please," my mother begs.

Traitor. Adulterer.

"She can't tell anyone," he spits out. "This is the only way."

"Please." She's sobbing. "You're not a murderer! Think of your daughter…"

I tremble, and finally the blow to the head comes down hard. I scream then go limp on the cold, hard floor. Before passing out completely, I fight through the pain, and I see them walking away. David is dragging my mom's body away from me, her sobs filling my ears.

Why Mom? Why me?

Two hours later, I start to regain feeling as my legs twitch slightly. My arms are sprawled out above my head, and I'm unable to move them. My cheek is against the floor, and it feels numb from being pressed against the cold surface for so long. The aroma of tuna from my dinner tickles my nostrils from the vomit I'm lying in. It smells like someone has died. Blood is covering my forehead, my eyelashes, and my eyebrows, sticking to me like glue, but I know I'm still alive, still breathing, still surviving.

Every part of my body is on fire—my head, back, and legs. They feel like they're burning. I fight through the pain and attempt to move my hand. Slowly, I reach for my head, and all I can feel is the wetness matted into my hair, and the damp, cold slime transfers onto my fingers—blood, sweat, and tears. My hand falls to the side and my whole body shakes uncontrollably; I think I'm having a fit. I stop. I don't know where I am.

I feel exhausted.

All I can do is listen and hope and pray someone finds me. I can no longer feel, no longer understand; all I can do is drift off to sleep.

I become conscious and my vision is hazy, my eyes burning, and I grimace at the pain in my head. It pounds hard against my skull, like a ticking time bomb, ready to explode. I notice someone entering the room.

Looking at me in awe, most likely terrified at the state of me, is Ashton Marston. I reach my arms out toward him, and I do the only thing I can think to do—I plead. He walks backward, his hazelnut eyes staring deep into mine, never letting me forget the eyes that saw but looked away. He leaves as quickly as he came in.

I whisper, "Help me, please." The door slams shut behind him.

I pass out.

A high-pitched scream like a banshee wakes me up.

Callie McGovern's at my side, breathing heavily. "Holy crap!"

There's the sound of footsteps around the garage. People whisper and hands touch me all over.

"Don't just stand there—call an ambulance you idiot!" Noelle demands. "Alyssa!" I hear her voice, but I don't respond. Her hands begin to shake me, willing me to move, but I can't. I can't move.

"Sweet Jesus, there's so much blood," Lindsey whispers.

David, Noelle's father, interjects, "How long has she been like this?" He's directing his next statement at his daughter. "Noelle, if she doesn't survive, this will be on you. This party was irresponsible."

"Dad, you told me—"

"Enough!" He shouts.

My body recoils. I hear a ticking clock; I think it's in my head, ticking away until my death.

Tick tock, tick tock, tick tock.

"What time is it?" Callie asks.

Noelle sobs. "Four a.m.," she chokes out. "She must have been here a few hours. Let's just hurry up and get her some help," she says aggravatedly.

I try to stay awake, try to scream to them that David did this, to tell Noelle her father isn't who she thinks he is, but my body becomes weaker by the minute and I drift back to sleep. Soon after, I become conscious as an angel speaks to me.

"Alyssa, stay with us. An ambulance is on its way," Conan whispers beside me.

I bring myself around and I smile inside. He remembers my name. He nearly kissed me. "I feel so weak." I think of David. "I know who—"

"I know, Darlington. Just hold on, okay?" He strokes my bloody hair. "Keep your strength."

"I—I don't think I can." I give him a long-suffering look.

Noelle grabs my hands. "Alyssa, don't you dare!" she screeches on the other side of me. "Me and you, best friends forever. We're graduating together, we're going to go traveling, go to college. Keep fighting, please. Help is on the way."

"I'm sorry," I whisper, barely getting the words out.

Noelle is leaning over my body, sobbing so hard, she's struggling to breathe.

"Darlington."

"Conan," I whisper back. I move my hand up to his face and trace his eyes, down to his nose and his lips. "In another life, you and I...we had a chance, ya know." I laugh but it hurts. Conan has my head in his lap. "Ever since I laid eyes on your cheeky smile, when we were just thirteen, I knew I was infatuated."

Noelle keeps a tight grip on my hand.

"Alyssa!" Tommy shouts through the crowd, pushing his way towards me.

"Henderson." I give a ghost of a smile. "Look after my dad and Mia, okay?"

He's nodding his head, tears slipping away from him.

And my soul is slipping away from me.

"No, no, no. Alyssa, it's not your time. I hear the ambulance—can you hear it?" Tommy says, shaking my arm.

I don't hear it. Instead I hear my heart thumping hard in my ears. I forget Tommy's question. "Conan?"

He strokes my hair, "Yeah?"

"Kiss me…" My eyes are closed. I struggle to open them and I wait. Will he do it? I smell his fruity breath before his finger wipes away a tear that's rolling down my face. He leans in and plants his lips upon mine. He turns my world upside down and I'm breathless.

I hear the ambulance. My limp body shivers under his touch. Noelle is clutching me, willing me to pull through.

"This is going to hurt me when it's over." I flinch.

"Nothing is really over until the moment you stop trying," Conan whispers. He kisses my matted, bloody hair.

"I'm sorry."

"Don't be." He says. Tears roll off his face onto mine. "Just rest—you're nearly there."

Whether he meant me surviving or not, I'm not sure, and I never will be.

"I love you," I say in a splintered voice to everyone clutching at me and willing for me to survive. I'm slipping away. At the end of the tunnel is a touch of white. I'm like a mere shadowy spot on a field of light...so beautiful, so warm, it's mesmerizing. It's safe. It's where I want to be. Nobody knows what death is, not really, but everything about it is so sure. There are no plans. No monsters. There's no fear, and I'm able to dry my silent tears.

In another life, Conan and I would have been a whirling love story. The kiss would still be upon my trembling lips. I'd have gotten my revenge on David, my dad would have finally seen my mother for what she really is, Tommy would have been free from his torturous uncle, and I would have watched Mia grow up to become a beautiful, caring young woman. I may have been blind from surviving, but I'd still have been living, still falling in love and making new friendships. It could have been real, but now, I'm above them all, and I hope they remember me as Alyssa Darlington, the beloved.

    Free-spirited. Kind. Adventurous.
    For here I am, no longer.
    I'm flying, soaring through the sky.
    I'm free.

THE END

Acknowledgement

I never thought I'd get here. I began writing this book years ago and never thought I'd actually get to this point. To have my first ever book out in the world for everyone to read is overwhelming but so exhilarating. I'd like to start by thanking you readers. If you're reading this, it means you've picked my book up and finally reached the end. For that, I'm grateful. I hope you enjoyed it as much as I enjoyed writing it.

None of this would have been possible without the support from my family. So let me start with my Fiancée, Kieran: you stand by my through everything. You encourage me. You support me and you love me. Next, my little boy: I wouldn't push myself if it wasn't for this little munchkin. I hope he's proud of me, as much as I am of him. To my mum and dad: for making me the women I am today. For supporting every dream, I ever had. You're wonderful parents and amazing grandparents. I love you. To my sister, Jessica Hobson: you are the best. She's the one and only person that read every single draft of Through Her Eyes. Standing by me through every struggle. Not only is she my sister, but she shows true friendship. I'm eternally grateful for everything you do for me.

Thank you to all my beta readers: Jessica Hobson, Alex Reid, Megan Spencer, Brandon L Moore, Asha Fields (Field Day Press), and Christie Davidson. Also, to my first rounds of professional edits by Caitlin Marie. I learnt a lot from your comments and feedback especially with the book being based in America.

To Claire Voet for my creative writing classes, I learnt so much in such a small amount of time. If it wasn't for meeting you, I wouldn't be here, where I am now at twenty-four. A very special thanks to everyone at Blossom Spring Publishing house, for taking a chance and seeing something in my writing and making all my dreams come true.

I'd like to take a moment and appreciate all my supporters and friends I've made through the writing community on social media. I've made friends for life. You guys are amazing, and I can't wait to watch all your dreams come true.

And finally, I'd like to thank someone who will never get the chance to read this because her life ended too soon. She showed me that life is too short and that everything happens for a reason. I wish you were here to get your signed copy, just like we always spoke about.

Today may not be the greatest day, but make sure you carry on seeing all the days ahead of you, because sometimes your darkest days may turn into your lightest days.

With love,
Sophie Fahy.

www.authorsophiefahy.com
Find me on Social Media:
Instagram: @authorfahy
Twitter: @authorfahy
Facebook: Sophie Fahy Author Page

www.blossomspringpublishing.com

Printed in Poland
by Amazon Fulfillment
Poland Sp. z o.o., Wrocław